FREEZING HELL

THE SMOKE AND ICE DUOLOGY
BOOK 2

HAYDN HUBBARD

Copyright © 2024 by Haydn Hubbard

Editing by Jessica McKelden

Cover designed by Covers by Jules (coversbyjules.crd.co)

All rights reserved.

No part of this book may be reproduced in any form or by any electronic or mechanical means, including information storage and retrieval systems, without written permission from the author, except for the use of brief quotations in a book review.

*For anyone who has felt like giving up on themselves.
Don't you fucking dare.*

CHAPTER 1
MADDY

I realize as I wake, a mess of blonde hair and vodka sweat, that I should probably know the name of the man who lays naked beside me. Next, I realize that I'm too sober to deal with that problem, and slink out of the hotel room, my heels in hand. I know I'm a walking cliché, sauntering back to my downtown apartment in the early hours of the morning. Know that the men lingering on the sidewalk have anything but my best intentions in mind as they all but break their necks to stare.

Let them fucking try.

I throw one a wicked grin, full of malice and reckless abandon. He shifts to the next foot, the others looking away as if they can sense that I have seen and survived much worse than them. Dated, fucked, and planned to marry much worse than them.

Donovan had his perks, I muse with cynical delight. Everything he threw at me would always be worse than some coward who hid in shadows, even if in the end, he wasn't much better himself.

Maurice, the doorman of my apartment complex, waves with a smile that is a mix of pitying and fearful. I wave back, nothing more than a single flick of my wrist in his direction before trudging towards the elevator.

The apartment was a gift from Mancini Security, the private security company owned by my best friend's fiancée. The name on the lease is the company, but I know it was Addie who begged her lover for a more secure apartment than our old one. Natalia conceded, as she always does when Addie is involved, but I know she plotted the move with her second-in-command the minute they found me bleeding out in the old apartment.

Again, having a psychotic, murderous ex-boyfriend does have its perks, one of them being a top-of-the-line penthouse with free rent and security. Nothing sneaks by Natalia, not between her two businesses and the gray area where they overlap.

Most know the woman for being the young founder of the successful security company, but the rest of us know the truth. We know that Mancini Security is only a cover for the Mafia organization she runs. It's how she was able to track down Donovan when authorities couldn't, and how she was able to save Addie before he killed her.

I push the thought of my best friend, unconscious and being dragged from our apartment, from my mind as I slide my key into the lock. The pins click with a satisfying pop as I plod into the room, ready for a scalding-hot shower and a few more minutes of sleep—sadly, not hours, as I have work soon, but five more minutes can't hurt.

"Good night?" a voice of smooth whiskey murmurs.

I pay the voice no mind, nor the man it came from.

Riven Barone, Natalia's second, sits completely at ease on my white couch, his arm propped on a pink pillow that reads "boss bitch" in swirling cursive. A few months ago, I would have laughed. Now, I just ignore him and creep towards my shower, where hot water promises some form of release that the man from last night couldn't deliver.

Before I can get there, though, a tall body of pure muscle blocks my path, his dark gaze cold and unfaltering. Christ, it's a sin to look that good. He's lethal and he knows it—and he isn't afraid to use it to his advantage.

When I first met Riven, I was dating Donovan, but I still noticed the spark between us. I chalked it up to rage—the man was infuriating, pushing buttons I didn't know I had. He did funny things to my heart, even as he glowered at me or offered a frequent snide remark. Now I only stare up at him, a cool darkness in my chest where that flutter used to be.

"You're blocking my bathroom," I say drily.

"Yes, I'm aware," he retorts.

"Could you..." I motion with my hands back towards the couch, or better yet the door. "Maybe not?"

"Maybe, once you tell me where you were."

"I don't owe you any explanations."

"No, but when you didn't answer your phone all night, Addie assumed the worst and sent me here. Imagine how she felt when I told her you weren't here."

Guilt flares in my chest at the mention of my best friend. Addie and I both moved to the city around the same time. We were fast friends who did everything together—we lived together, worked together, and survived almost being murdered by my ex together.

Donovan had a hidden obsession with Addie, one that we realized all too late. He had approached me at one of my photography galleries after seeing a photo I took of her. We dated and I fell in love with him while he fell in love with my best friend—who hated him from the start, by the way. He was a walking red flag and I was a girl desperate for love with a pair of rose-tinted glasses.

Still, when Addie started receiving threatening text messages and girls were dropping dead around the city, we never thought he was the killer.

I sigh in defeat. "Just tell her... tell her that I went to see a friend."

"Which friend?"

"I don't know, make one up," I snap.

Riven is Addie's friend, not mine, I remind myself. Even if he seemed concerned when I walked in the door, I know deep down it was all because he can't stand to see her hurt. And that's what would happen if she knew about my nightly escapades. She'd be hurt, and neither of us wants that.

It never used to be this way between us. We used to tell each other everything. Addie is the person who taught me that soulmates can exist platonically. There is no Maddy without Addie, I used to joke with her. But after Donovan...

I never resented her for any of what happened—not Donovan using me, my attempted murder, or even Riven's behavior now. Even though I desperately want someone I can pin this on, the only person besides myself that I can blame is dead. And Addie has been nothing but supportive, prioritizing my recovery over her own. She would be crushed to learn of my less-than-holy coping mechanisms when I have done such a good job of convincing her I'm fine thus far.

To be fair, I received most of the physical torture he dealt the two of us, but the mind games that he played with her will last a lifetime. The thought has me holding my side, the feeling of his boot in my ribs as they shattered fresh in my mind, even though three months have passed.

Three months since he beat me until I was barely breathing.

Three months since he stopped, only because Addie threw herself over me.

Three months since Riven found me, half dead in my apartment, and held me the whole way to the hospital.

We don't talk about that. We don't talk about many things, but we certainly don't talk about that.

And of course, Riven has to notice where my hands are, how they bunch in the fabric of my tight dress. I know he knows each rib that Donovan shattered, where the internal bleeding was, and how many stitches they put in my hairline.

"Do they still hurt?" he asks, his voice dangerously low.

"Not so much anymore."

It's a half lie. They hurt like hell when I walk up too many stairs, if I run into something, or when a memory washes over me. If I tell him that, though, He'd report it back to Addie—and the last thing she needs right now is to start worrying about me again.

Riven doesn't believe me—I know he doesn't—but he

bites his lip and sighs as he steps to the side. "We can talk after you've showered. You smell like alcohol."

I choose to ignore the slight and just take the victory.

The pain slightly ebbs as I step under the warm water in my shower. It's nice, living in a place where the water is automatically warm and I don't have to brave the cold for a few minutes before a semblance of warmth seeps in. It's a petty thing to be grateful for, but I'm grateful, nonetheless.

I keep my gaze trained on the cool white tile of the shower wall while I lather my body with soap. I don't watch as my hands trail over scar after scar, and flinch whenever they press against a raised mark.

My eyes are closed as I step out of the shower, fumbling for my towel. I don't open them until it's wrapped around my frame, and even then, I keep my gaze away from the mirror.

I used to love the attention thrown my way. I've always known I'm beautiful, but now, my appearance feels more like a curse.

My Tella's shirt feels like an embrace and sanctuary at the same time, covering all that remains from the past few months. The coffee shop itself feels like safety these days. I'm untouchable under its soft lights and the scrutinizing eyes of our boss, Daryl.

Addie and I moved to the city about the same time a few years ago. I lived a bit closer than she did and knew about the hefty price tag that came with all things urban here, so I quickly found a job working as a barista at Tella's. After Addie's dream of publishing her first novel was put on hold, she joined me behind the counter a few weeks later.

Daryl pretended to be annoyed by us, yet he always kept us on the same shift together, let me snag snacks from the bakery, and comforted Addie during her breakup—in the most standoffish way possible, of course. The middle-aged man didn't do feelings, as he's said and implied on multiple occasions. Still, he's like a weird, fun uncle at times.

My blonde hair now tied in a ponytail and all my dark circles covered, I push the bathroom door open. Riven has migrated to my counter, where he holds two mugs of coffee.

"You know I get free coffee at work, right?"

"Who said one was for you? Maybe they're both for me," Riven counters with an obnoxious slurp from one of the pink mugs.

I offer him a mocking laugh if only for pity's sake before accepting the other mug. It's black and bitter and I scrunch my nose. "Sugar."

"Say please."

"*Now*."

Riven grumbles under his breath but passes the sugar my way, the cream following close behind. He should know how I take my coffee by now, but part of me thinks he does it wrong just to get me to talk, even if I'm snapping at him.

"Addie is going to be at work today," I say between sips. "If you want to report back to her."

Riven sighs through his nose, something he does a lot these days, and fixes me with a stern look that can only be interpreted as, *"Really? We're doing this now?"* "Come on, I'll give you a ride."

I don't point out the fact that I can walk, mostly

because my feet are killing me, but also because I'm already running late. Wordlessly, I nod and follow him out the door, the lock snicking into place quietly behind us.

Addie is already behind the counter when Riven drops me off. Her curly brown hair is tied back in a low bun today, save for the few wild strands that escape around her face. Her blue eyes light up when she sees me, and she waves like we haven't seen each other in months. Daryl grumbles as he almost catches her elbow, but says nothing else as he stalks back to his office.

"Morning," I chirp, doing my best to plaster a smile on my face.

"Hey, glad you made it. Riven said you were at a friend's place last night?" she prompts, just an edge of suspicion lining her voice.

"A friend of sorts. More like a work colleague." The lie slips off my tongue easily enough. "We were trying to put together a portfolio for a prospective showing coming up in a few months."

All the worry disappears from her face almost instantly and her smile makes my heart ache. Just a few months ago, I thought I would never see that smile again, and it would be all my fault, yet here she is, rambling on about how proud she is of me.

You have no reason to be proud of me, I think with a bitter taste in my mouth.

Addie adjusted back to normal life quicker than I did —well, as quickly as one might after suffering what we did. If I'm being honest, she got the worst of it. While Donovan attempted to kill us both, Addie had to endure the months of stalking, threats, and break-ins, while I only had one night of hell. It's not fair—none of it is. Someone like Addie, someone kind and lovely, deserves a life without pain, yet she beams as if nothing happened. To be fair, she has Natalia, who we both know would die before letting anyone harm her fiancée ever again. Natalia and I get along fine, but we've never been closer than when protecting Addie.

"You good to take the register?" my best friend asks, just like she has every shift since we've worked here. Every time I say yes, even though I hate it. I'm simply better with people, and Addie's anxiety spikes any time she takes an order, so register duty usually falls to me.

"Yup."

"Oh, by the way, are you coming to dinner tonight? Natalia and Marco are cooking."

I grin. "You mean *Natalia* is cooking and Marco is eating as much as he can before she kicks him out?"

Addie laughs, a lilting sound. "Exactly."

Marco is Riven's cousin, who also works for Natalia within the Mancini Mafia, despite being part of the Barones, a rival Mafia family in the area. I never learned why they left and joined Natalia. Addie knows, but she insists it's Riven's story to tell, not hers. All I know is Riven's brother is leading the Barone family now, and the two of them haven't spoken in years. Something about bullets, family feuds, and a mess I don't have time for.

I let myself fall into my routine, a perfect smile planted on my pretty face. I laugh at jokes from men who aren't funny. I misspell a name or two on purpose, just for my own entertainment. I pretend I can't see Addie looking straight through my act.

Pretend, pretend, pretend.

My life is now just a string of events that I fake my way through, each day sinking further into the pit I've dug for myself.

CHAPTER 2
RIVEN

My damp hair sticks to my forehead despite the many times I've attempted to push it back on the drive to Addie and Natalia's. Natalia sent me to handle a minor uprising earlier, something that would otherwise be beneath me, but things have been slow lately. There were small fears of a rival group attacking many months ago after one of our own siphoned off weapons to sell to them. Natalia squashed that quickly enough, and things have been quiet ever since.

Well, quiet on the job front, anyway.

I stand on Addie's porch, lingering a second longer to admire the home they've built. The flowers in the flower boxes are dead now, but I smile, nonetheless. My mother had flower boxes just like these in her window. No doubt this touch was inspired by her.

Before I met Natalia, I was a hitman for the Barone family. My father was the head, and my brother, Malik, was poised to take the role after him, but in the last moments before his death, the title was passed to me.

Malik seized control before word could get out and placed a green light on me—I was to be killed on sight.

Natalia took me in, making me her second, and eventually, trusting me with everything. I didn't understand it at first—I still don't entirely. She could have killed me, made a strong ally out of my brother. I'm not sure what would have made my brother angrier—my father giving me the position or Natalia's massive "fuck you."

She is no stranger to family drama—if our blood feuds can be called something so trivial. From what she's told me, her father was not a stand-up guy, and being a female head isn't exactly traditional. Nothing about Natalia is traditional, but I like to think she sees a kindred spirit in me, and that's why she took me in.

Still, the action came with a price. Malik told my mother I was dead, and warned me that he could easily have her killed should she find out the truth. Natalia visits her in Rome in my stead, and she took Addie with on her last visit. From what I heard, my mother loves Addie, and Addie likewise.

I clear my throat and shake the thought from my mind. It's foolish to fantasize about something that can never happen. As much as I miss my mother, her safety is more important than my longing.

Addie answers the door after one knock, her curly hair piled high on her head and her apron covered in flour.

I raise an eyebrow. "I thought Natalia and Marco were cooking?"

"I thought I'd try to help."

"And how'd that go?"

Addie's face flushes red and she all but pulls my arm

off, yanking me inside. I tried to teach her to cook once as a surprise for Natalia. I heard that Natalia took one bite to be polite, but the garbage was fed the rest.

Addie peeks out the door behind me before shutting it. "Did you see Maddy? She said she'd be here tonight." She worries her lip with her teeth.

I push a finger against her forehead, smoothing out the furrow between her brows. "Stop frowning. I didn't see her, but she's probably just running late. Forgot to unplug her curling iron and rushed back to the apartment or something."

She laughs, her blue eyes glinting with mischief. "I'm going to tell her you said that."

I only grin and follow her into the kitchen, where Natalia and my cousin are finishing dinner. Marco is actually helping this time, not just stealing a taste of everything while Natalia does most of the work.

He waves me over and passes me a steaming platter. "Can you put this on the table? We're almost finished."

Natalia, with the sleeves of her work button-down rolled up, doesn't bother to look up as she barks, "Put a plate beneath it first."

"I won't damage your precious table," I promise, and do as she says.

Addie is filling wine glasses when I enter, her apron now missing. She accepts the food from me as another knock sounds from the front door. I've never understood the phrase "her face lit up" before now. Addie is practically glowing as she rushes to let Maddy in, despite having seen her only a few hours ago at work.

The two of them used to live together before Addie moved in with Natalia, and I know she misses living with

Maddy. The two have always been inseparable, and while I'm glad Addie has Natalia, I can't help but worry about Maddy living alone in that apartment.

Not that she ever seems to spend her nights alone.

"You're just in time." Addie beams, leading Maddy into the dining room. "We're just finishing setting the table."

"Actually, you're late," I quip.

Maddy rolls her eyes, purposely ignoring my comment. She looks better than she did this morning, now dressed in light jeans and a pink sweater. Her eyes are bright as she spots one of the photos garnishing the dining room walls. "That print came out beautiful," she murmurs.

I can't help but agree. It's one of the newer photos Maddy shot, a portrait of Addie and Natalia from their engagement shoot. Natalia's face is buried in Addie's neck, her arms around her waist as she lifts her up, Addie's face pinched with laughter. Maddy captured the moment perfectly, the light casting a golden glow across our friends, her lens focusing on the joy written across their faces. She had laid in the muddy field on her side for the shot, then laughed at the stains that refused to leave her clothes afterwards.

"Food's up, fuckers!" Marco hollers, and the smack upside the head that Natalia delivers resounds into the next room.

"Mind your manners," she mutters.

Addie takes her hand as they enter the room, Marco still grinning with a wink to Maddy. She smiles at him, and the sight does a funny thing to my heart. Jealousy is quick to smother that light feeling. She's never once looked at me like that, not as I protected her throughout Addie's stalker ordeal, nor as I found her in their apartment, nor as I held her hand until her parents arrived at the hospital.

Maddy turns and catches my sidelong stare. Bashful, if she can ever be described as such, she dips her chin and takes her seat beside Addie.

Addie and Maddy slip out to the front porch while I volunteer to help clean up dinner. Marco almost escaped with them, but Natalia grabs him by his collar and hauls him over to the sink. It's only once the water is running that she starts talking.

"There's something you both need to know."

Marco and I exchange knowing glances and shift so we can have one eye on the door. If Natalia has waited for Addie to step out, then I know it is something bad. Both Addie and Mads know of our Mafia involvement, and while they don't know the more gruesome details, I know for sure that they've seen the blood on Natalia before, especially when the three of them lived together a few months ago.

"Two Barones guys were caught trying to intercept one of our shipments earlier today. It seemed petty at first, and I intended to send a message back to Malik, but as it would turn out, he was sending one to me."

"Any casualties?" I ask, my mouth dry.

Marco is equally pale beside me. While the bad blood in our family is between me and my brothers, I know they didn't take it lightly when my cousin left them to join me. This message they're sending could be for either of us.

Natalia shakes her head, setting the last of the silverware away, then leans back against the counter, bracing her elbows in a stance that is both casual and powerful. Her shoulders flex beneath her shirt, her features tense as she levels her stare at me. "'Word has reached Malik that the youngest Barone brother has been seen over the past few months favoring a blonde. Sources have identified her as Madeline Yapon, former roommate of Natalia Mancini's Addison Collins, and ex-girlfriend of serial killer Donovan Larson.'" Natalia recites the message from memory, and my blood runs cold. "'Malik has chosen not to act at this time, but has stated he has a vested interest in her future, as her ties may someday tangle with the Barone family.' He has... *advised* me to keep her in my sight."

"That's bullshit. Maddy can't stand me, and I'm only there to make sure she doesn't self-destruct after all the shit that went down."

It's a half truth, half lie. The truth is that Maddy can't stand me, the lie being my motives. I'm sure Maddy thinks I'm there purely for Addie's sake, that I can't bear to see my friend get hurt again. While that may be part of it, that's not the whole of it.

To be fair, I'm not one hundred percent certain of my own motives yet. It's almost as if there is a magnetic force pulling me to Maddy. Maybe some part of me that sees myself in her. I know what it's like to go through loss and choose to deteriorate instead of heal. Maybe that's all this is—me seeing history repeat itself with a new name and face, and I'm determined to change the ending for her.

Or maybe I'm lying to myself. Who cares.

Natalia doesn't look convinced, but relents. That character trait is something that makes her such a powerful leader. She knows how to read people, how to push them to where they need to be, but also when to let it drop. "We know that, but Malik doesn't. And be that as it may, we have to make our plan around what he thinks the truth is, versus what we *know* it is."

"He's only going to see what he wants to see," Marco agrees. "Not to offend you, but you don't have the best track record of keeping a woman around, and all your friends are within the group. Maddy is a new blip on an otherwise unblemished trend, and if he can, Malik is going to want to exploit it."

"So what can we do? I can stay away from her, try to send another message?"

"No." Natalia shakes her head. "That will just tell him that he's right in his assumptions and he'll double down on his efforts."

I open my mouth to respond, but I'm cut off by the loud pop of a firearm and a scream.

Maddy.

CHAPTER 3
MADDY

The swing on Addie's front porch might be my favorite part of her new house. The whole home screams Addie, with Natalia's sleek flair shining through in the little technical details. The porch swing is decorated with pastel throw pillows in every color, and Addie had snagged a blanket on the way out to fight against the chill.

"I've missed Natalia's cooking," I groan, my hands on my stomach. "And I definitely should not have worn jeans tonight."

"I have sweatpants upstairs you can borrow," Addie laughs. She does that a lot these days. She's always been a happy person, but now it's like an invisible thread tying her down has been cut. She is freer with her love, despite all she has gone through.

My head falls heavy against her shoulder, and she allows hers to rest atop mine. I've missed this—eating meals together, then talking afterwards, just us.

"How've you been?" she asks a shade gently.

"Good. I've been doing good," I lie easy enough. "You?"

"I'm fine. Don't worry about me."

How can I not? My heart cracks within my chest. Everything that happened to her is entirely my fault. I brought Donovan into our lives. I left her alone with him multiple times. I told him when we returned from Italy that fateful night when he'd had enough waiting. Addie almost died that night, and it was all my fault.

Addie doesn't see it that way—she isn't the type. If anything, she'd feel guilty that I think this way.

"Can I ask you a question?" I ask after a while.

"Always."

"How do you... *manage* what happened and sex?"

It's a question that has been on my mind for a while now. Most of the time, it's not a problem for me, then there are nights like last night where a hand drifts too close to my ribs or they try to kiss me and I sink into myself. Donovan's voice lingers in my mind, calling me a coward, worthless, disgusting.

The lights are always kept off.

Addie sits up, her face softening as she searches mine with her gaze. She blushes and tucks a curl behind her ear. We share everything together, but even after numerous stories, she still blushes each time.

"It was hard, at first," she admits. "There were times I could feel Don—*his* hands on me when they were Natalia's. But she got me through it. She stopped when I said stop, she was always gentle, and she never cared if I cried."

My face must show my anguish because Addie's lips quirk up in a mischievous smirk. "Plus, she said I could sit on her face and suffocate her if I felt threatened," she adds. "Can't attack someone if they're passed out."

I choke. "Of course she said that."

"Where is this coming from? Have you tried having a partner since?"

There's so much understanding in her eyes that I have to look away. She wouldn't care how many men I've slept with—she never has—but if she knew *why* I do it... She's been through so much already, there's no use burdening her with my baggage as well.

"One or two. It's been fine so far. I just worry about you."

Addie's shoulders slump as she looses a breath. "Well, if it's ever not fine, you can always talk to me."

"You too." I squeeze her hand and say genuinely, "I'm glad you have Natalia."

"And I'm glad I have you."

The breeze picks up and we burrow deeper into the blanket she brought. We will need to go in soon, but the chill is almost nice, in a twisted way. I can feel every nerve in my body, every hair on my arm raise with gooseflesh beneath my sweater. Inhaling, I let the crisp air caress my lungs, reminding me that I am alive. Urging me to *feel* alive.

Addie tucks her knees to her chest, looping her arms around them and humming something under her breath. Despite myself, I smile. This fleeting feeling isn't happiness, I know, but content.

Just as my eyes begin to flutter closed, I hear footsteps crunching on gravel. Addie's hand slides to behind one of the pillows, discreet and smooth, like it's a simple, natural motion.

A man stands at the foot of the porch, a brown package in his hands. He wears a delivery uniform and the tension in Addie's posture loosens at least a little.

"Can I help you?" she asks, her voice light. That hand shifts forward, back to her lap. Something cool brushes against my thigh and I recognize the weight in her hand beneath the blanket.

"I have a delivery here for a..." The delivery man takes a second to glance at the package label. "Maddy Yapon?"

"That's me," I say, "but I didn't order anything."

"She also doesn't live here. You must be mistaken," Addie says slowly, the warning lacing her tone evident.

The delivery man doesn't balk, but instead smiles. It's an eerie thing, a kind gesture with an undertone of violence. "Am I?"

"Walk away," Addie warns.

My gaze darts to the lit window, the shadows of Marco, Riven, and Natalia visible. If we scream for help, how fast can they get out here? Will it be fast enough? If we run, can we make it inside? Can we outrun a bullet?

"Oh, I forgot one thing." The man steps forward onto the porch, the creaking wood covering the click from under our blanket. "The package is from Malik."

Then he lunges, a glint of a knife whipping out from beneath the box, the tip poised towards my neck. I hardly have time to scramble backwards as Addie lifts her gun and fires.

CHAPTER 4
RIVEN

Natalia is the first out the door, her gun raised and her eyes darting immediately to Addie. Her fiancée's face is pale and her lips a grim line, but she nods. The gun in her hands still smokes, and she doesn't lower it, not until Natalia is at her side, fingers cupping her jaw.

Marco rushes to the man bleeding on the ground, his fingers flying to the man's neck. He shakes his head once. Dead. Addie nailed him right between his eyes.

"Are you okay?" Natalia asks, but Addie has turned to Maddy now, whose hands are covering her ears.

My feet carry me to her on my own accord, my hands covering hers. "What happened?" I ask at the same time Addie cries, "Oh my god, I'm so sorry. He came so fast. I didn't mean to shoot so close to your ear."

Maddy looks up, dazed. Her lips part, then close, then part again.

"Can you hear me?" I ask.

Her eyes shift to mine and she lowers her hands, while mine linger. "Out of my other ear." She grimaces before turning to Addie. "It's okay. Better to be temporarily deaf than to be dead." She toes the knife that has fallen close to her. It's a long, wicked thing, not your standard-issue switchblade or something an ordinary crook would use. This shit was near military-grade.

"Who the hell was that?" Addie asks, her gaze on Natalia.

My boss has her arms folded, her face highlighted with worry. She glances to where Marco stands over the body, his brows furrowed. Almost as if he recognizes the man, but cannot remember where from.

I squint. The face is familiar, but distant. Like I might have known him in passing years ago, but memory has stolen his name away.

Maddy rolls her eyes. "That depends. Which one of you pissed off someone named Malik?"

I can feel the blood drain from my face and Natalia swears.

Addie spins on her heel, her features a mask of horror. "I thought he said Alec," she breathes.

"No, I'm sure he said Malik." Maddy frowns. "Who is he?"

Marco murmurs something like a prayer, as if he finally recognizes the man bleeding onto Natalia and Addie's driveway. Natalia's face is murderous as she glares at me, tucking Addie into her side—an instinctual movement, something she's been doing for months, but does more now after Donovan.

I drop my hands to my side and ball them into fists. "Malik is my brother."

I sit at the kitchen table now, Addie and Natalia across from me with Maddy as still as stone at my side. Marco left to deal with the body after I finally recognized the man as one of the Barones' hitmen. He was the one to take over my position after my brother placed a hit out for me. I shared the bloody story with Maddy, whose stare is vacant, as if she is still trying to wrap her head around it.

"I don't understand. If Malik wants Riven dead, why is he sending people to kill *me*?"

I was inside, just a few feet away. It would have been just as easy to break down the door and take a swing at me as it was to try for Maddy.

"That's what we're trying to figure out," Natalia admits. Her hand hasn't left Addie's since we were attacked. This house is supposed to be a safe place for Addie, after all she went through. It's supposed to be a place where she could put what happened with Donovan behind her and move on. I can practically see Maddy's guilt swirling around her mind. She hunches in on herself, as if trying to be smaller. Invisible. If she can't see the pain, then it can't see her.

"How did they even get past your security? I thought you had Lucas at the gate?" I ask.

Being engaged to the head of the country's most successful security firm has its perks, such as the armed gate Natalia had installed once Addie moved in. One of our men always stands guard, and the rest of the property is protected by a bajillion security cameras. I'm almost positive that this place is more secure than anywhere else in the country.

And yet the Barones got in.

"Marco called on his way out. Lucas is dead." Natalia shakes her head. "I have backup coming, but I want you to look into it tomorrow. You're more familiar with them than I am."

Shame burns the back of my eyes and Maddy drops her gaze to her lap, as if she knows.

"It's been years."

"Still, you and Marco are our best bet. I'll arrange a meeting with Malik in the meantime, and let him know how unappreciated his move on my home is. I'll make sure he understands the consequences should he continue."

A chill snakes its way up my spine at the cool indifference in Natalia's voice. After knowing the woman for as long as I have, I've come to learn not to be afraid when she's angry. No, everyone should be afraid when the light behind those black eyes dies and her voice flattens.

I can hardly keep the panic from my voice as I speak. "He won't care, Nat. We had this talk with him years ago and he warned us—"

"Enough." Natalia's cool voice slices through his words, but Addie's head swivels towards her fiancée.

"He warned you what, love?"

"It's not important."

"Natalia." Addie's lovely face is stoic as she glares down at the other woman. "What did he say?"

Natalia holds her stare, then sighs. "He warned us that by taking Riven, we'd be delaying the inevitable. He will come for his revenge, and when he does, there will be no stopping him, and all the other usual pretentious bullshit. It's fine."

"It's *not* fine. We need to take him seriously," I argue.

"I told you years ago that if he wants a war, I will gladly wage one. The Barones are strong, but if they cross this line, there is no amount of blood I won't be willing to shed to stop them."

A Mafia war, like something out of my nightmares.

My gaze darts to Addie. If this happens, she will be a target—Malik's first target, perhaps. Even the strongest fortress has a weak point, and Natalia's is Addie. I can't let her go through this again, not as she's finally healing.

Maddy must be thinking the same thing because it's her lilting voice that breaks the silence. "Can we maybe put a pin in that and go back to the fact that someone just tried to *kill* me?"

"We've covered that point, Maddy." Natalia's voice is droll, and she fixes me with a hard stare.

Maddy flips her off under the table. "Clearly not, because we haven't considered why me. Riven was right through that door. If they wanted to start a war, they would've gone for him, or Addie, or literally anyone else. I am *nothing* to him."

I flinch, barely, but she continues as if she doesn't see.

"So why me, if not to send a message? Perhaps you should figure out what Malik thinks he knows before, oh, I don't know, launching into a war?"

I smirk. "That might be the smartest thing you've ever said, blondie."

"Fuck off."

"Fine." Natalia sighs and pinches her nose. "I'll need to have a word and send a message of my own, but we will deescalate the situation for now."

I frown. She's not going to tell Maddy what we know? It's a minor detail, Malik thinking we're together, but it feels like something she should know. No, it won't change the fact that he's targeting her to get to me, but the idea of leaving the detail out doesn't sit right with me. It feels dirty, like I'm lying to her.

I open my mouth, but Natalia silences me with a glare. She suddenly looks much older than her twenty-eight years of age. She has always been an imposing figure, but now, sitting at her table, her head falling into her hands, she seems so small.

Addie traces circles across her palm, her expression pained. "What about Mads?" she asks softly. "We can't let them hurt her."

"I'm fine. Really, I can handle myself." Maddy's hands are already raising in surrender when Natalia lifts her head and narrows her gaze on me.

"Before you argue, I know this is a bad idea, but my hands are tied. A lowly hitman just cut through one of my better men. You'll need to watch her. You'll have the best chance against one of them."

"Not arguing," I say in a tone that is admittedly very much argumentative, "but since they're targeting her because of me, isn't the smart move for me to stay as far the fuck away as possible?"

We might have had this discussion earlier, but I still don't feel like spending more time with Maddy will solve this problem. If I stay with her, she's still a target and he'll know I'm trying to protect her. But if I leave her alone, then Malik will see through the act and come after her while she's alone, much to Natalia's point. It's a lose-lose situation.

Maddy nods. "I second that." A rare agreement between us.

"Again, they're coming after her anyway, so just be a bodyguard. You did that for months for her and Addie during the stalker situation. You can do it for a few weeks while I sort this shit out."

"And if you can't stop this?" I don't mean to let the mask fall, to reveal the bloody wounds I hide beneath my charms. I snap it back on as Maddy peers at me, and I raise a brow, my voice now laced with mirth. "How many do you want me to kill?"

Natalia's laughter is a dark rumble in the room. "As many as you can."

CHAPTER 5
MADDY

I knew Riven wasn't on good terms with his brothers—he himself told me as much, only for Addie and Natalia to constantly reiterate it—but this?

I've known for months now about Natalia's Mafia involvement. Addie confessed it to me in a teary panic after stumbling into one of Natalia's meetings. Maybe it was simply that I hadn't had a chance to process this bomb of information, but I never truly thought about what being in the Mafia would entail. Addie was hysterical, and not long after that, we were attacked, and I guess I simply never let myself think about it. Natalia is still the woman my best friend fell in love with, and perhaps the one person who loves her just as much as I do. And Riven is still a pain in my ass—nothing changed there.

I knew they were Mafia. I knew that their lives are shrouded with danger. I knew that it would catch up to us eventually. I knew, I knew, I knew, I try to remind myself, sitting in the front seat of Riven's car.

I took a cab here, but after the attempt on my life, Natalia deemed it unsafe to use public transportation again any time soon. So here I am, staring out a darkened window as trees slowly blur into city lights.

Riven says nothing, his knuckles white on the steering wheel. I shiver. Without glancing my way, his hand stretches out, turning up the heat in the car until the window fogs. The chill remains in my bones.

I came so close to death again. It was right in front of my face, and I was useless against it. If Addie hadn't been there... Well, I wouldn't have been outside without her anyway, so it's not the best idea to dwell on the what ifs.

"Are you okay?" Riven finally asks. His voice is thick and does nothing to slice through the tension in the air. It's the closest to sympathy I've ever heard from him, so different from his usual unflinching judgment.

"As good as I can be after cheating death again," I quip. "Maybe I can't be killed or something."

"Don't say that."

"Who knows, third time's the charm." The joke is dark, even for me, and I ball my fists to keep them from shaking.

Riven doesn't respond and silence falls heavy between us again.

I wish he'd say something, even if he just yelled at me. Anything would be better than this. I'm not used to this quieter side of him, different from the cool irritation he usually displays in my presence.

My phone lights up with a text message, catching my eye. It flashes like the knife the assassin held as he aimed for my throat, and suddenly, I'm in a different dark space, another man with me. Donovan's boot is in my ribs, my hands useless as I try to pry his fingers from my throat. I can't breathe. I can't breathe. I can't—

"Maddy." Riven's voice is sharp, and I jump.

My apartment. We're at my apartment, parked just outside the entrance. Maurice sits behind the front desk, his eyes slanted as he stares at his computer screen. A younger man walks past, his toddler holding his hand, tottering by his side. The sky is still dark, but the street is well illuminated with the pale yellow and white lights of the city.

"Thanks for the ride." My face flushes and I fumble with the seatbelt. Of all the places to have a panic attack, this is not it.

"Maddy—"

"I'll see you around." I open the car door, the lock clicking as it unlocks. The cold air whips my face and blows my hair back. Good, the sting is good.

"Let me walk you up," Riven argues. He's already moving to remove his seatbelt when I hold my hands up.

"The front door is five feet away. If someone manages to pick me off that close to home with you right here, then I'd say they've earned the kill."

I close the door before he can respond, walking quicker than usual. Maurice smiles and waves, and I wave back, a bit warmer than last time. I listen for a moment, and when I don't hear the sound of Riven following me, I head to my apartment.

The snick of my door closing behind me is almost a relief—*almost*, as I look around the darkened room. The place is spacious, far nicer than I could afford otherwise. It's large, but it's empty.

Setting my phone on the kitchen counter, I let myself wander in the dark, my bed calling my name. Work was brutal today, and even my charm couldn't soften the grating of Daryl's voice. The older man must have had the world's biggest stick shoved up his ass last night with the way he bitched all day.

Still, it's good to keep busy. Being busy means there's no time for memories to creep back in. No room for panic or thoughts.

The bed creaks as I throw myself down, rolling onto my back among the pink throw pillows. My bedding was one of the only things left salvageable after Donovan's attack.

I close my eyes.
Don't think about it.
Don't think about him.

I'm exhausted after the long flight back from Italy. Riven and Natalia just dropped us off, and Marco is stationed at the door. Addie is right across the hall, yet my eyes refuse to close. I count the lumps on the ceiling, and when that doesn't work, I try to judge which is the biggest, when something hits the wall in the hall outside.

I'm on my feet padding into the living room as the front door creaks open. I don't bother with the light or any weaponry. Marco is the only one outside the door, so he must be the one coming in. He must—he's Mafia, and one of Natalia's best men. We're safe.

"Marco?"

A slight odor leaks into the room as the door opens, and my eyes widen.

"What are you doing here?" I whisper as Donovan, my boyfriend of years, pushes open the door. He's in all black, a

look I've yet to see him wear, and wearing gloves. My eyes zero in on the knife at his hip. He doesn't brandish it.

"You were supposed to be asleep," is all he says before he lunges.

It all clicks too late—the way Addie's stalker had access to her schedule, knew when I was home and wasn't, how he got in without having to break the lock in the past.

I leap to the side, but it's not fast enough. Donovan's body slams into mine, sending my head careening into the corner of our living room table. Stars swim in front of my vision, but I won't let the darkness claim me. I grapple for his arms, my fingernails digging into his skin. Donovan pulls back, his face unrecognizable as he gets to his feet. I'm on my knees when the first kick lands against my stomach, sending me sprawling back to the floor. The next series of hits break bone, my breath rattling as my lungs try to inflate with my fracturing ribs splintering into them.

"All this time," I wheeze, "it was you!"

As if a cord has snapped, Donovan lunges, no longer content to bloody me with his boots. Instead, he leans over me, wrapping his fingers around my throat.

"You should've been my first kill, you worthless bitch," he whispers, right as Addie's door opens.

I'm vaguely aware of Addie screaming—I might be screaming with her—as Donovan is ripped off of me. Black dances across my vision. Stay awake, *I command myself.* Stay awake. *My lungs can't get enough air in. My body is shutting down in waves of pain. The next thing I remember is Natalia's voice, then Riven's face and—*

My eyes shoot open. The bedroom is too dark, the apartment too empty. My breathing comes in quick spurts, my hands immediately flying to my side where I feel each mended rib.

It's been a while since I remembered the full night. Usually, my flashbacks come in spurts.

The attack, I tell myself. *The attack must have set it off. There's no danger. You're safe.*

But I told myself I was safe then too.

Flicking the lights on does nothing to chase away the lingering panic. I left my phone in the other room like an idiot. *God.* I will my legs to move, and after a few moments, they do. I stumble into the kitchen, bringing a wave of light in my wake as I flick on every switch in the apartment.

My phone shakes in my hand as I type in the passcode. I read Addie's text first, the one that buzzed in the car.

ADDIE:

Text me when you're home safe!

Well fuck, I already failed at that.

All good. Thanks for dinner.

And everything else.

Always. Good night :)

I stall before reading Riven's messages, already knowing what I'll find.

RIVEN:

Did you get to your apartment alive?

> Blondie.

> If you don't answer, I will literally have to break your door down.

I roll my eyes.

> Leave my doors out of this. I'm in my apartment, very much alive.

No response to that, but a small checkmark appears to let me know he's read the message. I allow myself to click off of his name. My fingers hover over the screen and I pause. This is a bad idea—it always is—but what's one more to add to the long list of fuck ups I've made?

I scroll until I find an old name, one I haven't messaged in a while. I hit send, and receive a reply within a few seconds. *Come over.*

Disgust crawls up my throat but I still slip my shoes on. This is better than staying here alone, or calling Addie and worrying her more. God knows my parents wouldn't be particularly sympathetic to receive a call this late at night either.

The door clicks shut, and I wave to Maurice again as I head out. Something like pity flashes across his face and I grit my teeth. There's nothing left to pity in my heart.

My choice of the night opens the door after the second knock, even though I could see his shadowed feet beneath the door the moment I arrived. It's usually the same dance. I knock once and they wait to answer, as if giving off the illusion that they haven't been waiting. Then they open the door by the second so that I don't get impatient and leave before knocking a third time.

Brandon is a tall, lanky guy I matched with on a dating app a few months ago, right after the nightmares started. He's not terrible, just not exactly my type. Both times I've seen him, he's been dressed like he's in a frat, despite being out of college for years now. The first time we met, we didn't sleep together—well, more specifically, I did something for him and he did nothing for me. I didn't mind too much. Even if the sex was bad, at least I could spend the night focusing on how bad it is, rather than my memories.

"Come inside," he says in what he thinks is a seductive voice.

I oblige, refusing when he offers me something to drink.

This is perhaps my least favorite part of the night—the few minutes they spend awkwardly trying to be a good host while the only thing they want from me is my body. I can't say I'm in any position to judge, but I still let myself disassociate until my bare back hits his mattress. He doesn't have a headboard, and I have to crane my neck to stop from myself from bashing my skull against his wall.

I turn my gaze to his ceiling as Brandon climbs over me. Good, if he's on top, I can let my mind drift into nowhere. Just as I'm teetering on the edge of slipping away, he grabs my hips and thrusts into me, hard and without warning.

I leap up with a yelp, and he scrambles back with wide eyes.

"What's wrong?"

"I'm sorry," I huff, not actually feeling very sorry at all, "but have you ever had sex before?"

He looks taken aback by this, then his face blushes furiously. "Of course I have. This is how women like being fucked."

Oh my god.

I'm already off the bed, grabbing my clothes and pulling them on when my phone buzzes. Riven's face flashes back at me.

RIVEN:

Where the fuck are you?

I'm at your apartment, and guess where you aren't.

I am this close to having Natalia track your phone.

The first message was over ten minutes ago. I quickly type in the address as I finish zipping up my jeans and hit send.

"Who's that?" Brandon asks, still naked and standing with his arms crossed as if pouting.

"My ride."

Dear god, I wish I had worn something other than jeans as I take a few sore steps towards the door. I take back what I said earlier about bad sex being just fine.

"Don't be like that," he whines again, this time reaching for my arm.

I snatch it back, opening the front door to his apartment right as I see headlights turning into the parking lot. Riven slams his car door, already stalking for the stairs. A sigh slips from my lips and tension I didn't know I was holding onto suddenly releases.

"Sex isn't just sticking your dick in something. Stay away from women until you learn that."

I wish I had my camera, if just to snap a quick picture of the man's utterly gobsmacked face. It's pale and borderline green in the dingy apartment hall lighting, and I think that's a vein about to pop in his forehead.

Slamming his door in his face, I turn to find myself facing an absolutely murderous Riven.

CHAPTER 6
RIVEN

I shouldn't have left Maddy alone. It's been the one thought on my mind since I watched her blonde head disappear around the corner of her apartment lobby. I texted her, and of course, she took her sweet time responding. She probably thinks I was joking about breaking her door in. I wasn't. I was about halfway back to the apartment when she responded.

I sit in the parking lot of my own apartment complex now, the car turned off, my head resting against the steering wheel. This is stupid. I've been sitting here for ten minutes, waiting for what? A text? A call? *Come back*?

Don't be a fucking idiot, I think as I groan. Maddy is as stubbornly independent as they come, and I sure as hell am the last person she wants to talk to after the shit I've pulled her into.

A hitman.

My brother sent a goddamn hitman after her.

Malik has always been bold, conniving. He had to be, as the oldest of three brothers. Being the eldest didn't guarantee him the Barone throne, as we learned. He had to manipulate at every turn to get what he wanted, something that in the end turned my father away from him.

My father didn't refuse to hand Malik the title because he found the manipulation morally corrupt. No, he just didn't like that Malik had tried to use it against him.

Cas, the middle brother, was never smart enough to lead. He's the type to run in to a situation headfirst, meaning he uses his skull and not the brain in it. He's the perfect second to Malik, never questioning, and always following our brother blindly.

Where Natalia wants someone to challenge her, someone who is near her equal as a second, Malik wants pure submission, even when he's wrong. It's one of his main weaknesses that I know Natalia plans to exploit. Where she has me to call her on her bullshit, Malik has no one, and he hates that she refuses to bow to him. She is a woman, and to him, that's enough cause for her to be subservient. What followed next was a bloodbath.

Women are simply tools to my brother—tools for power, for prestige, and breeding. Disgusting piece of shit. My brother is ruthlessness in its basest form.

And now he has his eyes set on Maddy.

But what I can't figure out is why her? To any outsider, Addie would be a better target—the woman has practically become another sister to me. Natalia would be ideal if Malik's goal was to hurt me, but he'd have to get close enough to her for that. To an outside eye, it should look like my time spent with Maddy is simply me checking on a loose end, Addie's best friend. Hell, it's what Maddy herself thinks. She doesn't realize that half the time, Addie never calls me to check on her, that all of that is a lie. She doesn't realize the power she has over me, the magnetic pull that tethers me to her side.

Maybe it's because I feel guilty. I wasn't the kindest to her when we met. When she was being a good friend, trying to hold me accountable in protecting her best friend, I got snippy. I wasn't used to being bossed about by people, aside from Natalia. Every time she double-checked that I had done my job right, I felt like she was disregarding my authority. Now I know she was simply a woman terrified at the prospect of losing the most important person in the world to her. If I was in her shoes, I would have been so much worse.

She isn't exactly kind to me either, but I can't say I've ever deserved her kindness. She shines it on everyone, it seems—everyone but me. She's never had a shortened list of admirers either. She and Addie used to go dancing a lot, with me, Natalia, and Marco coming for protection. Every time I turned, it seemed like she had a new partner. Even at Natalia's gala a few months ago, she never lacked a dance partner. It made me... furious. I still don't know why, but something hot slithered up my throat every time I saw her dancing with them.

Fuck it.

I turn my car back on, reversing and heading back to her apartment. I'm there in a few minutes, knocking tentatively on the door. She's going to laugh at me for it when she opens up.

No response.

Not bothering to knock a second time, I slip the spare key from its hiding spot—she' s not very creative and we will have to fix that when we get back—and unlock the door. The lights are off. I check her living room, her kitchen, her bedroom. No Maddy.

My hand flies to my phone and I type furiously.

> Where the fuck are you
>
> I'm at your apartment, and guess where you aren't.
>
> I am this close to having Natalia track your phone.

No response.

Fucking hell.

I dial Natalia's number, cursing silently. This call is going to bring about a million questions.

Natalia's voice is muddled with sleep when she answers, and I already know if this isn't a goddamn emergency then I'm not seeing tomorrow. "You have thirty seconds."

"I need Maddy's phone tracked. She's not answering and she's not home."

There's a shuffling sound in the background and the rumple of sheets. I can hear Addie murmur and ask who it is. Natalia soothes her and types at the same time, when suddenly, my phone vibrates.

"Never mind. She just sent me the address."

Without a goodbye, I hang up, ready to have my balls nailed to the wall tomorrow at work. Some days, I wish I had a normal job. Those days surprisingly aren't when there's bullets whizzing towards me, but when shit like this happens.

I plug in the address and speed towards it. I'm out of my car and up the stairs just in time to see Maddy in front of this guy's apartment, that unidentified murderous feeling creeping up my throat again. She yells something about staying the fuck away from women before slamming the door in his face, and I might have laughed if I wasn't fucking furious.

She looks like a startled animal when she spins, coming face to face with my poorly concealed rage.

"Get in the car. Now."

We say nothing on the short drive back to her apartment. She didn't say anything when I found her in the hallway, and she doesn't look like she is going to say anything now.

We pull into the parking lot behind the apartment complex. This one is usually reserved for people who live here, but Natalia gave me a gate key the same day she gave Maddy hers. Once parked, she reaches for the door handle, only for me to click the lock button.

"I can just hit unlock on my door, you know." She points out the obvious, and I fix my furious stare on her face.

"How did you get there?"

"I walked."

"Jesus fuck, Maddy."

She slouches down in her seat, as if hoping that the leather will swallow her. She oddly looks like a child being scolded at the moment.

"Do you even hear how stupid that is? Someone tried to kill you hours ago. They were *sent* to kill you, at that, and you walked through the city in the middle of the night for what? Shitty dick?"

Her face burns under my scrutinizing glare. She looks humiliated, but I can't find it in myself to care. Okay, maybe I care a bit, but not enough to stave off the anger I feel.

"Don't you dare slut-shame me," she hisses. Forcing her own stinging gaze to meet mine, she lifts her chin as she seethes.

"That's what you think this is?"

"What is it then, if not that?"

"You scared the shit out of me. Imagine after everything that's happened, I come to your apartment and you're not there. What am I supposed to think?"

"What are you supposed to think?" she rages. "Why the fuck did you even come to my apartment?"

"Because I was worried about you. Is that so fucking awful?" I roar, every muscle in my body stiffening. "Is it so terrible to think that I might actually care what happens to you, while you don't seem to give a shit?"

She flinches—actually fucking flinches—and I pause.

Without another word, I unlock the door. She steps out, silently walking to the staircase. I follow her, and we say nothing, not until we are inside, the doors locked and the lights on. Here, I can see her face. I can read her, know when I'm pushing too far or just being a plain dick.

"Why do you do it?" I ask, borderline begging.

I need to know. I can't understand it, but I want to. She could have anyone in this city, and she settles for someone new every time. Not that I think that's a problem—she can fuck whoever she wants, even if the thought fills me with such unbridled rage I see red.

"That's none of your business."

"Why?"

She explodes, tears streaming down her face. "I can't handle it—the empty apartment, the nightmares, being alone with nothing but the memory of how it felt to almost die, and the terror of knowing Addie was next. If I'm not alone—and don't even *think* about telling me to talk to Addie—then I don't have time to think about it."

"Then why do you always go to them? Do you know how dangerous that is?" I press, not relenting.

"Because," she breathes, trying to calm herself, "I don't want men to know where I live, or to be in my apartment after what happened."

There it is—the truth behind the mask. My devastation must show on my face because she dips her chin, fucking hiding from me again. I should have known better. I shouldn't have pushed. I saw the bodies and what Donovan did to those other girls. I saw what he did to her. I have nightmares about it still, but to live in that moment constantly? It must be excruciating.

Then there's the last thing she said, about not wanting men in her apartment.

"You don't get anxious when I'm with you?" I say carefully. "Right?"

She exhales softly, the smallest of smiles lighting on her lips. "No." Then, "Besides, you're not a romantic prospect. Not a threat."

I hate the way those words leave her lips. I know when she says I'm not a threat I should be relieved, but I know the threat she's referring to isn't violence. There is no threat of us ever ending up together. I hold no sway over her that way. It's a truth I've always known, but I can't deny the sting.

"I'll take the couch then." I clear my throat, attempting to dispel some of the sourness that has cast itself over the room. "I learned my lesson leaving you alone last time."

Maddy half laughs at that, already walking towards her bedroom. "I guess you did." Then, "Good night."

"Good night."

I sprawl out across her couch, my arms tucked under my head as I try to bite back against the foul taste in my mouth. Even after her bedroom lights click off and I know she's asleep, her words echo in my head as if she is still saying them.

Not a threat. Not a threat.
Not a threat.

CHAPTER 7
MADDY

The green dress lands softly on my bed, draping across the edge of it. The coat hanger that used to hold it clatters a few feet away, my aim haphazard at best. My hip pops to the side, my hands resting on them as I glare at my closet. All these beautiful dresses and yet none of them fit the gallery venue's dress code.

I've been invited to an art gallery this weekend, showcasing the best pieces from the past year. None of my works are to be displayed, but I've been invited, nonetheless, and plan to use it as a networking event.

I've been to the venue once before, the Illustria, a modern building that doubles as both a wedding hall and an art gallery. I learned my mistake then, being the only one terribly underdressed. If the invite says business casual, they mean cocktail, and if it says cocktail, they mean black tie. This time, the invite reads cocktail attire in swirling font. The only thing I have close to black tie is the dress I wore to Natalia's company gala, but the draping pink gown might be too whimsical for such an event.

Fuck it, there's a mall nearby and it's my day off. Sure, I'm not supposed to go anywhere without a heavily armed chaperone, but I'll just call Addie and figure something out. Yeah, that can work.

Addie answers on the first ring, her voice breathless. "Hello?"

"Hey, are you busy today?" I explain the situation quickly, but can already tell by the pause before she answers that she's busy.

"Natalia and I have plans today, but take Marco with you." A pause, then, "Shit, no he's busy. Why don't you call Riven?"

My nose crinkles. "I would rather not go shopping with Barone, thank you. I'll go by myself."

"No, you won't. Call Riven or I will."

"Doesn't Natalia have anyone else? Maybe a woman?"

"No one she can trust." I can hear the exhaustion in her voice. I know she can't believe we have to do this whole bodyguard thing again. "Everyone is stressing out right now. Just take Riven. Please."

I sigh, giving her a small agreement before hanging up and dialing the number I know by heart now.

"Girls' day?" Riven smirks, leaning against my doorframe half an hour later. His sunglasses rest atop his head, pushing his hair back. Small black curls pop out behind the frames, and I fight the urge to reach out and twist one around my finger.

Freezing Hell

"Yes, ladies first." I motion for him to lead the way.

Unperturbed, Riven stalks down the hallway first, waiting for me to lock the door, then leads the way to a motorcycle parked out front.

"We are going shopping. What part of that makes you think a motorcycle would be a good method of transportation?"

Riven chuckles, low and dark, and passes a helmet my way. "Most women would be begging me to take them for a ride."

"Gag."

"Jealous?"

"You wish. Just wondering where I'll put a dress—you know, the whole reason for this trip?"

When I don't take the helmet right away, Riven stalks forward, placing it on my head himself. His gaze is scrutinizing as he checks the fit, his breath fogging the visor. I try to ignore how close his face is to mine, and blame the pink haze coating my cheeks on the heat of the helmet.

The visor lifts up, Riven's hands braced on either side of the helmet. His smile has the butterflies in my stomach doing backflips.

"There's that pretty face." He grabs his own helmet, securing it on his head before mounting the bike in one fluid motion. He pats the seat behind him. "There's storage in the seat. Come on."

I'd never ridden on a motorcycle before. A guy I dated in high school had a moped, but that was nowhere near as cool as the sleek machine before me. Riven waits patiently, his arms crossed over his chest in a way that makes his arms bulge beneath his black short sleeves. I can sense the challenging smirk beneath his helmet, daring me to admit my nerves. Fuck that.

Practically stomping to the bike, I toss my leg over the seat, albeit clunkier than his movements were, and lean forward until my chest brushes against his back. My arms wrap around his middle, and I notice with no small amount of satisfaction the way the hard muscle beneath stiffens at my touch.

"I swear to god, Barone, if this is just an excuse to feel my tits, I will kill you."

"Damn, you got me."

Before I can fire back a retort, the engine roars to life and we peel off down the road. I fly back with a small yelp, but Riven's hand immediately lands on my waist and tugs me forward. My slew of curses are lost to the wind as I tighten my grip around his torso. Riven's laughter rumbles through his core as if he can hear me.

About halfway into the drive, I loosen my grip, watching the other cars zip by in a blur of muted colors. I should have closed the visor before we started, but if I reach up to adjust it now, I'll slip off the edge. I'd rather not be a smudge on the road, so I settle for closing my eyes.

Riven taps my thigh with two fingers once we've stopped, my ears still roaring and eyes squeezed shut. When they open, I'm faced with the local mall, and Riven's amused glance.

Righting myself, I swing my leg over to dismount, stumbling only slightly. The ground feels like it is still moving beneath me, like stepping off of a boat for the first time.

Riven accepts my helmet, placing it back in its

rightful spot, then nods towards the looming before us. "Lead the way, Blondie."

Dressing rooms are the bane of my existence. I've never stepped into one where I didn't immediately cringe away from my reflection, even before Donovan. It's almost as if shop owners asked engineers for lightbulbs specifically designed to illuminate your every insecurity. At least one of the lightbulbs in this room is out, leaving me mostly in the dark.

This is the third store Riven and I have been to, a smaller shop tucked into the back of the mall. The other two stores were a bust, but Riven doesn't seem to mind. Nor does he seem to notice all the attention he's been garnering.

Every corner we turn, he has a new gawker—women turning to whisper to their friends, men studying him as if trying to figure out how to replicate whatever aura is drawing people to him. *He's unfairly hot, sorry*, I wanted to say.

Still, he said nothing of any of it, and followed me to each store like a loyal puppy. He sits outside the door now as I try on a final dress, a deep-red gown with a draping neckline and thin straps. I don't wear much red, and only grabbed it off the rack as an afterthought, but now that I've tried it on, I realize it fits better than anything I've tried yet. The bodice is the right amount of modest for the event, yet teasing enough not to age me. Getting the zipper up by myself was the only struggle, but I managed.

I check the price tag and mentally pat myself on the

back. Of course I'd manage to find the perfect dress while it's on sale.

Reaching my hand around to fumble with the zipper, I tug. Then tug again. And again. The zipper refuses to budge.

An awkward turn to look in the mirror reveals the zipper snagged in the thread, the teeth holding the red fabric hostage.

Okay, let's not panic. There are options in these situations. This is fine.

I try to pull the dress over my head first, but stop once it's halfway up my stomach. In no world will this beautiful fitted-waist ever slide over my chest without tearing. Curse you, universe, for gifting me with a well-endowed chest.

I try the zipper again, and after it yields the same result, I peek my head out of the door.

Riven sits with one leg crossed over his knee, engrossed in something on his phone. His head lifts when he hears the door creak open, and raises a brow. "Another bust?" he asks.

"Not exactly," I draw out with a wince. "I'm stuck."

Realization dawns on his face, and while I expect him to respond with a snide remark, I'm met with nothing but silence. He waves, motioning for me to step back from the door and slides in with me, closing it behind me.

With the door shut, the dressing room feels smaller, Riven's imposing presence filling the space to the point of intimacy. His back brushes the mirror, and mine the wall behind it, until we are standing chest to chest.

Riven glances down at me as like a dying man spotting an angel. Each look peels back every wall I've constructed until it's just me in my rawest form, vulnerable before him.

His hand alights on my waist, gentle, as if he's holding glass. "Turn around."

I do as he says, forcing myself to take small, even breaths. At the first graze of his hand against my back, I jump, and he pulls back immediately.

"You have cold fingers," I lie.

He scoffs, then his touch returns, leaving a scorching trail across each vertebra of my spine. In the mirror, I can see him focusing, his dark eyes narrowed and face pulled in concentration. I stare down at the ground, my face flushing red.

Riven's fingers make deft work of the fabric, carefully plucking at each thread that had gotten stuck in the zipper until the garment falls loose. My arms snap across my chest, catching the material right before it can embarrass me any further.

"Careful," I hiss.

"Sweetheart, if I see something I've never seen before, I'll throw a dollar at it."

"Asshole."

"Don't wear it out."

I don't need to look to know he is smirking. Asshole. Bastard. Prick, and every vile name under the sun.

"You can go now," I bite out again. I hold the dress tight against my chest, but I can still feel Riven's knuckles brushing ever so gently across my shoulder blades.

"You sure you don't need more help?"

The husky timbre of his voice sets my every nerve on edge and I find myself looking up into the mirror. Our gaze meets through the glass, the tension thick enough to shatter it. Riven's hand trails lower, to the small of my spine, and I turn to face him. That hand never moves. It stays, his fingers now splayed across my bare skin, his body mere millimeters from mine. He steps even closer, one of his legs slipping between mine as my back presses softly against the mirror.

I should say something to stop this. I should push him away, before he gets too close.

But I don't.

Riven's gaze is devastating. I've never been so close to his face before, never had the chance to see the tiny flecks of gold dancing amongst the darkness of his eyes.

He leans closer, his breath skittering across my lips like a caress. "Can I—"

"Hey!" A shrill voice comes from the other side of the door, accompanied by frenzied knocking. "I told you kids no funny business in the dressing room!"

Riven raises an eyebrow and mouths, "Funny business?"

My hand flies up to stifle my laughter as Riven disentangles himself from me then opens the door. The employee on the other side, a middle-aged woman with dark hair, still has her hand raised mid-knock when he steps out.

"No funny business, I promise," he says with a wink. "My girlfriend's zipper got stuck."

I do my best to ignore the way my heart flips at the word girlfriend. *It's because he's hot, Maddy. No other reason*, I try to reason with the treacherous organ doing gymnastics in my chest.

"I'm going to get changed, then I'll be out."

"Take your time."

I smile, face still flushed.

The employee's cheeks are painted the same pink as mine as Riven turns his charm to her next, apologizing again. She's quick to wave it off, and he turns to look back over his shoulder before I can shut the door.

"And Blondie?"

"Hm?"

"You should get that dress."

After I bought my dress, despite Riven's sneaky attempt to pay, we settle on lunch at the food court. I allow him to pay for my food this time, which he takes no small amount of delight in.

I've never met someone so happy to spend their money on someone else, but men are strange creatures.

Seeing Riven now, reclined in his chair wearing casual clothes and eating a burger, that might be the strangest thing of all. Riven has never been as formal as Natalia, and on occasion, I've seen him without a suit, but never wearing something as mundane as jeans. It suits him, and I'm not the only one to notice.

"Twenty-seven," I say, then take a long sip from my drink. "And that's just since we entered the food court."

"There's not even twenty-seven women here, let alone twenty-seven staring at me."

"Okay, first off, most of the people here are women, and second, oh my god, you are so blind."

Riven shrugs. "Why would I need to look at the women around me when the most beautiful one is right in front of me?" Then with a devilish grin, "You have ketchup on your chin."

"Oh, fuck off."

I wipe my chin anyway, just to be sure he's lying. He isn't.

I swear again under my breath, and Riven laughs, a full-body laugh that has him leaning back in his chair. He left his sunglasses back with his motorcycle, but his hair still stays pushed back, but for a single curl falling over his eye. He is easily the most beautiful man I've ever seen, and effortlessly so.

Riven reaches across the table and snags one of my chicken nuggets, the very ones he teased me for ordering, and pops it into his mouth with a grin. I swat his hand away when he comes back for seconds.

"What did you need the dress for, by the way?"

"There's a gallery showing coming up in a few weeks."

"For what?"

"Rich people? I don't know. None of my work is being displayed, but it's good for networking."

Riven frowns at that, but I'm not concerned. Events like these happen all the time, but I haven't been to one of this caliber since everything happened. Donovan used to be my plus-one to these things. He knew the right things to say, how to dress. In the end, he was the one making connections, but at least he was there.

"Do you want to come?"

Riven's knee hits the table with a heavy thud. "What?"

"I need a plus-one, and I can't exactly bring a hookup to a business event."

"I just thought you'd ask Marco or Addie."

Yup, that is suspicion lining his voice. Dear god, he couldn't make this easy, could he?

"Last I checked, Natalia told *you* to be my bodyguard. Besides, I've been informed that Marco is busy and the whole country knows Addie is with Natalia so she'd have no reason to be there with me."

"Fair enough." Then he adds with a sly grin, "Ask me properly."

Oh, fuck me.

I grab my final chicken nugget and extend it across the table halfway between us.

"Riven Barone. Will you do me the honor of accompanying me to a shitty work event?" Sarcasm practically drips from my voice, but Riven's smile only grows as he accepts the peace offering.

"Blondie, I'd be honored."

"You keep calling me that," I say, crossing my arms with a huff. "I have a name, you know."

"And now you have a nickname. Come on, Let's go."

He reaches down beside me, his hand brushing against my waist, as he picks up my bag. Involuntarily, the corners of my lips turn upwards, just enough for him to notice. His gaze is soft, softer than I've ever seen it, as we walk out of the food court.

My shoulders slowly drop as I walk beside him in comfortable silence. Today felt normal, good even, perhaps for the first time in a long while. I'm not foolish enough to think that all my damage has been unwound, or that this could ever be a thing. But if I'm honest with myself for even just a second...

In another life, I would have liked to have met Riven again. A life where he finds me first, before Donovan, and the mess of things that happened this summer. Maybe I could find him before his brothers and all the wounds they inflicted upon him. I could see us being happy then. Not now, but maybe in some alternate universe things work out that way.

Someone walks a little too close to my heels. When I turn my head, I catch sight of a girl, maybe a year or two younger than me. She's blushing, her phone in her hands.

Nope.

Nope, nope, nope.

Not on my one normal day.

Without thinking, I place my hand in Riven's, interlacing our fingers. For a moment, I am struck by how much larger his hand is than mine. His calluses scrape against my palm, but the hold is comfortable.

I hear the footsteps behind me stop, then continue away from us.

Riven huffs, and it almost sounds like laughter.

I move to remove my hand, but Riven's fingers curl around it, holding it in place. He says nothing, just stares ahead as I look up at him, the faintest smile on his lips. I find myself smiling too, and hold his hand the entire way back to the parking lot.

CHAPTER 8
MADDY

I hate working the night shift. Not because of the new threat of death looming over my head, but because of the sheer wall of boredom that I run face-first into every shift. During the day, there's enough business that I keep busy and entertained, but at night, there is no one but college students studying. Tella's has always been popular, thanks to a small university just down the road, but during the night, it's a breeding ground for blurry eyes, failed midterms, and red pens.

I got my degree online, using the money I made from tips during my first few years in the city. I'm no stranger to the feel of these wooden tables and cheap booths at the late hours of the night.

Usually I don't take the night shift, but Liam has to take the ACT tomorrow and begged me over the phone to cover his shift. Daryl only ever has one person on staff at night, so of course my boredom is coupled with loneliness. A deadly combo.

Marco dropped me off earlier, promising that Riven would pick me up and that Natalia has people monitoring this block. I waved him off with a gesture that can only be described as flippant.

Now I count the seconds on the clock backwards to pass time. Slowly, the hours blur together, and the last student leaves. Only ten minutes until midnight.

My shoulders pop as I yawn and stretch my arms above my head, my back curling like a cat. The only good news about all of this is that I don't have work tomorrow —that, and I'm tired enough that I might actually be able to sleep tonight.

I haven't met up with any of my nighttime calls since Riven picked me up from Brandon's apartment. Every time I reach for the phone, I see his stare and the murder written across his face. Not that I need his approval for who I sleep with and when, but I find myself caring more than I'd like.

So instead of distracting myself with my usual antics, I take to doom-scrolling on social media, trying to use the blue light to hypnotize my brain to sleep. It hasn't been working.

Then again, neither does yoga, painting, meditation, melatonin... or anything.

Hanging up my apron and clicking the lock into place on the front and back doors, I find myself sitting on the dark curb behind Tella's. I thought after everything that happened, I would be terrified of the dark. Sure, there are times it catches me off guard, but mostly I've come to a realization—even though I can't see threats in the dark, they also can't see me. The darkness is like a shelter.

A shelter similar to Riven.

Addie had a breakdown when she found out about

Natalia and her Mafia involvement. They had to work to overcome it, and Addie had to learn to love her violence.

Riven's violence has always felt like protection to me. His hands and past are bloody, and maybe a darker part of my heart yearns for that. It knows how far he'll go for those he loves. It sees how little his kills matter to him if it means saving one of his people. It wants him to do that for me.

Maybe I'm just fucked in the head, but I can't help but wonder what would have happened had Riven been the one on the porch with me that night. Would he have simply shot my assassin to get me out of danger as soon as possible, like Addie did?

No.

Riven would have taken his time with the death. He would have made that man *suffer*.

Footsteps shuffle in the shadows, and before I can stand, a man steps out. He is tall, perhaps the tallest man I've ever seen, with a body just as finely carved. His face is handsome in a wicked way, with hazel eyes and dark-brown curls.

His hands raise in surrender. "Sorry, I don't mean to sneak up on you. I just wanted to make sure you were okay." His voice is smooth, too, and drips with a dialect I can't quite place.

My eyebrows furrow in a look that I hope is menacing. "Why wouldn't I be?"

The man has no weapon that I can see, nor anywhere to conceal one, unless the world's smallest gun is in his pocket.

"You're sitting alone in a dark parking lot in the middle of the night."

"I'm fine. My ride is almost here."

The man sighs like he's relieved, then gestures to the curb beside me. "Can I sit with you until they come then? I'll keep my distance, don't worry. I'd just feel guilty leaving you here."

"Nothing to feel guilty about."

Still, the man sits next to me, a good few feet between us. He's curious, fiddling with his hands like he wants to say something.

I check my phone. Riven is running late. Of course he is. I text him back that there's a strange man sitting with me in the parking lot, then turn off my phone.

Let's see how fast you get here now, Barone.

A stiff breeze ruffles through my hair, gifting me with an involuntary shiver.

The man beside me startles, then a warmth drapes over my shoulders. His coat now rests heavily against my skin, blocking the wind and chill.

"You're being awfully kind to a stranger. It's not going to make me suck your dick."

The man laughs, a rich sound. "I'm being kind because my mother raised me to be, no strings attached."

"So you're a mama's boy." Sounds familiar, I think with a snicker.

The man's face falls. "You could say that."

"Do you have a name?"

"Sorry, she also told me not to give my name to strangers."

It's my turn to laugh. "Fair enough." I haven't offered my name either. My shoulders drop. I still don't trust him, but he hasn't tried to kill me yet, so I could stand to be a little less cruel.

I never used to be this way. I never used to judge people before I knew them, or make snippy comments, or scowl before I smile. I almost miss that side of me, the girl who didn't know better yet.

Headlights whip around the corner and the man stands up again, brushing off his pants as he does so. "Looks like your ride is here," he says as he takes a step away.

"Wait." I extend the coat to him, not raising from my spot on the curb. "Your coat."

The man flashes that tight-lipped smile again. "Keep it. It's going to be a cold night."

"That's kind, but no, thank you."

"Why?" he asks, not unkindly. "Do you have a boyfriend who would mind?"

"No, I just don't like owing strangers favors."

He shrugs at that and accepts the coat, slipping his arms into the sleeves and tugging it over his broad shoulders in one fluid motion. "There. Now you don't owe me anything."

"Thank you."

"I'll see you around."

With that, he disappears back into the shadows that he came from just as Riven steps from his car, his dark eyes scanning the lot. Relief washes over his face when he spots me unharmed, still sitting on the curb.

"Where is he?" he asks. Always straight to the point.

I rise, shaking my head at the way his gaze drifts over my face and form. "He left when you got here." Then, with a hand placed on his shoulder, "I'm fine. He just didn't want me waiting alone. Don't you know there's dangerous people out there?"

My joke falls flat, judging by Riven's scowl. Still, he lets it go with some reluctance, opening the door to his car.

"No motorcycle tonight?"

"It's cold. I didn't want you to freeze."

"Oddly considerate."

Riven's huff of a laugh is response enough as I slide into his car, clicking the seatbelt into place. He doesn't plug my address into the GPS—he knows the route between there and Tella's by now.

A few minutes go by and we miss the first turn, then the second.

"Hey, are you kidnapping me or something?" My gaze darts to his face, where the corners of his lips are upturned.

"Or something."

Well, I had a good run. Kind of.

A few moments later, we pull into the parking lot of a local park. It's in a nice part of town, well lit, with swings and a full playground. Lots of families move to this part of the city, as it's closer to the school and a safer area overall. Mancini Security is less than a mile away. My old apartment is nearby too. I haven't been back since that night. My parents packed everything for me, and I left my home behind.

I feel like I deserve a thank you note or something from the next tenant. I'm sure they got a hell of a discount on rent after all the shit that went down there.

"If you wanted someone to push you on the swings, all you had to do was ask, Barone."

"You're not funny."

"I'm hilarious." I grin and follow Riven out of the car.

He clicks the lock, then leads me not towards the park, but a dirt path that circles around it. It stretches towards the woods before forking, one path continuing through the open part of the park, and the other towards a man-made forest. We stick to the open path, walking in leisurely steps.

The night air is chilly against my bare arms, and I probably should have packed a coat, but the bite is good. Calming, almost.

"You use sex to cope right?" Riven asks just as I settle comfortably into the quiet.

"Excuse me?" I ask with a jolt.

"That's what you said. You can't stand to be alone with your thoughts, so you find these random hookups and you use them to escape your mind for an hour or two. Because you're having trouble sleeping at night."

Wow. Way to fucking call me out.

"Is this an intervention?"

"No, this is me trying to help." He sighs through his nose. "I can't say I know how it feels to have that happen to you, but I know about nightmares and self-destruction."

"I'm not self-destructing," I try, but my words lack the bite I intend for them to have. Maybe if Riven tried to have this talk with me a month ago, I would have torn him a new one, but now it sounds genuine—soft almost, despite coming from the wicked mouth of such a hard-cut man.

"Just try this for tonight. We can walk in silence. We can talk. You can yell at me, or do whatever you need to do, just don't shut down on me." Then, his hand reaches out, tucking a loose strand of hair behind my ear. "You've always shone so brightly. I can't sit by and watch that light fade."

I didn't bother to change from my ratty work shirt and an old tennis skirt after my shift, and I'm terribly aware of that fact now. It's not the chill that undresses me as his eyes sweep my form, gauging the distance between us.

"I—"

Tires squeal and tear through the quiet of the night. Riven responds quicker than I do, quicker than I knew was humanly possible. His body rams into mine before I even hear the pops of gunfire, throwing us both to the ground. His arms wrap over my head, cradling it during the fall and protecting it after. A bullet grazes my arm, warm blood immediately flowing down to my elbow. My skirt flips up, exposing me to the darkened night as Riven leaps to his feet. His gun is drawn, pointing towards the car. He returns fire, but it's already driving off.

"Malik." He swears low, then leans down towards me with his hand extended. He freezes.

His gaze isn't on the car peeling away down the road. No, he stares directly at my thighs where my skirt has lifted. Just enough to show the scars that lace my tan skin, high enough that I can still cover them with a dress. The angry cigarette burn marks, the bruises that somehow never fully healed. I covered them with makeup just fine when we were in Italy together, but I didn't expect this, so tonight, they're on full display.

"Maddy..." His voice breaks, and I can't handle it.

I can't fucking handle any of this.

I push him away from me as I stand, angry tears already burning at the back of my eyes. Damnit. I was so careful, only for someone to find out.

Only for *him* to find out.

I storm down the sidewalk in any direction. I don't bother to care that someone just tried to gun me down. I don't care that it's dark and I don't know where I'm going. I don't care about anything except getting away from Riven and the pity in his dark eyes.

"Maddy!"

"Go away, Riven. I don't want to talk about it."

"Tough shit," he growls, his hands gripping my shoulders and spinning me to face him. His jaw is set in a hard line, his lips peeled back in a near-animalistic snarl. His rage is dark, primal, and I can't recall a time I've ever seen him so thoroughly pissed.

"Who did this to you?" He swallows thickly. "Did *he* do this to you?"

"What do you think?"

It's a coward's answer. It's enough of the truth that I don't have to say more, but I won't admit what he already knows. I won't admit it to anyone.

I won't tell them how Donovan's abuse went deeper than any of them know. I won't tell them how long it went on, or that I just sat there and let him.

His lips part, forming the threat of killing Donovan, before closing them again as if realizing he can't. The bastard is already six feet deep, paying for his crimes against Addie and his murder victims, but not for what he did to me. Natalia and Addie killed him for the victims and each other, but no one knew enough to make him hurt for me.

"What do you need?" And then when I open my mouth, he speaks again, "That doesn't involve me fucking off, because that's not going to happen."

What do I need? Do I even know what I need? No, if I did, I wouldn't be standing here, scars burning my thighs and ribs aching before this beautiful man who looks truly broken.

"Just take me home."

Riven doesn't ask questions, doesn't do anything other than walk a safe distance from me. I can't tell if he's scared I'll break, or if he's too disgusted by what I let happen to me to even think about being close to me.

The ride to the apartment is the same, and I fixate on the clock blinking 2:32 a.m. I close my eyes against the light.

CHAPTER 9
RIVEN

Maddy took long enough in the shower that I finally succumbed to my own insanity. I pushed all thoughts of Donovan and her from my mind on the drive home, forcing myself to focus on the road in front of me and getting her to safety.

But now?

I can't stop my mind from wandering to all the times I've seen her after a date, her eyes duller than a woman in love's should be. All the times on our plane ride to Italy when she jumped if my knee accidentally brushed hers, or the way she defaulted to anger if I pushed too far too quick.

Then my thoughts drift to Donovan himself, as they often have in the past few months. Most nights, I beat myself bloody over being face to face with a murderer and never recognizing him. Then it shifts to the cold bodies of his five murder victims, and on bad nights, their faces mirror Maddy's, the night I found her dying in her apartment. How many times was I alone with the man, even for a second? And how many of those times were after he left Maddy's apartment, smelling of cigarettes, his hands stuffed in his pockets?

I am mere seconds away from internet searching how to raise the dead, just so I can kill him slower, when the bathroom door opens. Maddy steps out, a large gray T-shirt swamping her frame, a hint of green satin shorts peeking out underneath. My eyes narrow on the shirt, until I notice the feminine cursive logo in the corner. Right, so not another man's.

"Do you need anything?" she asks after a moment.

"Do *you*?"

I hate how small she looks. Her arms are crossed over her chest, her chin tucked as if she can shrink in on herself. *You don't have to hide from me*, I want to scream. I'm not used to her like this, not when she's usually goading me on, hurling insults as if it's her profession, and filling every room with that fiery light. The walls are down now, and all I want to do is take her in my arms and promise that no one will hurt her ever again.

But I can't.

It haunted me the entire drive back. I wanted to hold her, to comfort her, but I couldn't be another man who held her down. She probably doesn't want me to touch her, even with the growing friendship between us.

"My arm is fine. The bullet just grazed me." She switches topics quickly. "Did you get hit?"

"I'm fine."

"Do you want to use the shower? I can wash your clothes."

"I'm fine," I repeat.

"Okay," she breathes.

Raising Donovan from the dead and murdering him again will have to wait. Maddy stands in the corner of the living room, awkward like a stranger in her own home. Fuck, I shouldn't have been short with her. I can practically see the thoughts swirling in her mind, the way she's starting to think I'm disgusted with her, when the only person I'm disgusted with is myself.

"I'm sorry—"

"Don't." She silences me with a raised hand. "Don't you dare start pitying me, Riven, or I swear to god I will throw you out the front door."

"I'm not pitying you."

"Yes, you are. You got all dark and broody the minute you saw my scars and I'm telling you right now that if you're going to make this into a bigger deal than it is, then you can leave."

She is imposing, even in oversized clothes and her hair in a towel. If I saw only her face, I would guess she was marching into war rather than standing in her plush apartment with a balcony view.

I dismissed her as a vapid party girl the first time I'd met her, a loose end in a case I was working. Natalia had me by the throat the entirety of the Donovan case, and one slipup—one blonde and beautiful slipup—would have cost me my neck. So I wrote her off as a nothing, if only to convince myself to stay focused.

"I'm treating it like a big deal because it *is* one. I'm trying to wrap my head around how he could hurt you."

Maddy's answering laugh is dry and dripping with cynicism. "He killed people, Barone. Five women are dead because of him. How he could do this to me is very easy to picture, actually."

It's not easy at all. It's unbearable. I was in the morgue daily, staring at the bodies of his victims. Each died of strangulation—all except for one, whose throat had been slit. Every time I went in, I saw Addie's face, terrified that the girl I learned to love as a sister could be next. That fear was replaced with a new one the minute I thought Maddy was dead.

Bile climbs up my throat and I have to clear it before I can speak again. "I thought you were coping with guilt."

"I'm coping with a lot of things. Guilt, trauma, pain. Dating the wrong guy was like a three-for-one deal."

"That's not funny."

"I'm not trying to be." She shrugs. "But I will be clear with you—I don't need you to get all preachy on me. Nothing has changed."

Everything has changed.

Everything.

Seeing what he did to her woke up some long-slumbering rage in my chest, primal and threatening to scorch everything in its path. If I burned this goddamn city to the ground, there would be no one left to hurt her, no one left to make her feel as worthless as I know she does.

And Addie let it happen to her.

Addie—kind, sweet, and lovely Addie left her best friend with that monster almost daily.

Addie—who should have known what was going on.

Addie—who should have stopped it.

The rage within me grows until red flames lick at the corners of my vision.

Maddy releases me from my torment with a yawn. "Look, if we're done with this, then I'm going to bed. We have holiday dinner at Natalia and Addie's tomorrow night, and I have work. Are we good?"

How can she put up this front so well? How can she let her anger turn to indifference? I wish I could say it was the strength she so desperately is trying to show, but I know better. I've seen this pattern in myself, years ago, and sometimes even now. She simply doesn't care about it, herself, anything.

"We're good," I say slowly, rolling each letter over my tongue as if tasting the lie on them. "I'll see you tomorrow night?"

Maddy smiles for the first time since the park, now wearier but still bright. "Yeah, I'll see you there."

I nod, my mouth forming a hard line as I make for the door. Her voice is so soft I almost miss it, my hand on the doorknob.

"Riven?"

"Yes?"

"Thank you for tonight. You know, before shit went south. It was nice."

"You're welcome. Now lock your door," I say in response.

Her nose crinkles and she mocks a salute, holding two fingers to her brow before shutting the door behind me.

I wait until the lock clicks, then stalk to my car, but I don't drive home. I speed through the city to the Mancini-Collins home, the drive long enough to let my anger fester.

Natalia answers on the first knock, her eyes alert even though I can tell she'd been asleep. "You'd better have a good reason for banging down my door at this hour, Riven, or I swear to god—"

Pushing past her, I make my way up the stairs to where Addie is standing against the banister, watching the scene in sleep-muddled confusion.

"*You*," I growl.

She blinks once, then twice, her eyes widening. She points a finger at her chest. "Me?"

"She's your best friend! How could you not fucking do something?" I'm yelling now, but hardly notice it. My hands are on her shoulders, shaking her.

Realization washes over Addie's features, and her lower lip begins to wobble. "Maddy? What's wrong with Maddy?"

I can hear Natalia coming up behind me, her footsteps thundering. She's quick, but so am I, and I dodge her first attempt to grab me.

"What the *fuck* do you think you're doing, Barone?"

I ignore the lethal venom spitting from her voice, the murderous rage I know is paralleled in my own. Instead, I keep my eyes on Addie as her eyes begin to well up with tears.

"Riven, what happened to Maddy?"

"You were there with them, you let this happen. Now you have the nerve to play innocent?" I hardly realize the words that are spewing from my mouth, too filled with disgust for the woman I once loved like family to even recognize the bruises I'm leaving on her pale arms. Natalia doesn't miss this, and her second blow lands on my jaw, sending my head careening back into the wall with a sickening crack. The impact rattles the frames on the wall, and I know without looking that I've dented it.

Natalia's hands fist in my shirt, one arm forming a parallel across my throat, constricting most of my air. Her face is close to mine, nothing but predatory assessment in her soulless eyes as she seethes.

Addie backs up towards the stairs, her arms wrapped around her middle.

"If you ever fucking touch her again, I'll—"

"Nat, don't." Addie tries to come to my defense, but all it does is stoke the fire.

I glance over Natalia's shoulder with my eyes only, unable to move my head or neck from where Natalia still holds it pinned. I sneer at Addie, something I didn't know I was capable of doing until tonight. "You knew what Donovan did to her, for months, and said nothing. You saw the scars on her legs, the burn marks. You let him hurt her, you piece of—"

A swift chop to my throat steals all the air from my lungs, and I slump to the floor, Natalia's hold having been released. I don't care. I focus on the look on Addie's face, and dread seeps in.

She's crying, silent tears snaking down her freckled cheeks. There isn't an ounce of remembrance in the action. There is shock.

"He..."

Oh my god.

She didn't know.

"Addie," Natalia says soothingly, like one might speak to a startled animal.

Addie's hand flies to her mouth and she takes a step backwards. "I left her there with him. I didn't know. I..."

She's spiraling, and takes another step back. Back off the stairs, her foot slipping. Natalia lunges for her, but it's too late.

Addie slips, crumpling to the floor below us at the base of the stairs with a heart-stopping crack.

CHAPTER 10
MADDY

I wake up feeling hopeful for the day for the first time in months. I don't know why, but I get ready for work, allowing myself brief glimpses in the mirror. Okay, that's a lie—I do know why, and it might have something to do with Riven.

I never told anyone about what happened to me because in the grand scheme of things, it means nothing. At the end of the day, I got to walk away. I am alive while so many others are dead, so I should cut my losses and be happy with that.

The only problem is that's not how life works. I'm not happy. Most days, I am anything but.

Yet Riven knows now. He knows and he didn't push when I asked him not to, and yes, maybe a little push might be good for me, but in the moment, just having someone else to share the burden of this knowledge with was the first step.

It's been excruciating not telling Addie. We share everything with each other and always have, but this is a weight I can't bear to put on her shoulders. Already, she's been through so much, and I won't be the one to put more stress on her. My best friend is getting close to her happy ending, and I refuse to stand in the way of it.

Still, not having anyone to talk to has been harder than I thought it would be, and while last night I was horrified and furious that Riven found out, today, those feelings have morphed into something like relief.

My good morning takes a brief pause when I walk into Tella's only to find Addie not there. Daryl stands in her place, wiping down the counters for the day with a frown so deeply etched into his face I fear it may be permanent.

"Where's Addie?" I ask.

The older man flips the rag over his shoulder and sighs, like I should know this already. I probably should. "She's taking today off. Said she fell down the stairs last night and hurt her leg."

Panic flares in my ribs at that, and I have half a thought to bolt out the door and get a cab to her house. "Is she okay?"

"She sounded fine. That girlfriend of hers sounded worried, though."

Well, that much wasn't out of the usual.

"Natalia's her fiancée now."

"She's a pain in my ass. When you see her, tell her to stop fussing over Addie so she can get back behind the counter. My knees weren't made for this."

I don't ask what he means, too caught up in the fact that we open in ten minutes and Daryl never mentioned anything about a replacement. I swear to god if Addie left me working the morning rush alone, I might have to take back her "bestest best friend ever" mug.

My shift goes by surprisingly quick, with Kelsey coming in halfway through to sub in for Addie. She arrives halfway through the breakfast rush, blaming it on traffic while smoothing her bedhead. Aside from that hiccup, the morning runs smoothly, and soon enough, the hours are melting off the clock.

By the time the sun begins to sink across the sky, I am dressed and ready for dinner with everyone else. The Mancini-Collins house is lit up from within, and the porch creaks as I step onto it. I'm wearing thick socks within my ankle boots, but neither do anything to keep the chill from my frozen toes. I shift from one foot to the next, my breath crystallizing in the air in front of me.

I ring the bell once. Then twice. By the third time, I hear someone fumbling with the lock, then the door swings open to reveal Addie.

Addie on crutches, with a cast up her leg.

"What the hell happened?" I screech, rushing inside and gently taking her arms.

She winces and shrugs me off, not rudely, and crutches into the living room.

I shut the door and lock it, following close behind.

"It's nothing. I just slipped down the stairs."

"What did you break?"

"My fibula. It's a minor fracture and the doctor says it should only take six weeks to heal." She brushes me off with a wave of her hand. Her eyes dart to my lap, then back up to my face. Weird. "Anyway, I'll be up and moving again in no time."

"Daryl played it off."

"Daryl plays everything off. It's fine, really." Her eyes dart again, this time over my shoulder to where the bickering voices of Natalia and Marco filter in from the kitchen. No Riven yet, even though I arrived late.

"Is Riven coming still? When I saw him last night, he said he would be here."

Addie's face pales and she fiddles with her hands. Seriously, what the fuck isn't she telling me? She's never been good at keeping secrets from me, ever.

"No. He and Natalia had... a fight. So he's skipping." I don't miss the weight in her words, and the way her voice catches on the word *fight*. Something happened last night after Riven left my apartment, I just don't know what.

"Anyway, how are you?" Addie rushes out, now picking at a hangnail.

"Good. Are you okay? You're acting weird."

"Your ribs don't hurt? Or anywhere else?"

"Addison Collins." My best friend flinches at the use of her full name. "What happened last night? And don't you dare lie to me."

Natalia and Marco's voices grow softer, almost as if they are listening in on this conversation.

Addie's face drops to stare at her lap. My heart begins to pound wildly in my chest, a dull ache thrumming in my ribs. Please god, don't let this be what I think it is.

"I didn't know he was hurting you." Addie raises her head, tears dripping down her cheeks. "I'm so sorry."

Any illusion of healing I'd convinced myself of this morning shatters before my eyes. My hands shake in my lap and embarrassment burns my face.

They know.

They all know.

"He told you," I whisper. "He fucking told you."

"He thought I knew. He was so angry, Maddy, and I—"

"Wait. Did he do this to you?" I point to her leg, rage like I've never known filling every crevice of my body until I'm teeming with it. I'm like a live wire, waiting to spark something into flame.

"No! God, no. This happened after. I wasn't paying attention and I fell. Riven would never—"

"But he *did*. He told you."

"I'm so sorry."

"Don't. I— Just don't." I stand, not knowing where to go but knowing I need to be anywhere but here.

I trusted him. I fucking trusted Riven, and he turned around and reported back to Addie just like I used to fear he would. That's why he did all of this anyway—so our friend wouldn't be hurt. I should have known. He never cared for me, not really. I was just a problem to be fixed, another case to work.

Marco hangs his head in shame and pity as I breeze out the door, and Natalia opens her mouth like she wants to say something but thinks better of it.

Good. Now there's only the moon and darkness to see my tears.

I leave my apartment dark when I crash through the front door, collapsing on the rug in the center of the living room. Only then do I let myself sob, but now that I'm able to, no sound comes out, just a dry rasping. It's almost as if my body has used up all of its tears and cannot bear to give me any more.

Instead, I lay there, curled in the fetal position on my floor, one thought running through my mind.

How could he?

I was willing to make the effort, to try after last night. Maybe it was foolish of me to hope, but I didn't care.

I want to get better. I want to feel anything other than this despair.

But then there is this spark of fear, a tiny dose of dread that curls around my heart and squeezes until I feel myself clawing for it, as if I might rip it from my chest cavity myself. This tiny voice that screams at me, telling me that no matter what I do, how hard I work, everyone who has ever doubted me is right.

My mother and her dry, exasperated tone, explaining my worthlessness as if she is teaching a child why the sky is blue.

Donovan and his sneering timbre and the scent of cigarette butts searing through flesh.

My father, who never could understand how—after all he did for me, after all he sacrificed—I was this fucked up if I came from him.

I can hardly feel my knees as I wrap my arms around them, curling into myself as if being smaller will fix this. Insignificant and worthless.

For a moment, I think of calling someone, of picking up the phone a few feet away and dialing for Addie. Then, for a breath of a moment, Riven's name pops into my mind. My fingers splay, reaching... But despair grips at my wrist, shaking its head.

No.

It is a trap of my own design.

If I continue to lay here, I will rot. If I call for help, I'll hate myself for the burden I become. But if I say nothing...

Rotting seems like the best alternative.

My phone lights up, buzzing and displaying a familiar face.

Riven.

"You deserve this," Donovan sneers, *the bullet wound between his straight brows now clotted.*

There's a knock at the door.

"I know," I reply.

The ringing stops.

CHAPTER 11
MADDY

The bell above the entrance jingles its light tune as I push open the glass door of Tella's. My shoulders drop the moment the scent of freshly brewed coffee and warm pastries hits me.

Kelsey waves from behind the counter, her freckled face pulling into a smile. She and Liam are on shift today, a rare day off for me and Addie. Addie—who has already claimed a booth by the window.

"What's on the menu today?" I settle into the booth across from her. The worn blue leather crinkles as I scoot further inwards. Addie pushes a steaming mug my way, and I catch a whiff of herbal rose.

"I got you a rose and vanilla latte. Liam's latest addition to the menu. Daryl just approved it this morning."

Spring is starting to bloom around us, meaning Daryl lets us experiment with new flavors. It has become a yearly tradition, and whoever makes the best recipe gets to add it to the permanent menu. Addie won last year with a brown sugar espresso.

"What? Daryl didn't like my lavender latte?"

"No, just like he didn't last year, or the year before," Addie teases.

"One of these years, he will let me have my lavender."

Addie scoffs and wraps her hands around her own mug. It's just cool enough to order a hot drink, but warm enough to regret wearing a sweater by the afternoon. Disgusting weather.

"How've you been?" she finally asks.

Calling that a loaded question would be the understatement of the year. It's been two months now since I last saw Riven, an impressive feat on his part, given how our inner circles overlap. We haven't had any contact since he told Addie about what Donovan did to me. It wasn't his place, and while he tried calling once, he hasn't tried again since. I hate that he is where my mind first jumps to, and I swallow the sorrow in my throat with a sip of my latte.

I went to my photography event alone, wearing the red dress Riven and I picked out. I made a few business connections, and tried to drown myself in droll conversation to forget the ghost of a hand on my back, fixing my zipper.

Still, in these two months, no more attempts on my life have been made. Maybe Malik finally realized that I mean nothing to his brother, and killing me would be unnecessary stress. A small victory, I suppose.

"I saw my parents yesterday," I offer instead.

Addie cringes. "And?"

"And the usual happened. It started out nice, then it all became about my love life. They spent the whole dinner trying to set me up with their friends' sons. Apparently, my ex-boyfriend being a serial killer that tried to kill us is no longer a valid excuse for being single."

At first, my parents were supportive, perhaps for the first time in their lives. They didn't push me to date anyone for the first few months, but eventually, the novelty of Donovan's attempted murder wore off and they were back to their usual bullshit.

Addie winces. "Ouch."

"As if being single is the worst thing in the world."

"True," she hums, then adds, "Would you ever consider dating again?"

I think about that for a moment. I haven't considered the possibility before. While yes, I have had casual interactions and one-night stands, can I see myself entrusting my heart to someone again? After all that happened?

Yes, my heart screams.

Shut up, my brain screams back.

I'm quick to shove down the face that starts to appear in my mind.

"Eventually, but not any time soon," I admit, and it sounds unsure, even to my own ears.

"I don't think I could either, if Natalia weren't beside me the whole time."

"And what about you? The wedding is coming up soon. You have to have new news!" I nudge her with my toe under the table, and a shy smile lifts the corners of her lips. She's started twisting her engagement ring when she's excited or nervous recently, something she has been doing since I sat down.

I know she isn't asking about my life just to be polite. She's too kind to not be genuine, but her nervous tick has been begging me to ask her about her own life.

"Well, I got a call from my literary agent a few months ago, but I couldn't say anything until now."

"And?"

"And..." Her small smile bursts into a full-bodied grin now, "my book got picked up by my dream publisher! I was offered a contract for a full series, and I said yes!"

"Oh my god."

"I know!"

We might as well be screeching at this point, but I can't find it in my heart to care. This is something she's wanted for as long as I've known her, and now...

"I'm so proud of you," I say in earnest.

Her hands reach across the table to clasp mine. "Thank you."

We sit like this for a while, emotion clogging my throat as she tells me all the details. Addie can barely keep her voice down as she explains the process, how hard it was to keep this secret from me, that this is why she's cut back on her hours at Tella's, how shocked Natalia was. I have to laugh at that last bit. I've never seen Natalia truly shocked, but I know she must be so proud, just like I am.

Even as the small voice in my head tells me I'm falling behind.

Even as it shouts that I am failing.

Instead, I let the joy Addie emanates swallow it whole. After everything that has happened, she deserves this and all the good coming her way.

"So you get the girl, the dream, and the happily ever after," I say with no bitterness in my voice. Addie finally looks at peace, like a woman who is getting everything she's ever wanted.

"I wish my dad could see this," she hums. Addie's father passed when she was young, many years before we met.

I squeeze her hands, still entwined in mine. "He can see it all, and he's very proud of you."

"Oh, are you two pals now?"

"Yup," I say, popping the *p*. "He told me himself."

"And how'd you two meet?"

"Obviously I pulled out my Ouija board and made a call."

"Obviously," she laughs.

Liam comes by now, two new mugs in his hands. He's a newer hire, who started when Addie and I took leave. He's young, working to save up for college. His sandy hair and light eyes lend to his youth, not to mention he's still in that awkward teenage phase that we all try to forget going through.

"How does defeat taste, Maddy? I thought you'd like a refill."

"Is that any way to speak to your elders?"

"Elder? You're finally owning up to those wrinkles, I see."

"Try taunting me when you're tall enough to meet my eye, pipsqueak."

Liam's voice cracks when he goes to respond, and his face flushes scarlet.

Addie clears her throat with a pointed glance. "Don't tease him," she says, then to him, "And don't get too comfortable with winning. I plan on taking back my crown next year."

I smirk over the lip of my cup as he mocks a salute, taking our empty mugs back behind the counter where

Daryl waits. He fixes us with a withering stare and Addie waves. I blow a kiss. The older man rolls his eyes and retires back to his office with a grumble.

Things are good right now. This is what healing looks like.

So why does my heart still ache?

"Where's Riven been lately?" I ask before I can think better of it. Then I add, as if this makes me sound any more nonchalant, "He hasn't been haunting my doorstep in a while."

Addie's face darkens if only by a fraction. So she's still pissed at him too. Noted.

"Natalia has him doing something else for her right now since Malik hasn't made a move lately. Don't worry though, Marco has been watching over your apartment in the meantime."

"I'm not worried. He came in for breakfast this morning. It felt like old times."

Marco, unlike his cousin, didn't question me on where I was when I came home this morning. Instead, he waited outside my door, smiled, and asked if I had coffee inside. I pretended I didn't see his car trailing me as I walked back from last night's apartment, and he pretended he knew nothing. It was the perfect morning.

Except Riven would have been furious, and that thought has nausea settling into my stomach.

No.

No more talk of Riven. No more thoughts of him. Not his face, his actions, our memories. There was nothing between us to begin with, and there sure as hell is nothing now.

Right?

"Oh, Natalia's calling. She and..." Addie stops herself short. "They're back from the job they were working. I think I'm going to head out. Do you need a ride?"

"No, I'll be fine. It's broad daylight." I dismiss her with a wave of my hand.

Still, her face pulls into a frown. "But Marco was with them. There's no one at the apartment right now."

"Benny the baseball bat is there, and again, broad daylight. It's fine," I reply. "Say hi to wifey for me!"

I pull myself from the booth before she can argue, waving over my shoulder at Liam and Kelsey as I leave. Still, Addie's stare lingers on my back until I'm out of sight.

Maurice isn't at the front desk when I get back. Instead, a woman with sharp features and dark, slicked-back hair sits in his spot. She doesn't bother to wave or even look up, so neither do I.

The elevator ride up to my floor feels slower than usual, and my mind wanders back to the café. Addie said that Natalia, Marco, and Riven were back from their mission now, so they should be okay. So he's fine.

Still, what their little Mafia trio thinks is okay and what the average person thinks is okay are very different things. Natalia apparently had thirteen stitches on the day she met Addie and walked in to flirt with her like nothing was wrong. I'm sure one of them could be shot at this point and consider it a minor setback.

Shot.

The image of Riven, shot in the field and bleeding

out, seeps into my mind quicker than I can stop it. My breathing becomes labored before an ache in my ribs reminds me that I am furious with him and have cut all ties. I don't need to worry over him. That's not my job. It can be Natalia's, or whatever girl he goes for next.

I ignore the shot of jealousy that careens straight for my gut.

Instead, I focus on plucking my keys from my pocket and jamming it into the lock with what is probably a bit too much force. The door swings open and I step forward, only for a pair of hands to grab my arm and pull me in.

CHAPTER 12
RIVEN

Marco claims Natalia's couch the minute she pushes open her front door. "I thought you two dealt with all of the Russos months ago," he whines, draping his arm over his forehead.

Natalia rolls her eyes, grabbing a whiskey bottle from the cabinet. She offers the bottle to me first, then takes a large swig when I decline.

The sound of running water upstairs tells me Addie is home, presumably in the shower.

"We did too," I grumble. I take the chair opposite of him, sinking in as fatigue settles over me.

"They're dealt with now, that's what matters. I've sent someone else to clean up the mess—which, if I remember correctly, is part of *your* job description." She points her bottle at both of us as she seethes. "You're welcome."

"Thanks, Nat."

"Too little, too late, Marco."

"Aren't you supposed to be watching Maddy right

now?" The question slips out before I can stop it, and admittedly, it sounds a bit sharp.

Marco's head lolls to the side, and he stares at me with a raised eyebrow.

Natalia called Addie a few hours ago on the drive back. Our "work meeting" was a few hours from the city, so it took us longer than we would have liked to get back. At the time, Addie was just leaving Tella's, where she told Maddy the news about her book. It went well, judging by the bubbly voice coming through the speaker.

But that was hours ago, while the sun still shone. Now the city is bathed in darkness, only the moon outlining the road leading back to downtown. And the thought of Maddy alone in that apartment...

I think of her more often than I thought I would, and admittedly more often than I would like to. It's been two months since I saw her last. Two months since I saw her pretty face, heard her lovely laugh. Two months, and the last image I have of her is her photo on my phone as my call went to voicemail.

I fucked up. I know I fucked up. I don't deserve to even catch a glimpse of her, but I can't help but think of her. At night, I stare at my ceiling, wondering who is with her, holding her, fucking her. Do they know to be gentle around her ribs? Do they even care?

Does she care?

When sleep claims me, all I can dream of is her. Her voice, her lips. On the worst nights, we're back in her apartment, but the bloody body I find is cold, and she never gets a chance to tell me how much she hates me.

I can't decide which is worse—living in a world where

someone hurt her like that, or the world I live in now, where I'm leaving her at risk of it happening again.

You're doing this to keep her safe from an evil worse than that one, I remind myself. If I stay away, she'll be safe. Malik will lose interest and she will be free to live her life without worrying about anything like this ever again. It's the least she deserves after the hell she's been through.

"I asked one of the other guys to do it since I knew we'd get back late," Marco says carefully.

"None of them are half as competent as you are."

"And not even I hold a candle to you, dear cousin. So if you're so worried, go check on her yourself."

"Maybe I will." I rise to my feet, glaring at the challenge in his voice.

My cousin doesn't even bother to look concerned. Natalia, on the other hand, watches my every move warily, her black, calculating gaze peeling back the walls I've placed around myself.

Are you really going to do this? she seems to ask.

Instead of deigning them with a response, I grab my coat off the banister and walk out the front door. My car is still parked in the driveway and I slip into the driver's seat, ready to speed to her apartment when I pause.

Hey moron, remember that whole internal monologue you just had about staying away to keep her safe?

Fuck.

My head hits the steering wheel with a heavy thud. Any other woman, I would have forgotten by now. Any other woman, and I would have moved on to the next. But Maddy isn't any other woman, and I've known that infuriating fact for longer than I'd like to admit.

Freezing Hell

I don't believe in soulmates, but whatever fire the universe had pulled me from, it pulled her from it too.

In my pocket, my phone buzzes.

UNKNOWN NUMBER: SENT ONE IMAGE.

Against my better judgment, I open the picture.

Then I drop my phone and speed for Maddy's apartment.

There is no one at the front desk when I arrive. Go fucking figure. Malik never leaves a witness.

Cas had gotten my number somehow, and sent me a photo of Maddy, face down on her pink rug. A bruise had blossomed on her head, but there was no other sign of injury—none yet. Malik is too conniving for that. He wants me to know she's alive when I come for her, and wants to kill her seconds before I can stop him. It's all a game to him—the ultimate prize being my suffering.

Cas sent no explanation, no threats, just a silent, violent promise.

I'm sprinting up the stairs, nearly to her floor, when there's a heavy thud—like a body hitting the floor. No screaming. No struggle.

No.

I'm at her door in seconds, sprinting faster than I ever have before. I don't bother to clear the hall, nor check what I'm walking into before I throw open her door.

A body is on the ground, bruised and bleeding, as a baseball bat rams into it again, and again.

Cas.

It's my brother's body, as Maddy beats him, vicious and animalistic.

Silent tears stream down her face, and though her mouth is open, she is utterly silent as she beats my brother within an inch of his life.

Beats him with that goddamn pink baseball bat.

My arms are around her, hauling her away from the body when she swings that bat around again, slamming it into my side with a sickening crack. I refuse to let her go, even as all the air is robbed from my lungs. She has a hell of an arm, I won't lie. Cas's death must have been excruciating, and it's still better than he deserved.

"Riven." Recognition dawns in her eyes and her face drains of all color. "Oh, shit. Did I hurt you?"

"I can take a hit." The wheeze that follows makes me sound less than convincing, but Maddy doesn't say anything if she notices. The baseball bat falls from her hands, clattering to the ground. I kick it away, not caring much as I search her for injuries.

"Are you hurt?" I ask. I press on the side of her face and she winces.

"No."

Yes, she is—that much is becoming more than apparent as I spot the purple bruise blossoming across her cheekbone. Her arms sport matching marks, ten that look like fingerprints, and she's favoring her left ankle.

"Don't lie to me. You're better than that."

"Am I?" she challenges.

"Yes. You are. Now where does it hurt?"

Her shoulders finally slump in resignation and she points to that ankle. "I twisted it when they grabbed me. Arms will be sore for a bit, but I'll live."

Grabbed her. Fury boils low in my stomach at the thought of such a simple, possessive act. They felt free to grab her as they pleased. If Malik had come instead of Cas...

I kneel beside her, rolling up her pant leg to reveal her ankle twisted in an unnatural way, the skin a garish green color. I press on it, the flesh tender and puffed, but it still moves beneath my ministrations. Good, not broken then.

I rise to my feet again, Maddy staring at me curiously, if not warily, as I stand.

"And what about your face?" I ask.

"Oh, I think *he*—" she nudges my brother with the toe of her shoe, "—did that. I got hit with something when I tried to fight. Maybe his gun? It felt like metal. Anyway, I passed out after and the memory is kind of hazy."

Red clouds my vision and I nearly strangle the corpse of my brother, if just to release some of the violent anger thrashing in my heart. He *hit* her with his gun. He laid his hands on her. He hurt her. He...

He looks older now. His hair grew long in the past few years, and he has considerably more scars than the last time we spoke, though that same sneer is planted on his face, even in death. He still has my nose and Malik's jaw, the middle child, a perfect blend of the both of us. Where he lacked Malik's smarts and my charm, he made up for it with vicious cruelty.

And he's dead.

"I killed him." Maddy's bruised and blood-splattered hands reach up to cover her mouth. She doesn't cry, nor does she look panicked. She's in shock, surprised maybe that she could do that to another human, but it doesn't look like she's upset.

"No, you didn't."

Her hands drop and she stares at me in confusion. "Yes, I did. Oh my god, the cops... *I killed him.*"

"No, I did."

Before she can ask questions, I lift my gun and fire straight into my brother's head. Despite the bad blood and the hatred between us, I can't bring myself to look at his face again. It's my brother, my older brother, yet it's not. It's also just a body that I've shot, for no reason other than to comfort a woman who hates me.

"No cops are going to come near this scene, but if they do, they'll look at the bullet in his face first." It's a half lie. Any decent autopsy will show that Cas died from blunt force trauma, and that the bullet was fired post mortem, but no cops will come near this body. Natalia will ship it back to Malik, and he will know who did the damage.

"How do you know?"

"I won't let them. These things happen all the time in this industry."

"To high-ranking family members?"

"No, but I promise you, Maddy, no one will pin this on you. I'll protect you."

Her eyes lift to mine, and they burn with all the fires of hell as she asks, "Can you? Can you protect me from this? From *me*?"

The blood freezes in my veins at the ferocity of that gaze, the fury of a beautiful woman burned too often, and by none other than me. All the anger and words thrown in the past few weeks come flooding back. I'm the one who saw the scars lacing her body, the marks she's tried so hard to hide. I'm the one who betrayed her. I'm the one who told her best friend the one truth she never wanted shared. I'm the one who fucked up, and she paid the price.

"I will. I swear on my life," I vow solemnly, but Maddy isn't convinced.

She shakes her head, that devastating frown deepening. "No. You've never cared for your life. Swear it on mine."

"Maddy—"

"Swear it."

"I swear," I say, the weight of the words catching in my throat.

Maddy slumps at that, all the tension leaving her as if it was the only thing holding her upright. My arms encircle her waist, but she breaks the hold, pushing back. Those walls are up again, barbed now, but there's a door just waiting to be opened.

"Where were you?" she asks, and steps back. She stumbles over Cas's limp, outstretched hand. She flinches at the crunch, the broken fingers now added to the utterly broken body. She doesn't look at it, not as her whole body tenses like a tightly stung wire. If I try to touch her again, I know she'll explode and devolve into whatever madness is threatening to claim her.

"I was staying away. I thought that would be best, considering everything that happened."

"You mean when you told Addie about what Donovan did to me, then left?" Her voice breaks on the world *left*, and I finally see through the act she puts on, the door opening just slightly enough that I can catch a glimpse of the bloody wounds behind it all. There is a beating heart, still trying to open for everyone around her, while all the world does is continue to scar it.

And I saw those scars, then left.

"Yes," I say, my voice raw and as vulnerable as I can will it to be. "I thought you wouldn't want to see me anymore."

"I didn't," she says hurriedly. "I don't— I didn't until... God, this is hard."

"Take your time."

Maddy fixes me with a flat stare, and for the first time tonight, I recognize the woman in front of me. "I missed you more than I hated you."

A dry laugh rasps from between my lips, no more than a sigh in the dead room. "You missed me?"

"Don't get used to hearing it." A flicker of a smile lifts her lips, then her eyes widen, wild as they dart to the open apartment doorway.

I turn in time to see another man, Jaime, a Barone lower level I used to run hits with. He lifts his arm, a silenced pistol in hand, and fires. I lunge for Maddy and she does the same, our bodies crashing together in the center of the room. She lands on top, trying to cover my body with her own. Fuck that. I roll, covering as much of her as I can, one of my hands holding her wrists against my chest, the other cradling her head. She makes a muffled sound like protest, but I press my full body weight into her.

"Stay down."

Seven shots fire out in rapid succession, only one managing to graze my back. I grit my teeth. It's a small hurt compared to others I've sustained, but a hurt all the same. Maddy's face is panicked when she spots the blood, but I can't afford to let my gaze linger. I look over my shoulder to see if he's still there.

A click resounds and Jaime's face goes white as his pistol jams, and I pull my own gun from my waistband, firing back. He bolts down the hall, running until he's out of sight. I know he saw Cas's body, and will tell Malik before I can.

Let him.

"What the fuck were you thinking?" I explode, Maddy's body still pinned beneath mine. I prop myself up on my forearms, holding my torso above her but keeping her held below me. "When bullets start flying, you run away from them, not throw yourself over me."

My words seem to pass right through her, and she lifts her hand to my back, her fingertips ghosting the wound there. They come back bloody. "You were shot."

"*You* would have been shot, and killed. They were aiming for you."

"Why would you—"

"On your life, remember?" I force a grin to my face and hope it doesn't look like a grimace. "I won't let anything happen to you."

"Not at the risk of your own life," Maddy says. "Idiot."

As if I wouldn't lay my life down for her at any given moment. I nod, if only to appease her, then rise to my feet. She accepts my help, her arms shaking as I grip them, careful to avoid the bruises.

"What now?" she asks.

"I'm taking you to Addie and Natalia's. I need to double back and go find Jaime." At her confusion, I amend, "The man who just shot at us."

Maddy nods in recognition.

"I'll call in some guys for cleanup in the meantime."

"You have the power to do that?" Maddy's head tips to the side, her blonde hair cascading over her shoulder. It's blood-speckled and knotted, but I brush a hand over it regardless.

I huff a laugh. "Darling, I have the power to do much more than that. You really don't know what it is I do, do you?"

She shakes her head. "Can I come with some time?"

It's my turn to look at her confused. She's not displaying the morbid curiosity most civilians do when they think of Mafia work. Some people look at modern media—mostly romance novels and movies—and think the blood and gore are edgy. Some find the violence fascinating, but I find none of that in Maddy's pensive stare. She wants to understand me, all facets of me—including the killer in me.

"I'm not sure that's a great idea. It's not a great bring-your-kid-to-work-day occupation."

"Then it's a good thing I'm not a kid." Then, with her best puppy-dog stare, she adds, "Plus, I heard you brought Addie to the morgue. Are you picking favorites?"

She says it so innocently that I choke, my heart threatening to burst.

"She was being stalked and studying his other murder victims. It's a bit different."

"Technically, Malik is stalking me and has tried to kill me. Why is it different?"

I grimace as I think of what comes next. The blood that will spray, the guts that will splatter the walls. The knife in my hand. That's not something I want her to see any time soon—if ever.

"What I do... it's not a part of me I enjoy sharing with others. But maybe—that's a *maybe*, Maddy—I will find something less disturbing for you to observe."

"Thank you," she says with startling sincerity.

Where she used to flinch at my touch, she now leans into it as I bring a hand up to cup her face. The flinch only comes when my thumb brushes over the bruise, now a disturbingly dark black.

"Come on, we need to get some ice on this," I murmur, and to my surprise, she lets me lead her away from the bloody apartment. I focus entirely on Maddy as her steps falter, her adrenaline and shock failing her. My arms steady her as we walk to the car.

I don't look back at the body of my brother.

CHAPTER 13
RIVEN

To my surprise, it is not Addie that embraces Maddy when we arrive to the Mancini-Collins residence. Natalia steps forward, clad in sweatpants and a sports bra rather than her usual attire, and pulls Maddy into her. All the strength Maddy tried to force on the drive here fades as she crumbles into the other woman's arms, Natalia's hand resting on the back of her head. She whispers something to Maddy that I cannot hear, then leads her into her home, while Addie steps out onto the porch with murder in her eyes.

"Explain," is all she says.

So I do. I explain everything, from my fight with Maddy, which I assume she already knows about, to finding her and Cas tonight. By the end, Addie's face is fallen, her features suddenly looking worn. While Natalia and I have lived this way for our entire lives and have grown hard to the ways this job challenges us, Addie is new to it all. She's thrown away any chance of normalcy for love, and has done so willingly. Yet despite Natalia's best efforts to shield her from the worst of this world, the effects have aged Addie's soul drastically. I know it is here that her wariness stems as she worries for Maddy. She knows how it feels to be thrown into our world of blood and death, and she wants something better for her. She trusts Natalia to protect her, but wants to know if she can trust me to protect her best friend.

"I love you, Riven, but I loved Maddy first and I will *not* hesitate to end you if you put her in harm's way."

"I know."

"Do you have a plan to end this?"

"I do."

I don't. My plan starts and ends with Malik's death. How I intend to get there, I don't know.

Addie nods, seeing through my bullshit but too tired to call me on it tonight. "Marco is on his way. He told us before you arrived that he found Cas's accomplice. Natalia is sending you the address."

As if on cue, my phone pings in my hand, an address sprawling across the screen. I pocket the device and nod, tight lipped. Before I leave, I turn to catch one last glance of Maddy's silhouette through the front porch window. I consider Addie next, the purple smudges beneath her blue eyes, and the wrinkle between her brows. "Hey," I say softly. "You're doing good."

"Thanks, Riven." Her hands wrap around her waist before she heads back inside. "Make him pay."

"Gladly."

I find Marco parked in the shadow of the trees outside the warehouse Jaime and one other man are currently occupying. I park a few dozen feet down, far enough away that both cars are hidden. I turned my headlights off a few miles back, praying that I wouldn't stumble upon an unsuspecting cop or someone in the road. Not that it would be too much of a problem, but time is of the essence and I would prefer not to waste it.

My cousin is leaned against the dilapidated wood of the warehouse, close enough to a window that he can see in but far enough away that his presence remains undetected. He dips his chin in greeting as I idle beside him.

"Only two inside. I think they're waiting for pickup. Renner tracked them here an hour ago, so if I had to guess, I'd say we have ten minutes tops until backup arrives," he cautions.

"I only need five."

Marco nods again, and then waits for my signal before we slip in the back door. Usually, I'd like to announce myself with a bang, guns drawn and bullets flying. Not tonight. No, tonight I want to terrify him.

Men like us are used to the adrenaline pump of a good gunfight, and are hardly scared off by one at this point. Silence is a greater weapon—sneaking in behind them and putting a gun to their head before even their pride can convince them that they'll be the ones to walk away alive.

Jaime and a second man I don't recognize stand in the center of the room, still unaware of our arrival. The warehouse is otherwise empty, save for a single table and a few chairs in the middle—in other words, their choice of décor is fucking sketchy.

Marco advances in the front, and I pull up the rear

before we split off to stay out of their line of sight. I step up behind Jaime and he stiffens, but it's too late for him.

"Jaime, what a pleasure to see you again. It's been a few years," I croon, the barrel of my gun already against his temple.

In my periphery, I can see Marco has disarmed the other man, forcing him to sit. He nods, and Jaime sucks in a sharp breath.

"Not long enough."

"When I saw you last, you were just a low-level hitman who worked in my shadow a couple times." When he goes to grab his gun, I add, "Don't even try it. I taught you everything you know. Well, everything except how to miss."

"I still landed one shot."

"You grazed me."

"And you're still the bastard Barone," he spits, a glob of saliva splattering against my boot. Shame, I quite liked these boots. I'll remember this disrespect when I use them to wade through his blood later.

"Is that what Malik's told you?"

Their loyalty to Malik won't waver, no matter what I say. I don't bother explaining, just plant the tiny seed of curiosity in their minds and let it bloom into doubt. That's all I need—only one spark of distrust, and Malik's kingdom will fall. He isn't the only brother who can play the long game.

I disarm the man and drag a chair over, then point to it with the barrel of my gun. "Sit down."

"Make me."

A petty response, but I take it as an invite.

Bringing the toe of my boot up, I kick Jaime's knee in,

watching with a satisfied grin that must look maniacal as his crushed leg forces him to fall backwards into the chair.

"Any more requests?"

Jaime is silent.

"Good."

Marco inches closer to me, his aim still pointed towards the second man, but he waits in case I need backup. He plays the part of scary dog a bit too well sometimes, I think, as I spot the dark stain blooming across the front of the second man's pants. His wrists are bound now, so he isn't a threat, allowing Marco to come to my aid.

"You fired seven shots into Madeline Yapon's home." I pull a chair up to Jaime, sitting backwards with one arm braced against the chair back. On the table next to us, I slam my fist down, iron catching the light. Bullets.

The man's eyes go wide, and I can only grin.

"Seven bullets. Swallow them."

Jaime blanches, his lips pressing together in a way that is subconscious. "N-no."

Fine. Make this go the hard way. The longer you refuse, the longer I get to torture you the way you tortured her, I think. *Slow, agonizing fear, wondering if you'll survive.*

You won't.

I make a show of sighing, then nod to Marco.

In an instant, Marco's hand is fisted in Jaime's hair, pulling his head back while his other hand presses the barrel of a gun between the hitman's lips. I take my time rising and leaning over him, lavishing in every whimper of fear and pain his throat makes. His fear betrays him.

"You can swallow the bullets," I say in a voice I no

longer recognize, "or my cousin here can force-feed you. Your choice."

It should be alarming, how easily I slip into this killing calm. There is no anxiety, no second-guessing—only pure, unadulterated rage.

Marco removes his gun.

Jaime reaches for the first bullet.

It goes down easily enough, fear forcing his tongue to push it down his throat. He coughs once and swears something that sounds like a prayer. He gags on the second, but the third and fourth go down without much issue. By the fifth, he swallows easily, but the final one has him clawing at his throat.

I clap my hands together. "Now then, wasn't that easy?"

Marco releases Jaime's hair, leaving him whimpering a, "Yes," while Malik's second man sits in the corner, his wrists still bound. In a few strides, I'm by his side, cutting through the zip ties and stalking towards the door.

"Have a good night, gentlemen."

Both of Malik's men look at me like I must have lost my mind, letting them live after all they've done. Perhaps they think the youngest Barone has gone soft under Natalia.

Marco appears by my side with a frown. "That was only six bullets," he counts.

I pause, my face pulled as if in thought. "You're right."

Without warning, I brandish my own gun, firing the seventh and final bullet into Jaime's head. He falls back with a spray of crimson that flecks his friend's face, the second man hollering as the first dies. "There's the seventh, motherfucker."

Marco smirks, a wolfish action that would have every nerve in my body on high alert were he not on my side.

"You'll pay for this!" the second man shouts, his voice shaking.

Marco moves to shoot him, as well, when I stop him with a hand. As much as I'd love for my cousin to shoot the clichés from the bastard's mouth, I need a messenger.

"You get to live because you're going to give my brother a message. Tell him the next time, I won't stop at a hitman. I will target anyone and everything he loves until his empire crumbles around him, and when he is all that is left standing in the ashes, I will end him too."

Marco follows me to my car, still parked in the shadow of the tree line. I know his is not far but offer him a ride regardless.

"I'm fine. You've got to go get your girl," he says with a shit-eating grin.

I don't bother correcting him, but instead flip him a vulgar gesture that heavily relies on my middlemost finger before getting into my car and speeding off.

The drive is a blur as I navigate through the winding back roads and city streets until I end up back on Addie and Natalia's front porch.

Natalia lets me in, her dark gaze assessing me for any injuries. "Did you put him down?"

"Like a goddamn dog."

She nods and lets me in, pointing upstairs. "They're in the master bedroom. She doesn't want to stay here, but I don't want her going back to her apartment. Marco still has the cleanup crew there, and I'll need to replace the front desk manager with one of our people."

My inhale is sharp in my chest as I realize what she's asking. I don't particularly enjoy having people over to my apartment. Actually, I quite hate it, and the only two people I've ever allowed in are Natalia and Marco. Inviting Maddy feels like crossing a line into dangerous territory, a space where perhaps my forbidden fantasies of a life with her can exist.

"It's no problem. I can take her to my place."

"Riven—"

"It's fine, Nat."

"Don't fucking cut me off," she snaps, albeit with a begrudgingly loving undertone. "I'm not blind. When was the last time you showed interest in someone? Because I can't remember."

Great. First Addie threatens me and now Natalia. It's enough that I question whether they conspired to spring this intervention on me while I went and sorted out Jaime.

"What are you saying?"

"I'm saying to tread lightly. You don't get attached, so the stakes are already high. Now we're adding your brother into the mix? I'm just warning you to be careful."

This may be dangerous, but I level my gaze at her, challenging. I stand a few inches above her, but she cuts an imposing figure. Nonetheless, I square my shoulders. "I'll continue to do my job, but whatever happens outside of that is none of your concern."

Natalia's tattoos ripple as every inch of her tightens, the intricate artwork on display across her bare arms. Her restraint is almost admirable. "I'm going to let you walk away from that comment tonight, Riven. Take the mercy."

Maddy chooses the perfect time to walk down the stairs, now clean and clad in a pair of Natalia's sweats and Addie's shirt.

Addie squeezes her hand as they reach the bottom of the stairs where we stand, just barely out of the doorway. "I'll bring by your clothes tomorrow once they're clean. Don't worry, with Natalia around, I've gotten used to cleaning blood out of things," she says with a wink.

Maddy embraces her, murmuring a small, "Thank you," in her ear before turning and doing the same to Natalia. Natalia glances over Maddy's shoulder through the embrace, her face a mask of ice and warning.

"Come on," I say once Maddy disentangles herself. "Let's go home."

CHAPTER 14
MADDY

I've never been to Riven's apartment before, but according to Addie, almost no one has. She mentioned the subject warily, yet almost teasingly, when I told her I didn't want to go home. I didn't want to impose on her and Natalia either, and while Addie assured me I'd never be imposing, it still felt wrong to show up unannounced.

Not that I had much of a say in the matter.

"Only you would worry about being a bother after someone tried to kill you." Addie smiled, albeit a bit sadly, stroking my arm and tracing patterns across my skin with her thumb.

I didn't mean that I would go to Riven's place. I thought I would just get a hotel room for the night or something, but Addie had already texted Riven, and from what I had heard, he agreed that that would be best. I tried my best to hide my shock at that.

Riven—who hasn't spoken to me in two months.

Riven—who just saved me.

Riven—who told Addie about my scars and trauma.

Riven—who just killed someone for me.

The thought of him bloody and murderous shouldn't fill me with excitement, but it does, in some sick and twisted way that probably speaks volumes about my mental state.

Now he stands in front of me, holding the door open to the place no one's ever been, showing me a side of him he'd rather hide.

I step into the apartment, the lights flooding the room on some sort of motion sensor. "Fancy," I muse without looking at the rest of the room yet.

Riven steps in behind me, the door snicking shut. Something in it whirs, like some form of automatic lock clicking into place. He secures another deadbolt afterwards, and locks it with his thumbprint.

"You'll be able to get out, but not back in unless I put my thumb on it again. So don't leave if you want to come back, but also don't panic."

I thank him for his consideration with a small smile, then turn back to study the apartment. I don't know what I expected, but dark wood and gauche paintings were not the aesthetic I would imagine in his space.

The walls are white, like my apartment, but the crown molding is painted a mahogany color that matches the dark-wood flooring and cabinetry. His kitchen is the first place I go. One wall is dedicated entirely to wine bottles, then another filled with alphabetically ordered spices. I knew he liked to cook, but this kitchen is far more beautiful than anything I could have ever imagined.

I step out of the kitchen into his living room, where there's a brown leather couch and woven throw pillows scattered across it. The largest TV I've ever seen rests mounted on the wall across from it, a golden frame surrounding it while various images of paintings flicker across the screen.

On the far wall, I see a balcony, the door displaying another intricate set of locks. I used to think balconies weren't a threat if you were high enough up, now I'm ninety-nine percent sure Malik would find a way to scale that wall with his bare hands if he wanted to.

There's only one other door in the room, which I assume goes to his bedroom.

"Do you have a blanket? I'll take the couch," I say at the same time Riven says, "You can take the bed."

My mouth falls open. "Riven. I'm not kicking you out of your bed." Seriously, I am already intruding upon his private space. I'm not going to further burden him by making him sleep on the couch in his own home. "Besides, your couch looks comfy."

"Then you should have no issue letting me sleep on it. Take the bed, Blondie."

"It's your house. We aren't having this argument."

"Exactly. My house, my rules. Get in my bed."

We both realize what he's said at the same time, and my face flushes red while his hand goes to the back of his neck. Then I start laughing, folding over and clutching at my stomach. Soon, my laughter turns into sobs. Great, now he probably thinks I'm crazy.

Tonight has been a fucking nightmare, and the fact that I can still blush at something as simple as the slip of a tongue... well, I feel like I'm still human.

I'm still a girl. I can still blush and laugh, even if it ends in tears.

"Good night, Riven," I mumble through my slowing

cries, then march towards the one door we haven't opened yet.

He mumbles something that sounds like, "Good night."

I hardly have time to take in the details of Riven's room as I let myself stumble into his bed, not bothering to pull back the sheets, and fall asleep instantly.

I jolt up what feels like five seconds later.

I was back in my old apartment, but instead of Donovan's boot in my side, it was Cas's. My ribs begin to burn at the same time my cheek aches and my head spins.

A glance at the clock on the nightstand tells me it hasn't been five seconds, but more like two hours. Sleep muddles my brain and I have to squint to see the hands on the clock, since it's an analog and not a digital like I'm used to.

I freeze.

Where the fuck am I?

A quick glance down confirms my suspicions. I don't recognize these sheets, these clothes, or the room I'm in. The room has high, arching ceilings, with paintings of different Italian cities scattered across the walls and a potted plant in the corner.

I stumble out of bed blindly, running towards the first door I see, as my eyes slowly adjust to the darkness. Something snags the hem of the sweatpants I'm wearing and I go tumbling to the floor with a resounding crash.

Heavy footsteps rush over and light floods the room.

I'm about to scream for help, about to bite or kick,

when I see the concerned and sleep-muddled face of Riven, his hands reaching for me. The sight calms me just enough to take a breath and remember where I am and what had happened.

There was a break-in. Cas and one of the Barones' men tried to kill me. I killed Cas, and Riven killed the other, then he brought me here, to his apartment. I'm safe.

And I just made a fool out of myself.

"Are you okay?" he asks.

I'm still sprawled out across the floor, my palms flat against his hardwood floors and I just want them to swallow me. It's bad enough I forgot where I was and panicked, but I had to trip over a table and make a fool of myself too?

I swivel my head to eye the offending furniture with disdain. Motherfucker.

Riven chuckles with what sounds like relief. "If you're able to mean-mug my coffee table, I'd say you're fine."

"I'm fine, sorry. I didn't mean to wake you." I accept his hand up, relishing in the feeling of his calluses scraping again my palms. They're rubbed raw from the friction of beating Cas to death. My arms are sore, too, from the repetitive swinging of Benny.

I hope I don't have to throw out the baseball bat, since it's a murder weapon now. I've grown attached to the thing and the jokes Addie and I made about me protecting her with it if someone ever came for us. I never thought it would actually happen. Maybe in a few years, we can laugh about it, once time has dulled the sharpest pains of our memories.

Riven peers down at me from under a mess of dark

hair, his bedhead curls blocking most of his face. I want to reach up and touch them, to push them out of his warm eyes.

Riven always looks good—it's fucking annoying most of the time—but to be this attractive after waking up? It's just unfair at this point.

Dressed in just a T-shirt and sweatpants, I've never seen him look this hot, or relaxed. Maybe it's the casualness of the outfit that makes it so goddamn sexy. I can always blame my attraction on the outfit and not the man wearing it. That logic tracks, right?

It must, because my pulse is erratic right now, just from the act of him holding my hand to pull me to my feet. One of his hands slid to my back to act as a brace, and the feel of his hand there nearly made me jump out of my skin.

Seriously, get a fucking grip.

"Don't worry about it. I was already up," he lies.

I let him get away with it. Of all the fights we pick, I'd rather this not be one of them, especially as nausea roils in my stomach. Between the bad sleep, the nightmare, and the adrenaline crash, my body has decided that it's time I pay the price.

Do not vomit on Riven's carpet. Do not, I chant mentally like a mantra. I've made a big enough fool of myself tonight as it is. I refuse to end the night by ruining his apartment décor.

"Did you have a nightmare?" he asks.

I open my mouth to respond, but the bile threatens to rise again so I close my lips and press them tightly together. I push down against the center of my wrist, applying enough pressure to hopefully help the nausea subside.

Riven frowns and tells me to wait a minute for him.

Not long after, I hear a kettle whistling and somehow find enough strength in my legs to push myself to my feet and walk to his kitchen. Riven has two plates laid on the island, one with saltines on it, the other with some sort of shortbread cookie. He has his back turned to me as he pours the tea kettle over two mugs of something that smells minty.

"I thought you were Italian, not British," I tease, settling onto one of the stools at the island.

Riven rolls his eyes. "You must be feeling better if you can mock me."

"Just curious."

"My mom would make this for me when I had nightmares as a kid. She said peppermint tea is good for your stomach, same with saltines."

"And the cookies?" I ask, wanting to pry deeper but not willing to risk the fragile peace of him discussing his past.

"Good for the soul," he says with the smallest laugh.

I join in with him, reaching for a saltine first. I would love a cookie right now, but something tells me my stomach won't appreciate it just yet.

We sit in silence, just the sound of our chewing filling the tense space in between sips of tea. It's a few moments before I push my luck, reaching for my first cookie and staring him in the eye.

"Did you get nightmares a lot when you were a kid?"

"No, not until I learned about my dad's job. My mom did her best to hide me from most of it. Malik was supposed to be the family head, anyway, and if something happened to him, there was always Cas. She didn't want me getting involved if I didn't have to."

"Did you?"

"What?"

"Have to?" I clarify.

Riven sighs, a deep sound that makes me feel guilty for even asking. I'm selfish when it comes to him, I've learned. Maybe it's because I've never liked a mystery, but something about him makes me want to learn all of his secrets, all the things he's tried so hard to hide from the light.

"Eventually. My dad viewed her way of raising me as soft, but in the end, it's what made him name me head instead of Malik. Cas didn't have the intelligence to not lead the family to ruin, and Malik was too vicious. Even in this bloody business, my father knew there was nothing good in my brother, and that if Malik were head, he would drive the Barones into constant war. Which, to be fair, is what happened for a while, until Natalia came along to put him in his place."

"But your father was Mafia. I thought he'd be the type to want the blood and glory."

"I'm Mafia, too, Mads."

Heat flushes my cheeks. "That's not what I mean."

"I know," he says gently. "Most of the new families are in it for greed. They want the money and the prestige that come with it. They like being able to do whatever the fuck they want, and in that regard, I can't say I'm entirely different. The older families are all people who have been born into blood debts so deep they'll drown in them if they try to walk away. So they have no choice but to amass their empire for their own safety, like Natalia.

"Dad was prideful, but he was more paranoid than anything. He wanted the power, but not so much power that people would come for it. He wanted to be untouchable yet unseen. Malik wanted to usher in a new age of this city where the Barones run everything. He had a vision, and once he enacted it here, he wanted to take it back to Italy and start shit with the real heavy hitters, people my dad didn't want to fuck around and find out with, if you understand what I'm trying to say."

I did, unfortunately. I'd never seen it firsthand, but I'd heard stories, found them all during my internet deep dive when I found out about Natalia and the shit show Addie got us into all those months ago.

"What about your mom? What did she think? I mean, these are her sons and husband doing all of this."

Riven takes a slow, steadying breath. "She's not Malik or Cas's mother. Mom struggled with having kids when she and my dad first got married. He was too worried about carrying on the bloodline—again, paranoid—so he slept with someone, I don't know who it was, all before I was born. When she gave him one son and my mom still wasn't pregnant, he went back for a second, needing insurance. In case something happened to the first, he'd still have an heir to his empire. Then a year or so later, I come along. My mom had grown bitter towards my dad at that point and told him she wanted to raise me. He had Malik and Cas at that point, so he didn't care, not until things stopped going the way he wanted. I had only been in the family business for about a year when he died. He got shot by a smaller rival family and bled out before help could arrive. It was just me and Malik there at the time."

I don't mean to gasp, and I smother it with another sip of my tea. I knew his father was dead already, and I also knew that Riven was there when it happened, I just never knew it was such a violent death.

Now that I think about it, how do most people living this lifestyle die? I can't imagine it's a peaceful, old death. Will Natalia die young in the heat of gunfire, leaving Addie unprotected and widowed? Will Riven and Marco die, murdered as well?

The thought of them not living into a content old age is terrible, and my knuckles go white around my mug.

"I'm sorry."

Riven only offers a sad smile. "It comes with the business."

I really wish he hadn't said that. Now I'm failing to stop the images flooding my mind of Riven, dying as he looks now, still young and full of life. His hand failing to squeeze mine as tightly as it just did as the life fades from him.

I shake my head, peering up at him from under my hair that has fallen now to frame my face. "Why did you tell me all of this?"

"Because you asked?"

"No, I mean why would you bring me here, then answer every invasive question of mine, let me take your bed, and make me tea, and just be such a goddamn gentleman when you can't stand me?"

Riven goes deathly still, his face more serious now than it was when discussing his father's death and brother's betrayal. "Who told you I don't like you?"

"Your face, every time we're in the same room," I deadpan.

Riven has been kind to me lately, but I've chalked it up to him taking his job seriously. Natalia told him to protect me so he has been. The trip to the mall was so I wouldn't go alone. The walk in the park was so I wouldn't go to a stranger's house and risk getting hurt. Everything has been to protect me, but this is too much. He could have come with me to the hotel, or demanded I stay with Addie and Natalia.

But he didn't.

No, instead, he brought me to his home, his safe place, and has taken care of me in a way that I don't ever remember being taken care of.

"You really think that?" he asks softly, perhaps even a bit dejected. I don't know why it bothers him so much.

"I mean, I'm not exactly easy to handle."

"I like handling you just fine."

"Careful how you say that, Barone."

I mean the words to tease, but instead, Riven's eyes darken and he pushes off from where he leans against the kitchen counter across from me. In a few strides, he's by my side, and I swivel on my stool so that I'm facing him. His hands come to rest on my thighs as he steps between my knees, my face now only inches from his chest. I look up and he's glancing down at me with such ferocity that a blush rises to my cheeks instantly.

"You want to forget about your nightmare?" he asks. "Let me show you how much I can't stand you."

Heat pools low in my core, and I wet my lips. Is he being serious?

I stand, not liking how small I feel on the stool next to

him. He still towers at least a foot above me, but I mind it less when I'm on my own feet.

"You don't want that." I mean to say it as a statement, but it comes out more as a question. An embarrassingly breathy question.

"There you go again, putting words in my mouth." He tuts his tongue, and I hate the way I watch his mouth move. Hate how it makes me press my thighs together and my throat go dry.

Do I want to do this?

I'd be lying if I said I didn't find Riven attractive. The more time I spend with him, the more I find him devastatingly beautiful, something I never knew a man could be. He's shown me nothing but kindness when I threw attitude at him, and rides every wave of my moods with ease.

And he's here, in front of me, offering himself.

Slowly, I step forward, closing the remaining space between us. "Promise me this will mean nothing in the morning," I whisper.

"I promise," he swears. Then he takes my face in both his hands and crashes his lips against mine.

Riven is everything I imagined he would be and more. His mouth still tastes like the peppermint tea we were drinking, and it's soft as it slants against my own. His hands are gentle yet firm as they reach beneath me, cupping my ass and lifting me until I straddle his waist, wasting no time redirecting me to his bedroom.

That part takes me by surprise. I half expected him to take me on the couch or something. The bedroom feels too personal, too intimate for us. This is just fucking—nothing intimate or touching about it.

His comforter is no longer warm from my body when he drops me down on it, and I settle on my back with a heavy, "Oof."

I fumble with the waistband of his pants, tugging them down, quick and brutal. He's already doing the same, and soon, my shirt is gone, followed by my pants, leaving me only in my underwear. He makes a low sound of approval at the back of his throat at the sight of my breasts, nipples peaked. He kneads one between his fingers, calluses scraping them in a way that feels sinfully good. I moan, my back arching off the bed already and he's barely touched me.

"How do you want me?" he asks, now only in his boxer briefs, his hands pulling at the waistband of my panties. "Do you prefer the top?"

I shake my head. I'll take him any way he wants at this point. I just need him to shut up and fuck me, but goddammit, he's a gentleman, even though there is nothing chivalrous about the way he's staring at me right now.

"I want you right as we are," I say, throwing my head back as he lowers his face between my breasts, trailing kisses down my stomach. He kneels between my legs, then comes back up to continue his exploration of my body, one hand slipping beneath my underwear before pulling them off to toss to the side. I can feel the hardened length of him pressed against my thigh as he leans forward, his mouth taking mine as his thumb traces idle circles around my clit. I grind into his hand and he pulls back, leaving me whining.

"Harder."

"Impatient little thing," he murmurs, flicking his thumb across it again.

I cry out, almost embarrassed to be so turned on when we've only just begun.

There's no time to think on it, not as Riven pushes a finger inside of me, that thumb still circling, and then a second. I gasp his name, pushing myself further down the bed to ride his hand, my hips lifting for more pressure.

"Beautiful," he breathes, and I'm already close to release once he withdraws completely.

"Bastard," I curse, pressing my thighs together for any sort of pressure. I am so close to reaching my own hand down and finishing the job for him when he pushes my knees apart. He's slipped out of his briefs and positions himself at my entrance, looking to me for approval.

"Last chance, tell me you still want this."

"Yes. God, yes."

In this moment, lust casting my brain in a hazy fog, I've never wanted anything more. Riven takes my approval as I've given it to him, pushing into me slowly, still trying to be a gentleman and let me adjust. I don't want him to be sweet to me right now, though—I want him fully. When he pulls back again, I wrap my legs around his middle and pull myself all the way onto him as I throw my head back.

"So greedy for me, Blondie," he says in a tone that sounds like praise.

The sound of my nickname on his tongue while he's buried in me has me spiraling towards my climax, and Riven continues with a now punishing pace.

This is quick and dirty, casual sex that means absolutely nothing, even though I know it will ruin all other men for me.

Riven grunts, swearing under his breath, and I keep my legs wrapped around his middle, continuing to meet him for every stroke until I can't stop. My climax shatters through me at the same time Riven's does, and he leans down to swallow my cries with another kiss.

I've never kissed this much during sex in a relationship, let alone casual sex, but I let him anyway, losing myself in the taste and feel of him. He fits in me so perfectly in every way, like our bodies were made for each other.

I don't let the idea sit in my head too long, too afraid of what it might mean.

We stay like that for a moment, until Riven disentangles our bodies, leading me to the shower. He turns it on hot, just the way he knows I like it from all my mornings I come home post-hookup.

"Shampoo is in the bottom drawer, towels to the right," he says, then he's gone.

What the fuck?

I step under the stream of hot water and wash myself off. This is what I want, I remind myself. I never expected or wanted any of my other hookups to stay or cuddle—actually, I fucking hated it when they tried. So why does it bother me that I just had the best sex of my life and then he left me alone in the bathroom?

It isn't the quickest hookup I've had, but not the longest either. I don't think I've ever came so fast in my entire life, even by myself.

Stop thinking about it, I tell myself when I step out to find a new shirt and sheets on the bed. *It was just sex between two consenting adults who will forget about it tomorrow. Go to bed.*

Maybe it's because my brain is still fuzzy from sleep, or muddled by my recent orgasm, but I settle into the covers, closing my eyes. But I don't sleep. Instead, I wait and listen for the sound of Riven outside the door. He's walking around out front, the soft clang of pans telling me he's trying to quietly put our midnight snack away.

A smile lifts my lips, a smile that shouldn't be there. I can't keep this man, but after one night, I want to. I want him, and that just might be more dangerous than the death threats looming over my head.

CHAPTER 15
RIVEN

I don't expect to get a text from Maddy. It's been a few days since I last saw her, when she had curled up on my bed and fallen asleep from the shock of Cas attempting to kill her. Then, and after I fucked her in my home—something I did not plan on doing. But she looked so scared, and this was twice now that someone had hurt her and I hadn't been there to save her. Twice that someone else killed them before I could.

I took out most of my frustration out on the man who had shot at her, however. That helped more than I cared to admit. Seeing him swallow those bullets, and the fear in his eyes, was satisfying in a primal way.

I used to wonder if Maddy would balk at the violence in my heart, but after the other night, I know she wouldn't. As pure as she is, she is struck by that same violence. She is all that is beautiful in darkness, yet light all the same. She's my perfect hell—a paradox in a woman.

MADDY:

Are you busy?

No, what's wrong?

I'm about to shit myself over this meeting tomorrow.

Can you come over?

Wait

Not like that

You know what I mean.

omw

Locking my phone, I chuckle as I head for the door. Maddy mentioned over the phone that she has a big interview tomorrow with some artsy hotshot who owns a gallery. I'm supposed to drive her, and of course, I already ran a full background check on the guy she's meeting.

Austin Pembrooke. A lithe guy, the classically smart archetype who looks like he's better suited for architecture than photography. No prior arrests or outstanding warrants. He seems harmless, but I learned my lesson on writing people off too quick, and have opted to go with her regardless.

Maddy opens the door, her nails gritted between her teeth. I swat them from her mouth, noticing some bleeding and already bit to the quick.

"Stop that. The meeting is going to be fine and it's not until tomorrow."

"I know, it's just..." Her voice trails off and a low growl of frustration rises in the back of her throat. "It's stupid."

"It's not stupid."

"It is!" She throws her hands in the air. "I've done this hundreds of times. I shouldn't be this nervous."

"It's important to you," I say, laying a hand on her shoulder, then gesturing to the apartment behind her. "But can we continue this inside?"

Maddy swears under her breath and ushers me in. The sun has just begun to set and is halfway through its descent, casting her apartment in a warm golden glow. I've always loved how she put her personal touches all over the otherwise blank space. From the plants draping by her windows to the photos on the wall and the statement furniture, every inch of this apartment is a cozy place of solace.

"What can I do to help?"

She groans. "Distract me, please."

I raise an eyebrow, and she flushes scarlet.

"Not like that. Not this time."

Her words make my chest tighten. "If you insist," I tease, but not really teasing at all. If she gave me the word, I would take her in a second. The fact that I got to have her once was already more than I could have ever hoped for, but she'd consider letting me have her again? I don't know what I did in a past life to deserve this but I must have been a saint.

"I want to know about you," she says suddenly in a way that makes my heart drop. "I know about all the shit with your brothers, but I want to hear about your life from you. Not Addie, or Natalia, or Marco. You. Riven Barone." She pokes my chest with a well-manicured finger to emphasize her point, and I find myself rubbing the spot once she's done.

"I was named family head. My brothers tried to kill me. Natalia gave me a place to stay. My mother lives in Rome and thinks I'm dead because Malik said if she ever thought otherwise he'd kill her. Now I kill people for Natalia and babysit you, apparently. That's... pretty much it."

"What do you like to do in your free time?"

"What free time?"

"God." She tosses her head back as she laughs, her blonde hair cascading down her back like a golden waterfall. Her nose scrunches and she looks peaceful, young again, as if the weight of the past few months have all washed away. I want to keep that look for her face forever, to bottle this feeling so I can give it to her in doses when I see her pulling away. Selfishly, I want to etch the sound of her laughter into a vinyl, and play it on an old record player in a sunny kitchen. A kitchen that hopefully she'll be in, ready to record another track.

"You need a hobby," she says once she's done laughing.

"I do *not* need a hobby."

"You have no fun in your life!"

"What do you think *this* is?" I ask.

"Fair enough. I am a delight," she says, flipping her hair over her shoulder for dramatic flair. "But you need to do something for fun once in a while. Blow off steam. Something that doesn't involve guns and blood and crime."

"Do *you* have hobbies?"

Maddy stiffens at that, then stands up and leaves the room. My mind whirs to life as I try to think of what I said to upset her. She didn't look particularly upset, nor do I think I said anything. Maybe I hit a sore spot?

Before I can think on it too long, Maddy is back, a wooden box in her arms. She waddles into the room, trying to carry its hulking weight in front of her, the box an awkward size. Her face is slightly red as she sets it on the coffee table in front of me and grins, both sheepish and proud at the same time.

"I like to watch movies, usually kid cartoons or musicals," she says as way of explanation.

I reach for the box and see hundreds of DVDs, some at least fifteen years old, none gathering dust. Some of my childhood favorites sit in the collection, and nostalgia I didn't know I was capable of feeling crawls up my throat.

"Do you want to watch one?" I ask her, and mentally applaud myself when I see her face light up.

"Fine, but only if *you* pick the movie." She says it like I've twisted her arm. Maddy slides the box my way, then bites her lip with borderline giddy delight as I carefully sort through the collection. I watch her expression shift as my hand ghosts each new movie, and I stop when I see her eyes light up.

The movie I've landed on looks to be an animated musical, checking both of her boxes, as it tells the story of a lost princess and her dreams.

Perfect.

"I haven't seen this one yet," I say as nonchalantly as I can.

Maddy is practically vibrating where she sits perched

on the arm of the couch. "You haven't? *Tangled* is my favorite movie of all time."

I can tell, I think, but instead, I say, "Seems like we have our pick then."

Maddy bounces over to the TV, slipping the DVD in and grabbing the remote. She excuses herself to get a water while the opening credits roll, and when she comes back, she has a blanket draped over her shoulders, two bottles of water, and a whole tray of snacks.

"I thought I'd give you the full experience." She blushes. If she keeps smiling and blushing at me like this, my heart won't make it through the movie.

She settles beside me on the couch, completely at ease as she slowly tucks herself into my side. It's a familiar feeling, and she fits like she is made to be pressed against me, each of her soft curves filling in my hard edges. She tosses the blanket over both of us, the snacks in reach, and watches as the opening scene begins to play.

I'll admit the music is good, and the art style pretty, but I can't help but watch most of it through the reflection in her wide eyes while she absorbs every detail. She hits my arm every few minutes, explaining to me why this one line is so important, or asking if I got the joke. I do my best to keep up, but this Maddy is... entrancing. As much as I want to watch the movie with her, I can't seem to pull my eyes away.

Without turning from the screen, she says, "I'm going to turn this off if you don't start paying attention. I might even quiz you."

A nervous laugh rises in me. It's easy, being here with her. Everything feels natural, and dare I say normal.

Being with Maddy is like taking a deep breath in a forest after living in a smoggy city. She makes me feel alive, like I want to live and not just survive.

I pull my eyes from her and watch the movie unfold now, determined to understand this part of her world she's sharing with me. I won't deny that I find myself enthralled, laughing with her because yes, I did understand the joke, and no, I didn't miss the moment that one character looked at the other.

At some point, Maddy throws a chocolate candy at me, and I toss one back, only she catches it in her mouth then sticks her tongue out at me like a child.

"Very mature."

"Shh, you're interrupting my favorite song."

I roll my eyes but settle further into the couch, doing my best not to stiffen when she lays her head against my shoulder. As we reach an emotional climax, something wet plops against my shirt.

"Are you crying?"

"Shut up, Riven."

So yes, then.

The movie ends and we watch through the end credits, simply because she likes the song they play at the end. Maddy sits up now, and I immediately miss the warmth of her against my side, my fingers flexing as if they don't know what to do now that they don't have her shoulder to rest on.

"So," she asks, a sleepy grin on her face, "what did you think?"

"I think we should make this a weekly thing, but next time, you get to pick."

She yawns and stretches, her every joint popping with the motion. "Those are brave words, Barone."

"I'm sure you'll make me eat them." I stand with her, helping to clear away the remnants of our movie night. I didn't plan to stay so late, and the stars are now shining above the city in full force.

We settle into the silence as we clean, me taking over dishes while she puts away the blanket and movies. When she comes back, she's in pajamas, and I fight the heat growing in my chest at the sight of her long, tan legs as they stride to close the distance between us. She's in a matching set tonight, light purple.

"Have you thought of your 'something fun' yet?" she asks, hopping onto the counter to sit beside me while I finish up the rest of the dishes. I've rolled my shirt up to expose my forearms as I clean, and it is with no small amount of satisfaction that I watch her blatantly stare at them.

To be honest, I haven't given it much thought—I've been so consumed by our night. So instead, I say the first thing that pops into my mind.

"How about a concert?"

Maddy beams and pats my shoulder. "That's a great idea! There's a local festival happening in a few weeks now that the weather is getting slightly—I said *slightly*, not a lot—warmer. We can invite Addie, Natalia, and Marco. We can make a day of it. It'll be great."

"Just send me the details and I'll book the tickets."

"No way. It's your fun night so that means I pay."

"How does that math work?"

"It's not fun if you're paying for it, duh."

"It's fun because Natalia pays me well enough that I

could buy out the entire event," I say, flicking her nose with a bit of dish soap. "You're a barista."

Maddy flips a vulgar gesture my way, but shrugs as if to say *you win*. Not that she'll ever say those words out loud to anyone, least of all me.

"I should get going." I dry my hands off in a dish towel then face her properly. "I'll be back in the morning to pick you up for that interview. Don't forget to send me ticket information."

"Fine, fine. I'll see you then."

She shows me to the door, and I force myself to keep my eyes lifted. *God, don't be perverse.* Still, I let my gaze drift to her lips right before she opens the door. She stands with her arms around her in the open doorway, hugging herself slightly. I step out into the hallway.

"Riven?"

I turn around, stepping closer to where she still stands at the door. My arm braces the frame above her head and I look down, half in concern, half in curiosity.

"I just wanted to say thank you for tonight. And everything else." She says the last part hurriedly, almost stammering through a hazy blush she tries to hide by ducking her chin.

My thumb hooks beneath her jaw, tilting her face upwards so that she's looking in my eyes. "Always, Blondie."

It's excruciating, pulling myself away from her, but somehow, I manage the few steps back. I wait until she closes and locks her door to leave, then let the warmth I feel in my chest spread through the rest of my body.

Tomorrow.

I get to see her again tomorrow.

CHAPTER 16
MADDY

Smoothing my hands over my gray dress, I inhale shakily. Riven is going to bang down the bathroom door any minute now, but I needed another moment to collect myself.

A few weeks ago, I reached out to a gallery owner about showing him my more recent portfolio in the hopes of joining a showing he has in the coming weeks. I haven't had my photography displayed in a gallery since before Donovan, and as I am trying to get my footing again, it seemed like the right step.

Only I didn't account for the nerves that are eating away at my insides. These types of meetings used to be so easy—I would walk in, charm the owner, flash some photos and a winning smile, then walk out with a new showing date. I've been turned down before, sure, but the thought of it never bothered me until now. I've always had the "Oh well, there will be another one" mentality. Now the fear of rejection settles in my chest like a stone.

"Do I need to kick this door down?"

"If you break my door, I will break *you*." I swipe

another layer of lip gloss on and check my hair for a final time, taking longer than necessary to annoy the impatient man waiting for me.

Riven laughs. "You can try."

He is leaning against the frame when I open the door, one arm braced against the top as he peers down at me. The sight is devastating to my heart and I duck beneath his arm before he can see the blush on my cheeks.

"Nervous?" he asks.

"Nope."

"It would be more convincing if you tried squeaking less."

"Fuck you."

"Gladly."

I have to smile at that. It feels nice to focus on something other than the stress for a change. My hand slips into his, an action that feels slightly dangerous and a little too committal, but he squeezes it twice before we walk out of the apartment.

Riven keeps his sarcastic remarks coming the entirety of the drive, not so subtly keeping my mind from wandering too far into "what if" territory. He only stops when we reach the glass doors of the venue, his hand resting on the small of my back.

"You ready?"

I can only nod, my mouth suddenly dry.

Riven shoots me a look that tells me he isn't convinced, but opens the door anyway.

A tall, lithe man with glasses perched atop his pointed nose stands in the center of the room. He's younger than I thought he would be, perhaps only ten or so years older than I am. Most of the men I've met in this industry have been older, and the women are younger, but this man might have less wrinkles than I do.

"Miss Yapon, I presume?"

"That's me, and this is my assistant, Mr. Barone." I smile nervously. "Are you Mr. Pembrooke?"

"That would also be me," he says with a warm tone.

My shoulders drop from my ears and I let myself fully inhale.

"Please, my office is just this way."

We follow him through a series of glass corridors, beautiful artwork lining the walls in a sort of fragile beauty. I know we reach his office when I spot the grandiose double doors at the end of the hall, and a golden plaque that reads, "Chief Curator," standing stark in juxtaposition to the dark wood of the doors.

"Can I get you both a water or anything? Coffee?"

"We're fine, thank you." I try to be courteous and conceal my nerves as we step into the lavish office. This place is turning out to be far more glamorous than I expected, and I try not to regret not wearing heels or a blazer.

Riven pulls out a chair for me when Mr. Pembrooke motions for us to sit, settling behind his own desk with his hands folded. Atop the wooden surface, I spot my portfolio I sent him in advance, per his request, all my work spread out like evidence.

"I'll try to keep this brief, Miss Yapon, as I know we're both busy individuals."

If I was nervous before, then there are no words to describe the dread settling into my stomach.

"I appreciate your consideration, Mr. Pembrooke," I say, my mouth tasting like ash.

Next to me, Riven's frown settles deep in the lines of his face.

"As you know, our gallery showcases only the best, and while the team and I considered your pieces at length, we have ultimately decided that they have no place in this showing."

"I see. May I ask why?" I ask, at the same time Riven asks, "Couldn't you have said that in an email instead of making us drive across town?"

I nudge his shin with my toe, but there is no heart behind it.

"I can understand the frustration, Mr. Barone. We believe such matters are handled best in person, so we can answer questions such as the one Miss Yapon has brought to light." Mr. Pembrooke adjusts his glasses, that voice no longer warm and welcoming. "Your previous works are good, but they're dated, while your newer pieces are... dark. Too dark for this showing, I'm afraid. Photography is an art, simply put."

My fingernails bite into the soft flesh of my palms as I ball my hands into fists in my lap. "I am aware of that, sir."

"And art should make you feel something," he continues. "All I feel is that I've wasted my time looking at your work."

I think my heart cracks audibly, until I glance to the side where Riven has splintered the arm of the chair he's sitting in.

"Say that again," he growls, his voice dangerously low.

Pembrooke at least has the decency to look afraid, even as he straightens his tie. "Violence will not lighten the truth of my words."

"No, but it will make me feel better."

"Riven." His name falls breathlessly from my lips, and in an instant, he turns from the curator towards me. Pure rage lines the harsh contours of his face, turning his eyes to smoldering coals pulled straight from Hell itself. Pembrooke has good reason to cower behind his desk, his eyes still trained on the broken armrest of his wooden chair.

I shake my head. *Not now, please.*

Riven sighs, rising and offering me his hand before turning back to the other man with a sinister glower. "Your time is as worthless as the knockoff suit you're wearing," he snarls at a cowering Pembrooke. "If you're going to insult her by pretending to have class, you should at least dress the part."

With that, I let him lead me from the room, trying to hide my smirk at the way Pembrooke's jaw practically rests upon his desk.

"Was his suit really a knockoff?" I whisper as we walk through the hallways.

Riven raises an eyebrow. "Obviously. You can't stitch real tweed like that."

"Oh my god."

Riven opens the door with a wink and we walk hand in hand to the car, my heart still heavy but significantly lighter than before. Once settled in our seats, he glances at me, his face now pinched with concern. All the rage from earlier is contained now, hidden behind his eyes but still evident in his white knuckles.

"Are you alright?" he asks. "That was a shitty thing to say and I will gladly go back in there and kill him." He's serious—I know from the way his fingers tap against his hip, itching for his gun or maybe a more intimate weapon of mutilation.

"Please stop casually threatening to kill people," I sigh. "It's no longer funny now that I know you mean it."

"Fine, but do you want to talk about it?"

"Not really."

"It's not good to hold your emotions in."

I fix him with a dead look. "That sounds like something Addie would say. I'm not good with words like she is. I need action, images, something concrete to show that these words and feelings aren't empty."

Riven contemplates that for a moment, then braces his forearms against the steering wheel and resting his chin against his shoulder to look at me. "Give me an example."

"If you tell someone you love them then you cheat on them, which do you think they mean more?"

"Point taken."

"It's just that... what he said hurt because it hit too close to home. My camera is my way of using my words. My work, all of it, is the only lens I can offer that shows my world. And my world is dark right now, so of course my art will be too."

Riven sits up at that. As if on instinct, his hand reaches out and brushes a stray hair behind my ear. "That's nothing to be ashamed of, Maddy. Your work is beautiful."

The *you are beautiful* feels heavily implied, but I let it go, if only because my heart cannot take that right now.

Riven spares me from further embarrassment by whipping out his phone. "Why don't you host a private showing? A gallery that is just your work? I know a guy who as a venue, and he owes me a favor," he offers, his fingers already flying across the screen before pausing to look to me for confirmation.

A private gallery of just my work. The idea seemed so far away in the past that I never let myself actually consider it, but if Riven is offering...

"I love that idea."

"Really?" he asks, his eyebrows raising in shock.

"Yes, really, unless you weren't serious—"

"*No.* No, I am serious. I just didn't think you'd ever accept my help."

"I'm not above handouts. A connection is a connection, and if someone is offering to help, then I'll make sure I work to earn that help."

I used to have the mindset of having to do all the work myself, that accepting help meant I was cheating. Now I know life doesn't pass around handouts often, and when they do come about, it's best to accept them, then work to be worthy of it. Now, that doesn't mean I'm not going to put up a fight when my dad tries to pay the bill to hold it over my head, but for my dream to become my reality? I'll do just about anything for that to happen.

"You've already earned it," he says through a sad but knowing smile. "I'll make some calls today then."

"Thank you, Riven," I say, laying my hand on his arm. He knows I don't just mean for this, but for everything he's done for me, just being here.

He nods, covering my hand with his own. "Anything for you, Blondie."

CHAPTER 17
MADDY

I frown at the skies through the large glass windows at Tella's. The weatherman said there was a fifteen percent chance of rain today when I checked this morning. Fifteen percent my ass, I think as I look at the ominously dark clouds gathering above the city.

Marco warned me to pack an umbrella when he picked me up this morning, and seeing as I was already late, I didn't. Thank god Natalia has him running a hit for her today, otherwise I would be served the biggest "I told you so" at the end of my shift.

I half expected Natalia to tighten my security after the Cas incident, but if anything, she seems to have more faith in my ability to take care of myself. She was never strict about supervision while at work—since it would be too much trouble for Malik to send someone into the public eye in broad daylight—but even then, Riven usually stays during the first hour of my shift.

Riven was supposed to bring me this morning, but Addie had a meeting with her publicist and Natalia had him take her since it was so close to Barone territory.

That also means I'm opening shop alone, since Addie will be late. Lucky me.

The first onslaught of the morning rush leaves as swiftly as it comes. Usually, these are students at the local college, businessmen, or other city workers trying to get a quick caffeine fix before work. Our second round of customers are generally people interviewing, other college students who came to study, or friends meeting up. They sit and stay for a bit, leaving me with a small break from the constant orders.

The door opens, and my face splits into a smile when I see who walks through.

"I didn't think I'd see you again so soon," I say to the man who sat with me in the parking lot. He wears a dark trench coat today that stands in stark contrast to the light-gray dress shirt he wears beneath it. "What can I get for you?"

Now that his face is illuminated, I can see he is even more handsome than I originally thought, and unnervingly familiar.

"Hello again, Maddy," he says, looking at my name tag. His voice lacks the warmth it had last time, and my smile falters slightly. Whatever, maybe he's having a bad day. It's not like he owes me anything. Still, I plaster on my best customer service voice to take his order.

"What can I get for you?"

"Large cappuccino. Double espresso."

"You've got it." I pull out a Sharpie to write on the cup. "Do I finally get to learn your name?"

"Malik."

The Sharpie scratches against the cup. The man

doesn't flinch, just watches my expression with cool calculation.

"Alex?" I ask, hoping it's just a classic barista blunder and that the chatter of the café has made me hear him wrong.

"You know who I am, Madeline." Malik cocks his head to the side, assessing me still. "Aren't you going to make my coffee? I promise I'm a paying customer."

Fuck.

I quickly write his name on a new cup, throwing the other in the trash as I take a moment to collect myself. My eyes dart to the clock. Addie should almost be here, and Daryl is in the office behind me. Malik wouldn't try anything in front of all these people, would he? Natalia was confident about it and I haven't known the woman's intuition to be wrong yet. All he can do is intimidate me.

"That will be five dollars and ninety-five cents."

Malik pays, then walks down the other side of the counter as I work on is drink. His stare brands me and I fight the urge to be sick into his coffee.

You're okay. He's not going to do anything. He can't scare you if you don't let him.

"You're jumpier this morning."

"Forgive me for not being more welcoming to a man who wants me dead," I deadpan. Could this milk steam faster, please? I'd rush his order but something tells me he would have me remake it if it wasn't satisfactory, and I can't give him that excuse.

"If I really wanted to kill you then I would have in the parking lot."

"I don't know, the hitmen you've sent so far have been really convincing of your good intentions."

Malik laughs, and it sounds like Riven's but deeper, more twisted. It rasps against my skin like a perverse caress.

He lets me work in silence for a moment. I'm nearly done and reaching for a lid when he speaks again.

"How's my brother doing?"

One question sends a chill up my spine. The demeanor shifts, the similar face and stance. The voice of a man well acquainted with violence. Where Riven's dark eyes are warm with love, Malik's lighter ones are cold as he stares down at me.

"Riven's great."

"In what ways?" he asks, his elbows leaning against the counter as I pour his drink with shaking hands. "I bet you'd like what I have to offer better. Brothers share, you know."

Disgust crawls up my throat, but I force my voice to be calm as I say, "Ask Cas how that worked out for him."

Provoking a family head may be a bad move on my part, but I refuse to be thrown about by disgusting men any longer. I don't deserve it, and like hell will I let him continue to try and scare me. If he wants to kill me, fine. He can see his brother again.

Instead of rage flickering across his face, Malik looks amused, maybe even intrigued. "I would, but he's currently cooling on a table in the family morgue. The bruising is quite impressive. It will have to be a closed casket wake, but I imagine it will be an intimate, touching ceremony."

I snap the lid in place on his coffee, and shove it across the bar top. It stops mere centimeters from the edge, a bit splashing from the opening at the top. Malik traces his thumb over his name, printed in my neat handwriting.

"Thank you for visiting Tella's. I hope you have a nice day." My voice is sharp, as if I can force him to leave with my tone alone.

The bell above the door chimes, finally offering me an escape. To my relief, I spot a head of wild brown curls. Addie, catching sight of my face, hurries over, and I'm so focused on her that I miss Riven walking in behind her. It isn't until his thunderous voice cuts through the café that I realize he has arrived at all.

"Malik."

His voice is murderous, and the glare he levels at his brother is purely lethal. In only a few long strides, he is standing in front of me, his hands fisting Malik's shirt. For a moment, I think he might lift him from the ground.

Addie moves behind the counter, shifting so she's standing between me and the brothers, one hand reassuring on my arm, the other raised as if she might fight the eldest Barone herself should Riven fail.

"Hello, Riven." Malik smirks. "I was just introducing myself to your lovely friend. You know, most would consider it rude for you to not have introduced us already."

"I should kill you right now," Riven says. I don't miss the strain in his voice, the tremor in his hands that I know isn't just from rage. It's the same emotion he masks every day beneath his charm and confident bravado. It's sorrow.

This is the first time the brothers have seen each other since their father's death, I realize.

"That would be hard for even Natalia to cover up, and you know it. Walk away, brother." Then, over Riven's shoulder, Malik catches sight of Addie. Her offensive stance does not falter, not even with those wicked eyes upon her.

"Natalia's songbird," he croons. "What a surprise."

"The bastard head of the Barones. Why am I *not* surprised?" She responds evenly and with a coolness I wish I could mirror.

"I only mean to congratulate you on your engagement and upcoming book release. You must be quite happy."

If Addie is shocked that Malik knows about her publication, she doesn't show it. That information won't be released to the public for another week. Though with Malik's resources, I'm not surprised he knows.

"I'll be happy once you leave my job. If Riven doesn't kill you, I'll do it myself."

"And you're more than capable, aren't you? I did hear that it was Natalia's bullet that ended Donovan Larson's life, but it would be hard to miss the fact that he'd already been stabbed, wouldn't it?" His gaze slides back to me and my stomach churns. "A violent pair, the two of you. It must be why my brother and Mancini are so enamored."

Malik pushes Riven off of him, leaning around to grab his coffee cup. He makes a show of a sip, then with a flippant wave, he pushes through the door, disappearing amidst the winding sidewalks of the city, the shadows of the skyscrapers concealing him.

Addie turns to me immediately, her blue eyes blazing. "Are you okay? I'm so sorry I was late."

"It's okay. You had no way of knowing that would happen," I assure her.

The fight had drawn attention in the otherwise quiet

coffee shop, but the spectators were now turning back to their own drinks and business.

Riven hasn't moved from his spot yet, his fists clenching and unclenching at his side as if he can still feel the fabric of Malik's shirt in his hands. Like he's imagining driving those fists into Malik's face.

There's no line at the register, and with Addie now on shift, I take a moment to move to the front of the bar and lay a gentle hand on his shoulder. He flinches, then stops, as if he's trained his body to have no reaction to surprise and has only momentarily forgotten himself.

"Are you okay?"

Riven huffs a hollow laugh. "He's still the same after all these years."

"A tiger doesn't change its stripes."

"No, I guess not. Are you alright? Did he say anything to you?"

I cringe as I recall what Malik said, and wish the earth would swallow me whole as I repeat it to Riven. I leave out the part that Malik was the man to sit with me in the parking lot that one time. That's a stressor he doesn't need right now, not that it changes anything in this moment.

A muscle feathers in Riven's jaw, and for a moment, it looks like he has half a thought to go chase his brother down in the streets and make good on that promise to kill him.

"Look, it's fine. It was just to get under our skin. I have to get back to work now, but I'm off in a few hours. We can talk then. Are you going to be okay?" I ask.

Daryl has finally come out of his office to investigate, and while Addie is stalling him, I can feel his eyes burning through my back. One of these days, he is going to find our antics more annoying than endearing, and will finally fire us.

Riven looks hesitant to leave, as if him not being here in the first place is what caused this conflict. Nevertheless, he relents and fishes his phone from his pocket. "I'm good. I'm going to go talk to Natalia and see if we can get ahead of this. We've been picking up rumors that the Barones have a large shipment coming in soon. It would be truly terrible if someone were to leak its time and location to local authorities."

I feel a smile lifting my lips at the sarcasm dripping from his voice. "Horrible, but I thought it was beneath you all to involve the police?"

"Only when it doesn't benefit us. But by all means, if the cops want to do our dirty work, I will gladly slip them the information. An anonymous tip, of course," he says with a wink.

"Of course."

"I'll pick you up after work. Be safe." Then he leans in and kisses my forehead. The action is natural, as if it's instinct, and he walks away without another word. I, on the other hand, feel my whole face flush red. The crimson blush on my cheeks only worsens when I turn to find Addie grinning with wicked delight.

"How long has that been a thing, and why the fuck didn't you tell me?" she all but screeches when I join her behind the counter again.

Daryl sighs so deeply I think the whole city feels it, then returns to his office for some "peace and sanity."

Addie has been wanting Riven and I to get together since she met him, even while I was dating Donovan.

Granted, she and Donovan never got along, so I took her determination to ship us with a grain of salt. It's also the reason I haven't told her that I hooked up with her friend.

"Not too long. It's casual, and we aren't dating so it didn't seem important."

My best friend looks at me like I've just told her the most absurd thing in the world. Her nose scrunches and she gestures wildly with her hands as she speaks, as if she's trying to physically string the words together. "So you're casually hooking up with Riven—nice, by the way—yet he still comes in here and goes all stone-cold killer on his brother just for talking to you, then gives you the most adorable forehead kiss in front of your boss and your best friend... and you get where I'm going with this, right?"

"His brother wasn't just talking to me. He was threatening me and has actively sent men to kill me over the past few months."

"Details." She waves me off. "My point is, Riven's not the type to do that for anyone, and you're not the type to just let him."

Addie being my best friend is both the best and worst thing in the world. It's the best because she's amazing and I love her. It's the worst because she knows me too well and easily calls me out on my bullshit.

I take an order from a customer before turning back to her with a groan. "Okay, maybe—and this is a very strong maybe, Addison Collins—I might have feelings for him."

There it is—the ugly truth I've been hiding from everyone, including myself. I'm not sure when it happened.

At first, I could hardly tolerate Riven. Even from the moment I met him, I found him vexing. He came into our old apartment, swaggering and speaking to me as if I wasn't half as intelligent as he was. Then our annoyance turned into near rivalry. He had to outdo me in everything, and I always had to be right. It was a constant back and forth. Even when we went to Italy, spending a full day traveling with him was hell, but it was also ... fun. It was a challenge, like a game to see who could one-up the other at all times.

Then he was the one to find me when I was dying, while Natalia searched frantically for Addie. He talked my parents through what happened in a gentle voice when he thought I couldn't hear him. He thought I was still asleep while we were in the hospital, but really, I kept my eyes closed just so I could continue to feel the reassuring weight of his hand in mine. I knew that when I opened my eyes, my whole world would be changed, yet Riven would go back to treating me how he always had. While I grew to enjoy our banter, I needed his compassion then more than I needed the challenge.

Now there's a tension between us. I thought it was one-sided, but maybe...

"Riven obviously doesn't feel the same, though, so I'd appreciate you not saying anything. It's just a crush. It will go away on its own."

Addie pinches my arm. "You've gotten too comfortable lying to me these days. Stop it."

"I'm only half lying."

"If you think for one second that Riven doesn't have feelings for you, you're delusional. Have you tuned out everything I said?"

I roll my eyes. I want to believe her, I really do, but Addie has a tendency to see what she wants to see, and sometimes her dreams are too big for reality. It's something I love about her, but I can't let myself have that hope.

"I have been masterfully laying the foundation of this ship for months now. Do not let it sink!"

"I don't even want to know what that means." I laugh, but nonetheless watch through the window as storm clouds begin to roll over the city, and let my mind wander back to Riven's last words to me. *Be safe*, I mouth back to the universe, then get back to work.

CHAPTER 18
RIVEN

I pick up Maddy from Tella's, still fuming from both Malik's surprise appearance and the fact that we didn't find anything new today. She sits in the front seat of my car blasting some old pop song while I drive us through the downpour.

The storm that lingered all day finally decided to pop and drench the city, leaving it damn near impossible to see anything on these dark roads. We took a back road to avoid the traffic of downtown with the rain, not that it's much help.

In my periphery, I see Maddy stiffen.

"Stop the car."

"What?"

On instinct, I scan the darkness surrounding us for any threat. Lightning streaks the sky, but no other headlights illuminate the road.

"Stop the— Oh, for fucks sake."

A click.

Then Maddy jumps out of the still-moving car.

Shit.

Shit. Shit. Shit.

I've never slammed on the brakes harder than now, the tires squealing on the slick pavement. I'm out of the car with the parking brakes barely on, my finger lighting on the trigger of my gun.

Maddy has been all but swallowed by the darkness as she runs towards the side of the road we just passed. She rips her shirt off, pulling it over her head in one swift motion before kneeling by a shadow.

What. The. Fuck.

I'm sprinting now, my gun safely holstered as she meets me halfway. I peer down at the creature bundled in her now soaking-wet T-shirt—a small brown puppy. It's maybe only a few weeks old, a shepherd mix of some kind. My heart softens a fraction of an inch when I see her checking it for injuries. But I'm still pissed.

"What the hell were you thinking?" I hiss, wrapping my arms over her bare shoulders. "You don't jump out of a moving car."

"Take me to a vet," she murmurs instead, paying no attention to my lecture. Her fingers splay in the pup's wet fur as it cranes its neck up to lick at them. We're nearly to the car now, both of us soaked and Maddy's blonde hair stuck to her neck and shoulders.

"You're going to get sick."

"Riven." She raises her gaze to mine, nothing but fire in those brown eyes. "Take me to the vet or I will walk there like this."

There is no arguing with her on this, not as the poor dog shivers so hard that her arms jolt.

I open the door to my car for her before moving to my side and pulling a hoodie out of the back seat. I toss it her way as I slide in to the driver's seat. "At least put this on so we don't have to visit the hospital next."

"Or so the cute vets don't see my bra." She grins wickedly.

I glance down at the lacy red bra, the firm swell of her breasts beneath it, and...

"Don't push your luck," I grind out, my knuckles white on the steering wheel.

The puppy whines, snuggling closer to Maddy for warmth. I turn my gaze back to the rain-slick road. I am a competent driver, but these conditions make it near impossible to see.

We turn onto the highway, my GPS cheerily chirping out instructions that feel off in the somber situation.

"Oh, you poor thing," Maddy coos, her voice thick with emotion. "You're okay now, you're okay." I've never heard her so gentle before, so kind. She's always been sweet to Addie, cordial with Natalia, and stubborn with me, but gentle is a word I wouldn't have used for her before now.

A few moments later, we pull into the emergency vet, and Maddy is already sprinting to the door before the car is fully in park.

"Jesus fuck, Maddy!"

My voice dies in the storm and I swear lowly, locking my car and sprinting after her. I get inside just quick enough to see a vet tech leading her down a hall and ushering them into a room. I follow before the door snicks shut.

Maddy's face is grim as she lays the dog on the table. A second person, who I assume to be the vet judging by their white coat, enters and asks a few questions before she begins feeling the pup's abdomen. After nearly one whole painful hour of examinations, tests, and questions, the vet gives the poor animal the all-clear.

"She's maybe nine or ten weeks old, probably a Lab and German shepherd mix. She's lucky you found her when you did. Any longer and she might have become hypothermic."

"Did you find a microchip?" Maddy asks.

The vet shakes her head. "No microchip. We'll keep her overnight for observation then bring her to the humane society first thing tomorrow."

That seems like a happy enough ending to me, but before I can fish out my wallet and thank them for their time, Maddy interrupts.

"Or..." She glances my way. "I can take her. Is there any form of adoption paperwork since she's a stray?

The vet smiles softly. "No. She'll need vaccines—standard ones, like rabies. The shelter would pay for it usually, but if you're taking her home, it will come out of your pocket. We can also microchip her here now."

"Maddy—"

"Let's do it then." She takes the small pup's face in her hands and smiles when it licks her nose. "You want to come home with me? Yeah, you do? Okay then."

"Do you have a card we can put on file? I'd like to go get all the paperwork drawn up."

"Shoot, yes, it's in the car. I'll be right back—" She makes to go back to the car in the storm when my hand reaches out to grab her arm.

"Here, just use mine."

"Riven, no. This is something I want to do myself."

"Then pay me back later, but you're not going back

into that storm." I cross my arms, making a point of keeping the hand with my card on top, the card still extended towards her.

Maddy sighs, the wet hair stuck to her forehead shifting with her brows as she frowns, but nonetheless takes the card and extends it to the vet.

The vet accepts the card with a blushing smile.

Maddy looks up at me, her frown softening only a bit. "I will be paying you back."

"I'm sure you will."

"And you know we have to go back out into the storm anyway."

"No, I will. You will wait here with your dog while I bring the car around."

She throws her hands in the air, only missing my jaw by an inch. "How is that fair?"

"It's not, but that's what's happening." Then, because I know she isn't convinced and will follow me into the rain anyway, I add, "You don't want your dog to get wet again, and I'm not letting you drive my car."

That shifts her focus onto a new insult. "Why not? I'm a good driver."

"Your dog is gonna need a name, you know." I switch the topic again, hardly able to keep the humor out of my voice. "We can't just keep calling it 'your dog.'"

"I'll need a name for the paperwork, but we can leave it blank for now if you need some time to decide," the vet tech interrupts, reentering with my card and some more paperwork.

"Yeah, actually..." Maddy smiles softly. "Her name is Reece."

"Don't you think that's too many R's in one house?" I

tap her arm with my elbow, careful to avoid her ribs. "Riven *and* Reece?"

"You're assuming you're sticking around, but I suppose I'll have to get rid of one. I'd say I'll miss you but I was raised not to lie," Maddy teases, accepting the paperwork from the vet tech.

I place a mocking hand over my heart, but when she's not looking, I lean down to eye level with the pup. My hand lands lightly on her head. "Welcome to the dysfunctional family, Reece."

CHAPTER 19
MADDY

When I wake up, soft music is drifting from the kitchen into my bedroom. For a moment, I think I'm still dreaming until I realize the lyrics are in Italian, not some sleep-muddled language. A second voice, deep and male, hums along, assuming I'm still asleep.

Reece, now comfortable in my bed after living at home with us for a few weeks, stretches with the widest yawn I've ever seen her make. She's gotten big so quickly now that she's healthy, and last night, the vet gave her another exam before declaring she's perfectly on track. That good news coupled with an overall good day led to some celebration last night—celebration that had us shutting Reece out of the room. She did not care for that at all, but quickly forgot all about it when we let her sleep in the bed.

I slip out of bed, tying a robe around me as I walk. Not that it's anything Riven hasn't seen before, but I'd rather not give my neighbors a full show just in case he left the blinds open this morning. My apartment may be on a high floor, but I've learned the hard way that the complex across the way has a direct view into my apartment.

I don't know when Riven and I decided that sex between us wasn't a one-time thing. It just seemed to keep happening. I'd have a nightmare, and instead of seeking out someone else, I found Riven, who was more than happy to oblige.

I do go get tested routinely, as I always do anyway, just to be safe, but we continue to use protection, regardless of our semi-exclusive deal that isn't an ideal situation.

Riven still hasn't noticed my approach as he stands at my kitchen island. He has a book open in front of him, his eyebrows pinched in concentration. I take a moment to admire the view. I would wake up to his tan abs every day if I could. My arms slip around his waist, my face resting against his bare back, and his soft chuckle rumbles through the embrace.

"Morning," he rasps, his voice still fogged with sleep.

I hum a barely human response, nearly falling asleep again against his warmth.

"There's coffee on the counter," he says.

I hum again.

"And cocaine next to it."

"Oh good, I'll need it," I respond to the tease, only half joking as a headache blooms behind my eyes. I can practically see Riven's amused expression in my mind—the crinkle in the corners of his eyes, his straight brows subtly rising, and that charming grin lifting to his face.

"You just woke up. How can you already be in a bad mood?"

"I'm not in a bad mood yet, just preparing," I huff,

disentangling myself from him. "I'm meeting my parents for brunch."

Riven turns around at that, spreading his legs apart just enough for me to step between them as he leans his back against the counter. His hands find my hips, brushing ever so lightly against the soft fabric of my robe, concern written across his features. "I forgot that was today."

"I wish I did."

"Why do you go then?"

The question is genuine, not judging in the way others might be. It's the very question I ask myself every Sunday as I mentally prepare for the onslaught of questions and borderline emotional abuse.

"Because they're my parents and I love them," I answer truthfully. "I just don't always *like* them."

Riven nods, then reaches one of those hands up to tuck a stray stand of hair behind my ear. My heart does traitorous backflips at the motion, and I try to focus on anything other than that. In moments like these, where it's just us, soft in the morning light, nothing but skin between us, it's easy to imagine a different scenario, another morning, where maybe we are more than what we are.

I've tried to shove down this desire for months now—not the lust or attraction we share, but the feelings that have developed with it. Feelings I can't afford to have because they sure as hell are not reciprocated.

Riven and I are friends now, and have a good, mutually beneficial thing going on. There's no need for me to go and ruin it by telling him I think I could be falling in love with him.

In my defense, it would be harder *not* to fall in love with him. He's wickedly clever, considerate, and underneath that harsh exterior, he is *good*. He is so good, it hurts sometimes, how genuine he is, and how despite everything, he still believes in the good in people. For months, I could only see the worst, but even now, after all he's been through, he still believes, deep down, that people are capable of so much goodness. He believes there's still something good in my heart, and he's started to show it to me as well.

And have I mentioned he's incredibly hot? Like the legitimately jaw-dropping, heart-eyes, drooling type of attractive. And he's shirtless, in *my* kitchen.

Still, I remind myself, whatever butterflies are stirring in my chest are unrequited. Don't ruin a good thing.

"I'm going to go get dressed," I say suddenly, and force my feet to walk away from him.

Riven nods and doesn't mention the fact that I still have well over two hours before I have to leave. He would know, considering he's my ride. I told him I could take the bus, but that was apparently out of the question, so we settled for him dropping me off a bit early so he still has time to get to Natalia's. They caught a new lead on Malik's whereabouts that they plan to explore today. It honestly works out better that way anyway. If my mother saw me with Riven, I would never be able to convince her that we weren't dating, and there is no way I'll reveal the truth of our relationship to her.

I step into my bathroom, a soft jumpsuit in my hands. The weather is slowly warming, but not enough for my cold blood.

My fingers fumble with the knot of my robe for a

moment before the fabric falls loose. The garment slips to the side, revealing angry burn marks and scars. My breath hitches in my throat.

I've been getting better at forgetting they're there. I'm too focused on Riven and what he's doing when we're in bed to really notice them anymore, and as long as my gaze doesn't dip when changing, I can forget that they exist entirely. Even when I do spot them, it's merely a dark stain on my morning before I move on, but for some reason, this morning is different. Maybe it's the stress of seeing my parents, or the bitterness that accompanies my feelings for Riven, but the memories linger, and suddenly, the scars are engulfed in searing pain.

Involuntarily, I gasp, stumbling backwards until I hit the wall, sending things clattering across the floor. My ribs burn, and my hands reach up as if pushing on them will make the pain lessen.

"Maddy?" Riven calls from behind the door, his tone frantic.

I can't find the breath to respond, so I leave my mouth open, gasping even as he barrels through the door.

"What's wrong? What happened?" His hands go to my ribs first and I flinch, and he immediately drops them. I can see the loathing in his eyes, both for Donovan and himself—Donovan for putting the flinch there, and himself for causing it today.

Desire to tell him it's alright overrides my panic for just a moment, long enough for me to take his hand and lay it flat against my side. I try to convey how much I trust him, but all that comes out is a soft whimper as I school my breathing.

"Breathe," Riven commands.

"I'm trying," I grit out.

"Try harder."

"Fuck you."

"There's my girl," he says.

Usually, those words would make my heart flutter, but today, it sinks. He says it so easily, so casually. His other hand slips underneath my robe now, pressing his palm flat against the scars there as well.

"Are these hurting today?"

I nod, closing my eyes and letting my head fall back with a heavy thud against the wall. This is ridiculous. I've been doing so much better lately.

"Want to talk about it?"

"What's there to talk about?"

"Quite a bit, Maddy."

"Look. I know you're probably going to tell me these scars are proof that I'm a survivor or some shit, but I really can't handle that right now, so just don't."

"I wasn't going to," Riven murmurs, tracing over one of the burn marks with his thumb. "This is your body, and these are your scars. You want to keep them as some token? You keep them. You want them gone? I'll call every doctor and surgeon in this goddamn city and they'll be gone by tomorrow. It's your choice, your past. It's not mine to decide."

My throat clogs with emotion as I consider the possibility. Will there ever be a day that I don't look down and see them? Would my pride even allow that?

"I want them gone." I choke on the words. "Not now, but soon. I want them *gone*."

Riven only nods, nothing but unwavering understanding in those warm eyes, and my heart breaks a bit.

"I'll call in some favors today. We can start with a consultation. In the meantime..." He sinks to his knees. "Let me show you exactly how I feel about you and these marks, since you won't let me tell you."

I open my mouth to protest, but before I can, his lips press over the blemish closest to him, a tender caress against my skin that has my heart hammering. Is he going to...

"I have to meet my parents," I rasp as he moves to another scar, this one closer to my inner thigh.

"We have time."

"I've never done this before," I blurt out.

That's enough to make him pause. Before the embarrassment can settle in, Riven's eyes darken. As if that isn't the most attractive thing I've ever seen.

"You've never had someone go down on you before?"

I shake my head.

"After how many years with— Christ. Do you want me to stop?"

"No," I say, perhaps a bit too quickly. "No, just maybe not in the bathroom? I don't know what I'm doing and it's embarrassing." I begin to pray that the earth will swallow me whole. After however many men I've been with... It feels almost ridiculous to feel embarrassed, but Riven's frown deepens.

"The only person who needs to be embarrassed is any man that's ever slept with you." He says it with such conviction that I start to believe him, and let him lead me back to the bedroom. My robe slips from my shoulders as I do, nerves bundling in my stomach—but the good type, this time.

Riven pauses, stopping at his bag that lays resting against the door. "Are you nervous?"

"A bit."

"About which part?"

Maybe it says something about my past partners, the fact that I am so incredibly turned on by the fact that he is asking and talking me through it.

"It feels more vulnerable, I guess. Like you'll have power over me."

Riven's answering chuckle is dark. "Sweetheart, you have all the power here." He leans down and reaches into his bag, pulling out two long strips of fabric that resemble corset laces.

I raise a single brow. "I don't want to know why you have those."

"Tie me to the bed," he says, ignoring me. "I won't have my hands, and you will have full control."

Holy fuck.

I can't pretend my hands don't shake as I accept the fabric from him, watching with wide eye as he lays back against the bed, his hands already raised. I walk to him, heat pooling in my gut as I climb beside him. Riven takes one of my nipples in his mouth as I lean over him to tie the laces, his tongue flicking punishing circles against the sensitive bud.

"Is this too tight?" I ask, already breathless and hardly able to focus.

Riven takes a moment to answer, and I can feel him smiling around my breast as he moves to the other one. "Perfect, Blondie," he murmurs against my skin.

Tease.

Deciding I've had enough of his taunts, I push myself

back, pulling myself from his lips as I move down his body so I'm straddling his hips. I can feel the hardened length of him pushing against the shorts he left on, and slowly work myself over it.

Riven swears long and low, his teeth gritting. "This wasn't the deal."

"You said I was in control," I remind him. I move in slow, taunting circles, my desire heightening when I see the effect I have on him. A muscle in his jaw feathers as a soft moan slips between my lips.

Riven's body bucks as if seeking mine, the laces around his wrists snapping taut. "If you don't get that perfect ass over here and sit on my face right fucking now—"

"You'll what?" I pant. I love toying with him like this, seeing him unravel from just how badly he wants me. "You seem occupied right now."

I palm at my breasts, moaning softly at the rough scrape of my skin over my pebbled nipples. Riven's eyes track every motion as I arch my back above him, my head tipping back so all he can see is the smooth plane of my stomach and my breasts as I toy with myself.

Snap.

Riven's hands shoot out, tearing through his restraints, and grip my thighs. His fingers dig into the soft flesh of my leg, pulling me forward 'til I straddle his face, his grip holding me in place. He plunges his tongue inside me, no warning or slow start. He fucks me with his mouth as I gasp, and it's all I can do to reach forward and grip the headboard.

"Riven," I whine, his name nothing more than a breath upon my lips.

His fingers dig deeper, leaving delicious bruises where he claims me.

My thighs clamp around his head even as I pant, "I'm going to suffocate you."

Riven only presses down harder in response, perfectly content in dying between my legs. His tongue slips out from my center, moving to circle my clit in slow, tantalizing strokes. I cry out, my knuckles white on the headboard. His fingers reach up from behind to pump in and out now, pressure coiling in my core.

"Come on my face for me, sweetheart."

That's all it takes for release to shatter through me completely. I'm panting, still keeled over when Riven pulls me down, letting himself sit up so he can see my face. He leans forward, softly kissing me. I can taste myself on him.

"You taste sweet." He grins. "Now you need to get ready for your brunch."

Fuck.

CHAPTER 20
MADDY

I'm seriously regretting my decision to wear my hair pulled back as I sit in a corner booth with my parents at brunch. It's gotten to the point where I can't tell if the headache is from how tightly the style pulls against my scalp, or my parents themselves.

Sunday meetups have been a tradition for me and my family since I moved to the city. I'm an only child, and they're helicopter parents whose claws are sunk in too deep to let me out of their sight for too long.

Technically, I am an adult. I have a job, I support myself, I'm working towards my dreams. If we were to look at parent-child relationships as a contract, I've been cut loose from my end of the deal. But they're still my parents.

The restaurant my mother chose is all glass and gauzy white curtains. The pale winter light filters through weakly, leaving the lit candles doing nothing much for lighting, yet providing the expensive ambiance I know my mother loves.

I brought flowers this time, an apology for our last

meeting—not that one was owed. My father pitched a fit that I wouldn't let him pay for me. I didn't want that hanging over my head, and in the end, it made my mother cry. The flowers are for her. I think my dad would reject any apology that isn't ten pages long, double-spaced, and twelve-point Times New Roman font. It's the literature professor in him.

Usually, they set into our routine round of discussion right away. *How's your job? Are you dating anyone? Why don't you do something with your life?* Today, they at least let me get through ordering first, so hopefully by the time we get to, "You should move back in," I'll be able to drown them out with the sounds of chewing Belgian waffles.

"So," my father starts.

Oh, here we go.

"Are you still working at that coffee shop? What's it called?"

"Tina's?" my mother tries.

"Tella's," I correct gently. "And yes, I am."

"And it's paying well?"

"It covers rent and all my expenses, so I'd say so." I take a bit more tone that I usually would, but leave out the part where Natalia is taking care of my apartment. Without rent to factor in, most of my paycheck goes towards my savings or fun. Maybe a bit more fun than they'd like to hear about.

"You know—"

Stop.

"My friend Lawrence—"

For the love of god.

"He has a position at his company available right now.

It's just a desk job—secretary—but it's corporate and will look good on a resume."

And there it is.

"It would look good on a resume for someone who wants to go into dishwasher sales," I say slowly, "but not so much a photographer."

Plus, your good buddy Lawrence is an absolute sleaze, Dad. I'm sure he has more positions available than secretary, but why else would he want a pretty blonde sitting around? He's made that much clear the two times I've met him in passing.

"You should be investing in your future. Sometimes life doesn't work out the way we want it to. It never hurts to have a backup plan."

And didn't I know it, I think with a mental eye roll.

"I'd rather not have this fight again."

"So," my mom interjects. Mom to the rescue. However, my grateful gaze sours as she continues by saying, "Have you been seeing anyone?"

My brain immediately conjures up the image of Riven on his knees in the bathroom this morning. My fingers fumble with my phone in my lap as I try to distract myself from the memory and the subsequent heat rising to my face.

"Like a therapist?" I try, again attempting to send help-me eyes to the waiter.

My mother, either oblivious or uncaring, shakes her head. "As in a date."

"No."

"Why not?" she presses.

"You know why not."

She sighs, as if I am being the unreasonable one.

My hands ball into fists beneath the table, shaking in my lap.

"Seriously Madeline, this again? It's been *months*."

"I'm sorry that I'm not healing fast enough for you."

"Don't take that tone with your mother."

"I—" Embarrassment clogs my throat and I close my mouth, my chin dipping and eyes burning. Suddenly, I'm thirteen years old again, sitting at the kitchen table being berated for not having the top grade in my class. My grades were good, great even, but they weren't the best, and that was unacceptable. Then I'm fifteen, my mother untucking my hair from behind my ear to hide the acne dotting my chin at a formal dinner. The shame is the same now as it was then, and all the other times that came before this.

"Excuse me, I need to use the restroom," I mumble before exiting the booth and making a beeline for the bathroom. I realize when I get there that I left my phone and purse on the booth. With no way to throw out an SOS call, I find myself in front of the mirror, placing cool water on my neck and forcing myself to inhale. *In for three, out for three.*

"They're just doing it because they love you and want what's best for you," I try to reason with my weeping heart. It's out of love.

But is it?

It has to be. I can't handle it otherwise.

Inhaling one final time, I plaster a smile on my face and head back to the table.

Only for my smile to drop when I see who is standing there, talking to my parents with a tight-lipped grin.

Riven's hands are in his pockets, his shoulders

dropped in a way that looks almost casual, but I can see the muscle tightening in his jaw as he talks to my parents. My father looks a bit sweaty and uncomfortable with the fact that Riven is standing while he is still sitting, but Riven has him blocked in the booth. My mother, on the other hand, looks about ready to swoon—a real nineties-cartoon swoon.

My hand lights on Riven's shoulder, and I fight the urge to dig my nails in. His features loosen as he spots me, and I raise a brow. He mouths, "I'll tell you in the car."

"Natalia and I finished early, so I thought I'd come pick you up," he lies smoothly. "I'm terribly sorry if I've imposed or interrupted. I didn't realize the time."

My mother looks stricken. "Is Natalia your girlfriend, Mr. Barone?"

I cut him off with a look. "No, Mom. She's Addie's fiancée, remember? She and Riven work together at Mancini Security. How do you know his name?"

"Please, call me Riven," he interjects, brushing over my earlier question.

My mother blushes, and I want to die.

"Addie and Natalia are like sisters to me. I helped work the serial killer case a few months ago."

"Oh yes, Donovan. Tragic, really. None of us saw it coming," my mother says at the same time my father finally speaks.

"So you're a businessman then?" A topic he can finally relate to.

"Yes, I'm the head of management for all personal security clients."

My father has the decency to look impressed, almost pleased, even.

The food arrives and my mother asks the waitress for a box.

I frown and look at her fresh plate of food. "What's wrong? Why do you need a box?"

"Oh, it's for you! Riven said you two had plans this afternoon, so I figured you'd want your breakfast to go." My mom winks at the word *plans*, and I can already see the wedding invitations she's mailing out in her head.

Sorry, Mom. For once, I'd like to join you in your delusions, but it just isn't going to happen.

For the first time in the conversation, Riven looks unsure. "I can give you more time if you—"

"No, no, it's fine, right, Mom? Dad?"

"Right." My father clears his throat in the way all men do once they reach his age—wet and uncomfortable—and my mother politely cringes. "I'll handle the bill this time."

"Thank you," I force out.

"Have fun!" My mother waves, and Riven takes my hand in one of his, my freshly boxed breakfast in the other.

"Okay, I'm seriously freaked out now," I say once we get to the car. "Do you have a sixth sense for when I'm in trouble or something?"

Riven huffs a laugh, then holds up his phone. My own face flashes back at me with a timer counting down our ongoing call. He hangs up now that we're seated, but the call looks like it started a few minutes before I went to the bathroom.

"Butt dial," I say as a way of explanation.

"I figured, but I also thought you might need an escape."

"How'd you know who my parents were? There were plenty of older blond couples in that restaurant."

"I met them at the hospital after that night. Plus I saw your purse on the booth," he says as he starts the car. "So I reintroduced myself. Don't give me that look, I just told them we're friends. We started talking while we waited, then you came back, and you know the rest."

I let my shoulders slump and fall back into the comfortable leather seats. He's saved me once again, in a new way this time.

Riven lets me pick the music we listen to on the way home. I even catch him humming along to a few songs that he swore he hated only a few weeks ago.

"Did you find out what Malik's doing?" I ask at the end of the song.

Riven's features form a hard line and he shakes his head. "Not a clue. He's still trying to kill you, from what I've gathered, so don't let your guard down."

"Well, at least he's consistent."

"That's morbid."

"I was going for hilarious."

Maybe I should be more concerned by the fact that the head of a Mafia family is targeting me. Any sane person might have crumpled up sobbing—and not that I would blame them—but I can't find it in my heart to be worried. Riven has been by my side the entire time, his looming presence a comfort. With him, I feel like I can rest. I know I'm safe. I can let my violence find peace in his own.

It might be greedy to want more, but I don't care. I

want every lazy Sunday morning with him, his quick wit, and protective glances. I want every broken piece of his heart and to piece it back together, like he's done for me. I want him—all of him, in all his wicked ways, and his kind soul.

I say nothing, want crawling up my throat until it's suffocating me as we arrive at the apartment and make the trek upstairs. Reece comes bounding forward when we walk in, her tongue sticking out the side of her mouth and her tail wagging furiously.

Riven's voice is a low, affectionate rumble at the back of his throat as he pats her head. "Hey, good girl."

My heart does a back flip.

Unable to take it anymore, I move to stand in the living room, facing the portraits I've recently hung. Some of them match the ones in Addie's house, while some are simply old pieces that hold a sentimental grip on my soul.

Riven's footsteps stop just behind me, his breath warming the back of my neck. He comes beside me and copies my stance, his arms crossing as he traces where I stare. "Are any of these in the showing next month?" he asks.

"No, I don't have those selected yet."

Riven and I have been working tirelessly to organize my first gallery showing, from venue selection to caterers. The only thing still missing is the actual display.

I haven't decided which pieces to include. Some feel too raw, too new, yet I know those are exactly the type of images I need to show. Then there are some I have of Riven that he hasn't seen yet, photos I snapped when he wasn't looking. There's one from Natalia's company gathering all those months ago, his face obscured by a glass and the light around him forming a golden halo. He looks like a dark god, some being too devastatingly beautiful to be mortal.

Then I have self-portraits, something new that I have been experimenting with. I know they need to be shown, but I need one final push to do it.

"You don't have any new ones of Addie?"

"No. She used to be my main muse. It was easy when we lived together, you know? But I don't think I could ever ask her to model for me again, considering that's how he found us."

"And that doesn't bother you ever when you're working?"

My lips purse in thought. "No. Being behind the lens is like taking back control. I choose what angle the world is viewed at, the colors I allow the viewer to see. Whatever happens only happens because I let it."

The silent pause that follows hangs too heavy between us, and I'm shifting to face him when Riven breathes, "You're incredible."

I turn my face from him sharply. He says it so reverentially I can't breathe.

"You shouldn't say things like that."

"Why?"

A low growl of frustration rises in the back of my throat. How can he not see how confusing it is when he says things like this? When he looks at me like I've hung the stars? I can't help but get this false confidence, this utterly stupid hope that maybe he feels even just a fraction for me what I feel for him.

"What are we?" I look at Riven now, look at him fully.

If he is going to reject me, then he can do it looking into my eyes so that my mind can't twist this memory into something it isn't. There will be no what ifs. Riven either wants me, or he doesn't. I won't wait for him to draw out his decision.

His face is pinched, as if he's in pain but poorly concealing it. Every hard line of his body is stiff, as if he might shatter if I reach out and touch him. "I thought we were friends," he says carefully.

Bullshit.

"Friends don't act the way we do."

"We've never been the traditional type," he argues, not cruelly. "There is literally nothing traditional about us, from how we met to where we are now."

My heart begins to sink like a stone in my chest. Reece whines and pushes her wet nose into the palm of my hand, standing on her hind legs to do so.

He's avoiding giving me a direct answer, stringing me along in ways I didn't think he was capable of. Or maybe my own broken heart has molded the narrative to fit the dream I have, one where we can be happy. One where he loves me too.

"I need to know a real answer, because I can't do this again, Riven." Hot tears roll down my cheeks despite my best efforts, and I don't bother wiping them away. Riven steps forward, but I stop him with a single hand. "I've done this before. I won't deny my own involvement in this... situation, but I can't—I *won't* fall in love with another man who doesn't love me back. I have come too far to let myself get hurt like this again."

"Maddy," he breathes, but I'm not finished yet.

My voice cracks, resolution lining my words. "I love

you, Riven, but I won't lose myself for the sake of loving you."

A shuddering breath. Then Riven's hands are cradling my face, his forehead pressed against mine. He kisses my nose, my cheek where the tears have begun to dry. "Give me permission to make you mine, Maddy. It's all I've ever wanted."

"Then you..."

"How could I not love you?"

I laugh, and it breaks into a choking sob. "You have to say it the right way for me to believe it."

"The right way? Hell. I love you, Maddy Yapon. I fell in love with you despite my every effort not to. You have me, in whatever way you want me, in whatever way you need me. Let me have you, because you already have me."

If I opened the door to the walls I built before, Riven has come and completely torn them down now. His arms are wrapping around my waist, his mouth against mine as I fist my fingers in his hair. I attempt to draw him further into me, both of us stumbling until my back hits the wall behind me, in between two of my prints.

"Dumb... fucking... idiot," I say against his mouth between kisses. "Say it again."

Riven's mouth is frantic as it finds mine, kissing me in a way I've never been kissed before—possessive, urgent, worshipping. "I love you."

"Again."

"I love you."

"Agai—"

"If you would stop talking now, I'm trying to kiss you," then, "and I love you."

One of Riven's knees slips between my legs, the

weight of his body pressing and caging me against the wall a welcomed comfort. Everything is him. All I can taste, smell, and feel. Everything is so distinctly Riven, it hurts.

I wrap my arms around his neck, letting a whimper slip from my mouth as his lips trail downwards towards my neck. We've kissed before, but this time feels new, as if the moment is driven by the pure need to be so deeply intwined with each other that we cannot tell where I start and he begins. I need to feel his heart in my chest, his breath in my lungs. I need to see me from his eyes, to love myself the way he loves me. Somehow, I know that he needs it too.

"Riven," I pant when his hand slips to the zipper on the back of my jumpsuit. "The window."

"Let them watch and see who claims you."

My head tips back, my jumpsuit falling from my shoulders to expose the black bra beneath. My fingers fumble for the buttons of his shirt, tugging until they come undone, and let it fall to the floor behind us. I reach for his belt next, palming him over his pants as I unfasten it. The groan the motion elicits is delicious and I bring my lips to his jaw, forcing him to pull his head back from my neck. He moves to take my lips again but I turn my head to the side, traveling further down until I reach the finely carved column of his throat.

I have finally succeeded at removing his belt, and I push his pants down with urgent fervor. The length of him springs free, already hard and pressing against me. I continue my motions, sucking on his neck and stroking until his hands snap up to grip my wrists.

"If I come, it's going to be inside you, after you've come already twice."

Suddenly, an old pop tune comes on and I recognize my ringtone, my phone still in my pocket. It vibrates a little too close to where I'm sensitive right now, and the sound it elicits from me is borderline humiliating.

"Leave it," Riven growls as I reach for it.

I switch it off, but it buzzes again. And again.

I shoot him an apologetic look, biting back my own groan of frustration. Natalia's name flashes across the screen.

"It's about the event, I'm sorry," I pant, trying to compose myself. Natalia has been planning my gallery for me and it opens this month. She's been blowing up my phone nonstop and the last time I didn't answer, I was greeted by her nearly kicking down my door.

"We'll finish this later," he promises with a look akin to murder in his eyes.

I nod, my mouth dry and my core aching.

I try to answer as smoothly as I can, and while Natalia drones on about flowers and investors, all I can think of is Riven's hands on me, his mouth—the very one that just told me he loved me.

Shit.

I am in such deep, unending trouble in all the ways I've fallen for this man, violently and headfirst. It might kill me, how much I love him, and yet I know that death will be worth every second spent with him.

CHAPTER 21
RIVEN

If Maddy and Addie take any longer getting ready for tonight, we'll miss the opening of the festival. Not that Natalia, Marco, or I particularly care, but Maddy will whine if we miss it. She's the only one who knows the first band playing, and while I recognize the tune of some of their songs from our drives together, I can't say I'm their biggest fan.

Maddy and I have very different tastes in music—shocking, I know. It's weird how well we work together given the vast differences between us. She likes upbeat pop-y songs, show tunes, and sometimes folk music, meanwhile I prefer something more mellow, or occasionally indulge in a country song. I tried to say once that folk and country are the same thing and Maddy looked like I told her that a close friend had died. "I will never be able to look at you the same again, Barone." She mocked fainting, the back of her hand pressed dramatically to her brow. I only managed an eye roll, used to her antics by then.

"We're ready, we're ready," Addie chirps as they descend the staircase in a flurry of hurried footsteps.

For someone who fell down the stairs not too long ago, I half expect Addie to be more careful than this, not borderline sliding down the railing.

"How do we look?" she asks, spinning with a bright grin on her face once they reach the bottom. Addie wears high-rise denim shorts with rhinestone fringe across the pockets that slaps at her thighs when she spins. A white scarf is tied around her chest, with her curly hair forced into pigtail braids, half hidden by the obnoxiously large cowboy hat on her head.

Maddy stands behind her, wearing a light-blue halter top and low-rise jean shorts. The toned planes of her stomach are exposed and I find my gaze drifting lower and lower until the impatient tapping of her foot brings me back.

"Have you ever even ridden a horse?" Marco asks with a pointed look at their matching cowboy boots. For someone who claims she hates country music, Maddy sure does look the part.

"Yes," Addie replies.

"At a fair doesn't count."

"Yes, it does!" Her voice in incredulous, borderline exasperated, and an octave higher than usual. I laugh at the blush in her cheeks as she grabs my cousin by his collar. "At least we look the part. You're literally wearing what you wear every weekend."

"That's the point. I have to go back to stuffy suits on Monday. Let me be comfortable today, Collins."

"You didn't feel like dressing up with them, Nat?" I ask, lightly elbowing Natalia's ribs.

She fixes me with a scowl that I can only take half serious from her getup. More subdued than the others, she wears ripped jean shorts and a white T-shirt paired with a baseball cap, none of which were items that I knew she owned.

"Did *you*?" she asks, staring at my own shorts and tee. We almost match, minus the shorts, which is a comical thought in and of itself.

I almost forgot about the music festival until I got an email a few days ago with the e-tickets attached. Maddy and I made these plans what feels like a lifetime ago, and I never thought I'd be attending it with her at my side, this time in a relationship rather than the casual sex we'd been having.

I bought the tickets of course, because again, my girlfriend is on a barista's salary. What she doesn't know is I purchased VIP, meaning we have access to a banded-off section at the front of every stage, with free drinks, food, and private bathrooms. Call me a snob, but if she's dragging me to a music festival in the middle of the city park, we're going to do it in style. When I mentioned going to a concert with her, I thought of air-conditioned arenas. Spring came crashing in with a heat wave, and the temperatures today are supposed to soar.

Addie warned me Maddy tends to forget to drink water at events like these, and with the alcohol she's sure to be consuming, I make a mental note to always have a water bottle on hand for her. I've never gotten to see drunk Maddy before, and I'll admit I'm looking forward to the experience more than I thought I would.

The entire city must have turned out for this event, and I am more than grateful I decided to book VIP. When we arrive, we're ushered through a private entrance and led to a section roped off with seats and food stands. The man at the front explains we'll have to swipe our wristbands to be let back in, then tells us to have fun.

The girls don't wait long to take him up on his suggestion. Addie and Maddy came back double-fisting drinks, dragging Natalia with them to carry snacks. They join me and Marco at the table we've found in a shady area, and display all their goods with satisfied smiles.

"Have I told you recently that I love you?" Maddy asks, her mouth half full with a fried mozzarella stick.

The Italian half of my heart recoils at the sight, while the other half kicks into high gear at the sound of those three words leaving her lips.

Maddy is less guarded using them with me than I originally thought she would be. Sometimes I feel like I hear it every five minutes. It could be something as simple as making her coffee in the morning and instead of, "Thank you," I get, "Love you." Granted, that might be her reaction to anyone bringing her coffee in the morning, but I'm going to choose to believe I am just that special.

I initially thought I would hear it from her once every few days, if that. Her scars with love run deeper than just Donovan, I know now. I try not to think of how little she might have heard praise or love from her parents. Still, she gives love as freely as someone who has never been burned before, and I constantly find myself further impressed by her.

The hours fly by, and soon enough, we're reaching the

second-to-last act, right before the headliner. Marco is surprisingly tipsy at this point, a sight that is truly amusing to me. My camera roll is now filled with blackmail, but Natalia is unfortunately sober. Something about Addie being drunk and not willing to risk her safety in a crowd, combined with her high alcohol tolerance and other nonsensical shit.

Maddy is absolutely plastered, and having the time of her life.

She is magnetic as she moves through the crowd, her hips swiveling as she dances her way between other people until we're at the barricade in front of the stage. I'm not entirely sure how we got here, as I've entirely been focused on her and the feel of her hand in mine.

We dance the entire show—and by we, I mean Maddy. She's electric, captivating, and before I realize it, the performance is almost over. What I haven't missed, however, is how the lead singer's eyes stay glued to her the entire time, even when I have my arm wrapped protectively around her middle. In fact, that seems to amuse him, if his raised eyebrow is anything to note when I press a kiss to her cheek.

He says something to his manager after the encore before walking backstage, and the manager sighs with an expression that can only be described as "not again."

To confirm my suspicions, the manager exits the stage, but instead of heading back with the rest of the band, he walks over to where we stand pressed against the black barricade at the front of the stage. Maddy is drunk and borderline giddy with excitement when she points it out to me, like the man isn't standing right in front of us.

I imagine this is the dream for many teenage girls at one point or another in their life. To be standing in a crowd of people and have the singer's eyes only on you? I think I've heard Addie murmur something about fan fictions starting that way before. Maddy seems more excited about sharing the experience with me, and frowns when the manager tells her that the singer is only interested in bringing her backstage.

"Sorry, but I'm here with my boyfriend," she shouts over the roaring crowd.

Boyfriend.

I hate how that word sounds in her mouth. A boyfriend is something you have in high school, or when you're still trying to figure out how dating works. A boyfriend is temporary. I'll have to replace that title soon with something that makes her irrevocably mine.

God, I've had her for a week and suddenly I want her for all of the weeks still to come. I want to tell her and this snobby manager that she's mine for more than just this moment, and that I don't ever plan on letting her go, but I know the look that will pass over her face. Fear. Terror that another man will come along and try to make her decisions for her. She'll walk away, and I don't know if I'm a good enough man to let her.

"He knows. I don't think he cares," the manager says, and I'm not sure if she's talking about me or the singer.

Maddy seems to understand, however, and her expression sours, her hand tightening its grip on mine. "Well I do, so go tell your boss he can fuck himself. If he doesn't want to, I'm sure anyone else out here would, but it's not going to be me."

A rustle in the backstage curtains reveals a head

poking out, and I choke back a laugh. The lead singer is looking on from behind the curtains, hiding behind his personal assistant like a child. Now that he's out of the stage lights, he looks young, like an immature brat who isn't used to being told no.

Maddy seems to notice, as well, and lifts her fist in a high diagonal towards him, her middle finger extended. Once she's sure he's seen her and he looks as affronted as she hopes, she spins on her heel, dragging me with. She pulls me to one of the chiller sections back in VIP, settling heavily on a linen papasan cushion.

"Easy," I murmur in her ear once I settle beside her. My lips ghost her temple where she has a vein popping and I feel some of the tension leaving her as I do so. It's adorable, seeing her this worked up over something that I would usually be the one getting angry over.

"The fucking nerve of that guy. I mean, did he not see you were right there? Bastard. Shit face. Cock-sucking—"

"I doubt he's had anyone turn him down before, boyfriend or not." I cut off her obscene tirade.

A middle-aged woman and her husband look less than impressed a few seats down, but one glare has them moving further away.

"Well, congratulations to him. I guess he has one now."

"And what made you say no?" The question comes out more as a growl, what is meant to be teasing suddenly layering the air thick with tension.

Maddy's grin turns mischievous as she leans closer, her breath skittering across the shell of my ear. "Because I have you." Her whisper is a caress that matches the slow stroke of her fingernails up and down my arm. "And I know his type. He would never bloody himself for me like you would, and that is just one of your traits that I find very attractive."

Fuck. Me.

She can't keep talking like this or I might lose all composure and take her in a darkened corner right here and now. But she's drunk, and I would never take advantage of her like that. I'm about to tell her as much when she springs to her feet.

"Come on, there's still the closing act!" she chirps as if she wasn't singlehandedly responsible for me getting a hard-on in front of the judgmental old couple from earlier.

"Give me a fucking minute."

Maddy smirks, then flounces off back into the pulsing throng of people, her blonde hair streaming behind her like a flare.

Maddy has found Marco, Addie, and Natalia near the front of the crowd by the time I catch up. Natalia is tying Addie's wild curls into a high bun, trying her best to avoid the glitter smattered across her fiancée's face. When she turns to face me, I notice she is sporting matching glitter. Another glance confirms that Marco has it on his face as well.

"That's a good look on you two."

"I can and will kill you, Barone," Natalia threatens, though it's hard to take her seriously through my borderline giddy delight.

Addie notices my arrival and throws her arms around

my neck, her top knot now firmly secured. "Riven! We thought you would miss it!"

"Never." I smile. "And how much have you had to drink tonight?" If her red cheeks aren't indication enough of her intoxication, the way Natalia has to hold her back from hugging me again surely is.

"Not enough!"

"More than enough," Natalia corrects.

Addie pouts while Marco laughs behind his own cup. He extends one my way, but Maddy promptly steals it. She narrows her eyes at me as I feign shock.

"What? This last band is your type of music, not mine. I'm going to need this to have a good time."

"Sure," I deadpan, and Maddy giggles. Truly giggles like a child.

Okay, so maybe she has had enough tonight as well. Still, I can't force myself to play responsible adult. Not as her hips begin to sway and she lets her head fall back with pure joy written across her face. She dances along to the pre-show music, a few people joining her.

One man in particular gets too close, to which she spins away into my arms, sloshing some of the drink onto her shoes. She's too busy laughing at the mess to notice the icy glare I give the man from over the top of her head, my arm now wrapped securely around her waist.

"Let go, I want to dance," she says.

"If you want to dance, then dance with me."

"You can't dance."

"Not the way you like to, no. But I can hold you just fine."

The final band taking the stage cuts off her response and her body presses into mine. I try to focus on the music and the band in front of me, but all I can see is the way the flashing lights outline her darkened silhouette in the areas where our bodies do not touch. I can smell her clean scent over the stale concert air, packed with sweat and writhing bodies. I want this moment captured in my brain forever, and I take the time to memorize every angle of her body, the feel of her curves in my hands, and the way she laughs when Addie kisses her cheek, pressing some of that glitter onto her face.

For the first time since my childhood, I forget who I am. There is no killing, no blood feuds, no ghosts haunting every corner of this city.

I press a kiss to the top of her head, tasting the sweat that beads along her hairline.

She tilts back until I have clear access to her lips, capturing them with my own. "I love you," she says with startling clarity for a drunk person.

"I know."

"You're supposed to say it back, dummy."

"I'd die for you."

She tilts her head curiously at my declaration. "What was that?"

"I love you too."

CHAPTER 22
MADDY

Having Natalia plan my first gallery showing might be the best decision I've ever made. Her attention to detail is what makes her such a great leader, and in turn, a great event planner. I went to her company gala last year for their ten-year anniversary, and noted then how exquisite it was. I called her a few weeks ago after Riven booked the venue, a beautiful old building downtown, and asked if she would be willing to help me manage the event.

Instead, in typical Natalia fashion, she took over the full role of event manager and coordinator, handling everything from invites to catering. The only thing I had to do was supply the prints—and answer her million phone calls.

The venue Riven booked is lovely. It is an old, refurbished library in the heart of downtown. The owners left the bookcases pressed against the walls, but cut out the backs and painted them white to create ornate window frames, resulting in a large glass window spreading sunlight through the old shelves. They expanded it a few years ago in order to be able to accommodate weddings, and in turn, added sky-to-ceiling glass walls, each casting the main hall in brilliant light.

I walk into the oldest part of the building first and find Natalia fussing over florals, a frazzled-looking assistant at her side. Natalia stands tall, a light-blue suit hugging her figure. It's a nice contrast to the black I know she prefers, but my dress code specifically said light colors. I did so in order to create contrast between the attendees and the dark-lit photographs that will be hanging, giving an air of othering.

My own dress is a pale-yellow satin that falls loose around my ankles, cinching at my ribs. The long sleeves flow past my outstretched fingertips, like the blooming wings of a butterfly. It's a color I'm not normally comfortable in, but something about it felt right enough to push myself out of my comfort zone.

"Is something wrong?" I ask.

Natalia crosses her arms, a hint of her tattoos peeking out from under the collar of her white button-down. "Nothing for you to be concerned with." Natalia brushes me off with a wave of her hand, then turns back to the assistant. "Fix this. Now."

The assistant rushes off, floral display loaded in his arms. Natalia turns then, and I notice the pastel blue lightens her dark eyes enough that they almost look brown in the light.

She raises an eyebrow, shooting a polite, appraising look my way. "You look nice."

"Likewise. I'm sure Addie is a fan."

A slight blush warms Natalia's ears, and she untucks her short black hair to hide the evidence. "She's off with the caterer right now. They're setting up the hors d'oeuvres in the back room. She's arranging the trays and making sure the servers are in line. Marco is out front with our bouncer checking on security, just in case. Malik shouldn't show, but I wouldn't put it past him to try."

"Sounds like everyone has a job but me."

"Your job was to provide the art, which is lovely by the way. We are here to make sure everything runs smoothly."

"Speaking of everyone..." I trail off, letting my gaze dart around the room. "Where is Riven?"

I had arrived at the venue alone, opting to accept the ride that Natalia sent. The driver was one of her men, of course, and he was polite enough, but not the best at holding a conversation. I'm sure he knows who I am to Riven and Natalia, and that fact did nothing to loosen his tongue.

"He's on his way. He had to sort out something last minute, but he's coming."

"Okay." I smooth my hands over my dress, hoping my sweaty palms don't mar the satin. I spent admittedly too long in front of the mirror before this event. I always try my best to look presentable before an event, but today feels bigger. Important. I highly doubt that today will bring many new connections, but I still took the time to style my hair in large Hollywood waves and swiped on an extra layer of lip gloss before leaving the house.

"I'm going to go track down Addie and send the servers out. We open in five minutes. Are you going to be okay on your own?" Natalia asks. Where Natalia and I have never been as close as we are to Addie, she did live with us for a while when Donovan was at large on his killing spree. We grew close enough then that I'd call the woman a friend—an odd friend, sure, but a friend, nonetheless. She stares at me now with that assessing look I've grown so familiar to, and I force a nervous smile to my lips.

"I'm fine. Better than fine, even. Go ahead."

The woman nods, then stalks off in the direction of the back room.

I take a deep breath, then walk into the main hall of the venue. There on the walls, surrounded by pastel-colored flowers and green vines, is my photography. Each image is printed on large canvas, some on metal, and hung so that they loom over the otherwise bright room.

I stop at the largest canvas that sits in the center of the room, the light haloing behind it. My own face stares back at me, my first self-portrait. My features are gaunt, half obscured by a thin strip of gauzy curtain, but the contours of them are still visible through the fabric, even if only a dark splotch on the image. I had doused my hair in gel, pressing it in swirling patterns against my face, my mascara dripping down my chin and bare shoulders. The curtain covers my breasts, but my collarbones are hollowed. My lips are parted as if sighing, and water clumps my eyelashes together in a faux makeup look. I am sorrow personified until you catch the slighted raise of my brow, a single beam of light catching my eyes. Hope flickers there, resilience I didn't know existed within myself until I looked past everything else.

I withheld this photo from the original prints I showed Pembrooke. At the time, it felt too personal, too raw to share with someone else. Now I know it is exactly the side of healing I need to show—the single spark of light that makes the sorrow of the rest of the collection worth the suffering.

People slowly filter in. Some I recognize from Natalia's event, while other faces are new. I see Pembrooke among the crowd and excuse myself to the back room. I won't need to show my face for a while, at the risk of appearing too eager. Instead, I find Addie in the back, finishing up her task. She wears a lilac gown that drapes over her chest in a cowl neck, then tapers down to a slip dress. It's a color she wears rarely, but looks lovely in. It makes the strands of auburn amongst the brown of her curls more visible. She wears her hair half tied back with a jeweled comb, one I recognize from her nightstand in our old apartment.

Her hands come to rub up and down my arms, a smile planted on her pretty face. "How're you doing?"

"Nervous," I admit. "But I'm working on it. It's good to feel nervous instead of just sad."

"I'm proud of you." She says it so earnestly that my heart clenches.

The only thing missing now is Riven.

I try not to let the fact that he's late sting, but it's hard not to. He's been there with me since day one, and now there's an empty space in the room where he should be. The ghost of that space floats around the hall, winding between the patrons.

I take a moment to peek my head around the door. The servers are flitting around the room like hummingbirds, their white uniforms blending with the walls and contrasting with the bright colors of the gallery observers. Some platters hold champagne flutes, others hors d'oeuvres straight from Italy, courtesy of Natalia.

Most patrons take advantage of the refreshments, while some hold pen and paper. I recognize one of the latter as a reporter for the city's largest newspaper, and my breath hitches in my throat. Slowly, I recognize more journalists, then a minor news anchor who seems to be doing a report on one of the pieces Pembrooke refused. This could be the breakthrough I've been waiting for, and for just a moment, I allow my hopes to lift.

Then Pembrooke spots me, still cowering in the doorway.

He smiles at me, his face kind and inviting as he raises his champagne stem in greeting. Steeling my nerves, I paste an equally pleasant expression on my face and make my way to him.

"Mr. Pembrooke." I dip my chin in acknowledgement towards the photography hanging from the walls before him. "I hope you are enjoying the gallery."

"I am, Miss Yapon, and please, call me Austin."

"Then you should call me Maddy."

"Alright, Maddy," he says. "I'll be blunt. I regret the way we left things the last time we spoke. I've been looking at your work, and seeing it hung has shone a new light on your skill. Now, we have a showing next month and I've listed a few pieces here that we would love to showcase in it."

I open my mouth, but before I can respond, one of the event assistants approaches. The young woman fails to hide her grin, but my eyes go straight to the envelope in her hand.

"I am sorry to interrupt, Miss Yapon, but I have urgent news."

I squint at her name tag and take the envelope from

her. "Thank you, Lily." I scan the words quickly and before I can stop it, a laugh slips through.

Austin lifts a single brow, and I fold my hands in front of me.

"I'm sorry, Austin," I try to force an apologetic tone through my budding smile, "but I am afraid this collection is no longer available."

"Excuse me?"

"A private collector has just purchased the entire collection, so I will be unable to give any of these images for your future gallery. Please reach out to inquire about my work in the future, but please stay and continue to enjoy the showing."

I turn on my heel and march to the back atrium where I know I can find the buyer of my collection, as the letter said I could. We kept this area sealed off, per the venue owner's request, so that none of the antiques become damaged during the event.

Riven stands in the center, a bouquet of pink calla lilies in his hand. He's wrapped the fragile flowers in brown paper and tied it with a matching pink bow, the same exact shade I painted my bedroom in the old apartment.

"Sorry I'm late. I couldn't figure out which shade of yellow tie matched my complexion best."

He is, in fact, wearing a yellow tie, but I know he was finalizing the sale of my art. There was supposed to be an auction for the pieces at the end of the night, unless a private buyer decided to pay the obscene price Natalia placed on my work at the beginning of the event. I couldn't figure out why she did it, but now I know.

"You're ridiculous."

"—ly rich and sexy? Yes, I know."

"Try adding full of yourself to that list."

Riven's answering grin is brilliant, and it sets loose a horde of butterflies in my stomach. My heart does backflips in tandem with their fluttering, and I feel like an electric wire ready to snap at the smallest touch, but in the best possible way.

"You bought my collection," I breathe, not bothering to hide the joy from my voice.

Riven places both his hands on my hips, placing a tender kiss to the top of my head. His touch shocks my pulse into overdrive, and I want to both marry and kill him right now.

"Well, I knew Pembrooke would show and I just couldn't let the bastard have the last word," he says coolly. "Besides, Addie told me you threw a self-portrait into the mix, and like hell I was going to let anyone have a photo of you hanging in their house. Buying it simply means I don't have to kill whoever would have had it."

"Mhm," I hum, not even caring that he's serious about the murderous bits of that statement. Is it bad that I've grown used to it? Probably, but I don't want to think about that now.

"You're perfect," I say, gently touching his face.

He turns his head to the side to kiss me again, this time on my palm. "I wouldn't go that far. You can stick with ridiculously rich and sexy, though, if you'd like."

"Shut up," I laugh, pushing away from him. "And come on, I want to enjoy the rest of this perfect day."

"You seem to like that word."

"What?"

"Perfect."

"Well," I say, already leading him back to the main room, "I suppose things just feel that way right now."

Riven doesn't respond to that, just lets me drag him around the venue, talking to investors, gallery owners, and booking four more showings in the coming months. He stands beside me for all of it, nodding and playing nice, even when Pembrooke shows his face again. Riven comments on his lack of tweed suit and the man's face turns a horrid shade of scarlet before he excuses himself to find refreshments.

Addie is helping the servers again, Natalia managing some high-level investors, and I catch Marco sampling the snacks even as my best friend swats at his hand.

Perfect, I told Riven. I don't use that word to describe many things, but as the sunlight filters in, scattering across the images of my pain and healing, and Riven's hand is heavy in mine, I can't help but think that there is no better word to describe today.

CHAPTER 23
MADDY

The next morning, I wait in the lobby of Mancini Security while the secretary calls for Natalia. I wipe my sweaty hands against my jeans, already regretting my morning coffee as my stomach twists with nerves. Riven and Marco are with Addie, who is stalling them as I meet with her fiancée.

The clicking of heels on tile draws my attention upwards.

"Maddy," Natalia greets me. "I'll admit I thought you'd still be sleeping this morning."

"I wish," I say, rolling my neck out. In hindsight, I probably could have scheduled this meeting for later in the day, not the early-morning hours after a late event. "Though this is more important."

Natalia nods and opens her arm to the side, gesturing for me to follow her. I walk down the winding halls, still familiar after the past few months. Everyone we pass dips their head in greeting and respect, and I wonder how many of them are truly just security workers and how many know the truth.

Natalia's office is just as I remember it, all bulletproof glass, pristine iron, and minimal decoration. Now there are a few photos on her desk, all of Addie, either by herself or with Natalia. There's also a mug that reads, "World's Best Boss" that I know she didn't buy for herself.

"You want to talk about Riven." Natalia jumps straight to the point, never one to waste too much time. "Is something wrong?"

"No, not exactly. It's about his mother."

Natalia's dark eyes narrow in warning. "What about Cecile?"

I know Cecile is just as much Natalia's mother figure as she is Riven's. Natalia visits her annually. From what Addie's told me, Natalia didn't have the best relationship with her own parents—and she was the one to kill her father herself—and she's now fiercely loyal to Cecile.

"I think it's time she knows the truth about Riven." I swallow thickly. "That he's alive."

A chill settles in the room, and a muscle feathers in Natalia's jaw. "There's a reason she doesn't know."

"I know."

"Do you?"

"I do," I say confidently, "I know everything, and I think it's worth the risk. You've already thought about relocating her to the city to be safe, because you know Malik won't hold up his end of the deal. There's only two ways this ends: with Riven dead or Malik."

Natalia nods and she looks, dare I say, impressed? Not by anything I've claimed—of course, she's known this all herself for months, maybe years, however long this shit has been going on. She's impressed by my confidence, the way I don't shy from the blunt truth. It's something we've always bonded over—our ability to make people uncomfortable by being brutally honest.

"Malik already sent someone to kill her after you killed Cas. My guards intercepted them in time and brought her here. She's living in my old apartment right now."

My mouth drops open and dries. "Does Riven know?"

Natalia tilts her head to the side, not at all in the puppy-like way I've seen from Addie. No, this is the action of a serpent, calculating her next move. In the end, she says plainly, "No. I was waiting for the right moment. Perhaps a certain blonde to come see me and let me know her intentions."

"My intentions?" My heart sinks in my chest.

I've never gotten a good glimpse of the politics of this life. Every day with Riven has felt like a fairy tale so far—a very dark and twisted fairy tale, but a fairy tale at that. I'm starting to fall for him, but how much of this will become our life? How much will he keep from me, just for the sake of playing the game?

"With Riven. I need to know if you're worth the risk."

"What do you mean?"

"Did you know I offered to replace Riven with a new guard a few weeks ago, right after the Cas incident? I planned to remove him anyway before you two fought two months prior, because I found someone else to replace him, and risking both of you was probably not the smartest decision I've made lately. He came to me when he went to pick you up that night, requesting to be reinstated as your guard. He told me if I said no, he'd do it anyway, so I should make the right fucking choice. So I need to know, what are your intentions?"

"We haven't gotten that far yet," I answer honestly. In my mind, I think I know the truth, but then I think back to all the times I've almost died. I took all of the Mafia shit in stride until now. I narrowly escaped being murdered by my last boyfriend, and that was enough to traumatize me for months, if not the rest of my life. Am I so willing to walk back into the same fire that burned me, for the sake of a man I hated less than a year ago?

Natalia groans. "Blood is just blood in this business. It doesn't matter if you bleed the same. Maybe that's not how it used to work, but it's how it works now. My family died a long time ago. There's no one close enough to me to be able to hurt Addie, or anyone who would want to. But Riven has family—brothers who would do anything to hurt him, even if it meant hurting you in the process. So Riven is putting his life on the line every day to protect you despite knowing they'd just as gladly kill him. That they're trying to kill him through you."

"What does this have to do with me?" It's a dumb question, I know, but I can't stop my mind from reeling at the ultimatum she's delivered me.

Natalia slams her hands on the table. "Because you can either choose to walk into hell with him or cut the rope so he can focus on saving himself. If you release him, he'll force himself to let you go, and not only will your life not be in danger, but his risk will drop as well. We'd be able to focus our efforts on protecting him instead of worrying about you. But if you choose him, he'll protect you with his life, and you'll be one of us."

"What would happen to me?" I breathed, my voice cracking at a whisper. "If I let him go?"

"I'd have someone watch you until the threat passes,

or continue on if you or Addie expressed the desire for it."

"You're willing to do all of this for Addie?"

She shrugs as if it's simple. Like she's offering me a tissue or a piece of gum. "I love her. I want her to be happy, and she wouldn't be happy without you." Then she smirks. "And maybe I've grown fond of you, Yapon."

I know what I have to do. I've always known.

Then my shoulders are shaking, my body wracked with heavy sobs. Natalia doesn't move from her position behind the desk, not as I bite my fist hard enough to draw blood, trying to hold back the scream clawing its way up my throat.

I need to let him go. I can't live in this world, this life—but more importantly, I can't keep letting him risk his life for me.

But a life without Riven in it... a life without his banter, those warm eyes that become dappled in the sunlight. The way I felt safe for the first time in my life when he wrapped his arms around me, even as the bullets flew.

I need to let him go. But I can't. He is the tether that holds me to life, and I need him as desperately as I need oxygen. Maybe I'm selfish. Maybe all that is good in my heart died months ago, but I can't force myself to say the words I know I need to.

Instead, I sniffle and wipe at my eyes with the back of my hand. "Is Hell nice this time of year?"

Natalia grins, like that's the answer she was hoping for. "For sinners like us? Never."

I laugh, the sound a broken rasp from my raw throat. "Great."

The other woman, used to my dramatics, settles in the chair behind her desk, typing something into her computer. "I'll arrange a dinner tomorrow. I've all but run out of excuses anyway to keep Cecile from seeing our new house. She and Addie miss each other terribly, and when Addie found out this morning that Cecile is here..." Natalia breaks off. The look on her face is the closest thing I've seen her wear to embarrassment. "It didn't go well."

"I can imagine," I say with a shit-eating grin. Addie angry is truly a spectacle. You'd think she's too adorable to be intimidating, and sure, you might laugh the first time you see her face get really red, but that woman knows all the most painful places to land a blow—physically and psychologically. Thankfully, I've never been on the opposing side of her rage. Roommate squabbles? Sure, but the lethal rage I saw directed at Malik in Tella's? Never.

I'm lucky to have the four most terrifying people I know in my corner, and despite the heavy weight pressing against my back, I know I can shoulder it. I'm not alone anymore, Riven showed me that, and I'll be damned if I let him walk through life thinking the same destructive thoughts I used to.

Just wait one more day, Barone. I'll carve our way to a happy ending, starting with yours.

CHAPTER 24
RIVEN

Natalia called an impromptu dinner earlier today, with no explanation other than Addie has been begging her to make a new recipe she found online for her, and wants all of us to join in the experience. Not that I'm complaining—Natalia's food is only second to my own, and mine second to my mother's.

I knock at the front door and receive a shout from inside that it's unlocked. Strange—and irresponsible considering all that's been going on these past few months. However, I guess they were expecting me.

Pushing open the door, I let myself in, making sure to lock it afterwards. As far as I know, I'm the last to arrive, and we don't need any more guests at this table.

I can hear the soft Italian music playing in the kitchen when I walk in, the type my mom used to play when she taught me how to cook as a boy. The soft melody combined with the scent of garlic in the air hits me like a wall, and I fight the urge to stagger back.

It's been so long since I've seen my mother. I miss her every day as if she were dead, but I know not seeing her is for the best. I can't afford to be selfish, not when it could cost her her life. I couldn't do that to her. I'd never be able to live with myself.

Still, sometimes memories like these creep up on me and I find myself wondering if living like this is worth it. Not the keeping my mother safe part, but the games, the lies, and the web I've spun so deeply around myself that I'll never escape. My mother was the first victim of this life, but who will be next? Marco, my cousin who sided with me over my bloodthirsty and vindictive brother? Maybe Natalia, the one person who has never turned her back on me, giving me chance after chance, regardless of what happened? She's my sister—not by blood, but by something deeper, an invisible tether that links our souls like we were pulled from the same flame. Or what about Addie, my newest family member, who barreled into my life so unexpectedly that I nearly stumbled?

Or will it be Maddy?

Fiery, beautiful Maddy with a temper that matches my own. Every challenge I've thrown her way, she's blocked and countered with her own like we're entangled in some twisted dance. And I love it. I love *her*, and if something were to happen to her...

No. I won't allow anything to happen to her. I will die before I let that happen.

I follow the sound of the music, inhaling deeply as I round the corner into the next room.

There, in the kitchen, is my mother. She is laughing with Maddy as she tries to show her the correct way to knead the dough for whatever they're making, her eyes crinkling as the flour puffs up in my girlfriend's face. Addie sits at the counter next to them, and nudges

Natalia at my entrance. I hardly notice, feeling like I'm in a daze.

This is a dream, a cruel and beautiful hallucination induced by too much heat and not enough sleep. My mother is in Rome right now, under heavy guard per Natalia's orders. She has a beautiful house with flower boxes and family photos from when I was a kid. Photo albums hold the rest of what frames can't.

One of those albums sits on the table beside six glasses of wine. Marco points at one of the images, his face pinched with joy. I recognize it as one of us as kids, our laughter frozen in the photo.

My mother turns around, plate in hand, and our eyes lock.

I watch the seven stages of grief play out on her face as she takes me in—my curly hair that used to match hers in color and volume, my new scars, the muscling of my weapon of a body, no longer the soft boy she sheltered. She takes in all the ways I've grown that she's missed. She can't believe it any more than I can. It's only then that I notice that any photos with me in them have been turned around and hidden from her. They haven't told her yet that I'm alive, despite me being here.

The plate drops to the ground and shatters upon impact.

"Cecile." Maddy moves to rush to her side, but my mother is already bending down to pick up the shards.

"Sorry, amore, I thought I saw a ghost. This city gives my old heart trouble with my memories," she says, still staring at me. She's in a haze, just as I am. Only the sight of her reaching to pick up the ceramic shards with her bare hands has me breaking free of my trance, and I rush to her side, catching them in mine.

"Careful, Mamma."

She looks up at me then, as if my voice has broken whatever had taken ahold of her. Her hands shake in mine as she stays crouched near the floor, and I have half the thought to pull her to her feet when she begins to weep.

"You're alive."

Silent tears snake their way down my face and the others blur to the background. We rise, and her thin yet sturdy arms wrap around my neck, mine going around her waist. She sobs into my neck as I inhale deeply.

She's changed so much since I last saw her—the lines etching her face are now more prominent, her eyes sadder than I've ever seen them, and I swear she's shrunk some, but she still smells the same. Home—she smells like home.

"How are you here?" I mumble as rage suddenly overtakes me. I whirl on Natalia. "Why is she here? Malik is going to kill her. She's not supposed to know I'm alive."

But it's Maddy I come face to face with, her brown eyes narrowed in determination. "It was my idea, Riven, so if you're going to shout at anyone, shout at me."

Anguish tears into my heart, shredding it with iron nails. She knew—she knew the risk and still brought my mother into this danger. I can't forgive her for this. I can't—

"Malik already tried to kill her," she says softly, her hand finding and squeezing my own. "After... after I killed Cas. Natalia brought her here, but it was my idea to let her know that you're alive. He's coming after everyone you love and I just thought if he isn't going to uphold his end of your deal, then you shouldn't either. I'm sorry. I should have said something, I just—"

My lips are on hers in an instant, pulling her close for a slow and tender kiss. I try to pour everything into it—the love I feel, the relief that's washing over my body in waves.

When I pull away and turn around, my mother is smiling like she can already hear wedding bells.

"Are you four having a joint wedding?" she asks, confirming my suspicions.

Maddy blushes furiously, and I suppose she hadn't explained to my mother who she is to me, aside from being Addie's best friend.

"No, this," she says, motioning between us, "is pretty new."

"Don't lie to an old woman. God will send you to hell."

"Mamma," I gasp, but Maddy laughs and I catch the mischievous glimmer in my mother's eyes. She winks and Addie brings in a broom.

"I'll clean this up. I think you two need to have a talk. Maddy, help me finish dinner?" Addie asks.

"Um, no," Natalia interjects. "Maddy can help *me* finish dinner while *you* finish cleaning that up. Don't look at me like that, my love. Let's not sour the night with food poisoning."

Addie pouts, pushing the shards into the dustpan with a broom. "I'm getting better."

Natalia smiles and presses a tender kiss to her temple. "Yes, you are."

That seems to appease Addie enough for her to stop her grumbling.

My mother laughs, so full of light now. She lets me lead her to the library, where I lean against Addie's desk, risking her wrath as I allow my mother the only chair in the room.

She sits gingerly, as if she doesn't know how to use her body anymore. She looks at me like she can't bear to look away, yet it seems like she's seen a ghost all the same.

"Where have you been?" she finally asks, her voice breaking. Her tears have since dried but I can see them still lingering, just looking for an excuse to break free. She switched back into Italian, more comfortable with the language, and I do too.

"Here, in the city with Natalia and Marco. They've been keeping me safe."

Her eyes drift to the scars lacing my exposed skin. They're newer than the ones she remembers, those having been left from wounds she dressed herself, while these ones have been cared for by my sloppy hand. "Have they?"

"Yes, from as much as they can. And they've been protecting you. I've been protecting you too. That's why I stayed away. After Father named me head of the family, Malik ordered everyone to kill me on sight. That's when Natalia rescued me."

My mother frowns. "She told me that you two met in passing and were friends."

"We are friends. She's become a sister to me. I love her, Mamma, but the rest is a lie we were forced to tell you. I'm sorry. Malik said he'd kill you if you ever found out. At the time, you were the only way to hurt me.

Natalia was, and still is, untouchable, and he needed to hurt me, so he went to you. I'm so sorry."

She rises now, her hand cupping my cheek while her thumb idly brushes away my tears. I lean into the touch. I forgot how good it feels to be loved so unconditionally. I never knew love like this from my father, and my mother was ripped from me too soon. I thought I'd never know this feeling again. Maddy is different. As much as I've grown to love her, the love we share is a different type, thank god.

"You have nothing to be sorry for. Don't ever apologize for this, or anything ever again, Riven."

"Even if I ruin everything?"

"Well, I hope I raised you better," she says with a laugh. "But even then, you are my son. I love you more than life, so don't you ever apologize to me for anything."

I've cried too much today, and to be entirely honest, I can't remember the last time I cried at all. I know Addie would tell me it's good for men to cry, and maybe she isn't wrong, but I was raised differently—not by my mother, but by my father and my brothers. Men like me don't show any signs of weakness, because then it can be exploited.

But this is my mother—my lovely mother I've missed so terribly.

"Now, you said at the time I was the only way to hurt you, but it's different now, isn't it?" she says with a knowing glance. "The blonde girl, Maddy."

I laugh despite my watery eyes. "She's hardly a girl, Mamma."

My mother waves a dismissive hand, the corners of her eyes crinkling again. "You love her, don't you?"

For a moment, I expect this conversation to deepen, and I steel myself against the words I'm about to say. I've never been ashamed of Maddy, and I never will be. I love her so deeply that it feels as if she's taken a piece of her soul and imbued it in mine. We've become so intwined that if someone could study the love in a human heart, they wouldn't know what belongs to me and what is hers.

But I've never loved anyone before, not that I told my mother about. I loved one girl once, then I had to leave her a month later. Malik caught wind and had Father send me away on a lengthy job. When I got back, he had claimed her, and they stayed together for months despite Malik's cheating. I never told her about our life, our family.

Then she became one of Donovan's victims—a fact that I've shared with no one yet, not even Natalia. Seeing Anna's face, cold and blue on the morgue table after being apart for years... It's not a way anyone should ever have to see another person, let alone their first love, and all it did was heighten the nightmares I have now of finding Maddy the same way.

"I do. More than I've ever loved before," I admit solemnly. "And that fact terrifies me because now he's after her. He's already tried to kill her three times, and I'm scared that next time, I won't be able to stop it."

My mother nods like she's deep in thought, a crease forming between her graying brows as she pinches them together. Aside from the stray gray hairs and newer lines set in her face, she still looks as youthful as she was during my boyhood. I remember Natalia telling me that my mother once told her not to worry about wrinkles because she has good Italian genetics.

"And have you protected her from the other three attempts?"

"No." I let my head fall. "Not all of them. The first one happened here, but Natalia has increased security since, if that's even possible. Addie saved her then. The second time, I managed to cover her in time, and the third, she saved herself. Cas broke into her apartment with someone, and tried to kill her. I got there, but if she hadn't fought back, I would have come back to a body."

My mother nods again, this time pinching my cheek. "Then it sounds like you have nothing to worry about."

Thinking back on those nights, the last thought in my mind is that I have nothing to worry about. I eye her incredulously, the shock making me flinch. "What do you mean?"

"I mean that she has such a support system around her that you don't need to carry this all on you. Addie will protect her. Natalia, and Marco too. And it sounds like she handled herself just fine against your brother, of all people. You're carrying the weight of the world on your shoulders again, my love, when all they're asking for is your hand. Stop trying to bear it by yourself." Then she sighs, for the first time since we met looking her sixty-nine years of age. "I know your father tried to tell you something different. I know, despite my best effort, he tried his hardest to convince you that the fate of the world and this family was in your hands. I know your brothers tried to tell you you were unworthy and nothing more than a weapon. I am telling you now, as the only one out of the four that loves you, that you don't need to be anything other than who you are. You are good and kind, and should never let this world freeze your heart.

Above all, you are my son, and I know you will do what is right."

I pull my mother into another hug now. I've missed this. I've missed it so fucking much—her hugs, her voice, how she always knows the right thing to say. Suddenly, I feel like a little boy again, running into his mother's arms after kids at school called me a fatherless freak.

I've let the world harden me the past few years, and never knew why I feel so deeply when everyone around me is so apathetic. Natalia began to thaw that ice and chip away the rock walls surrounding my heart. In her own odd way, she had invited me to do the same, until there was a crack in that stone. Then came Marco, and Addie, then Maddy.

Now my mother tears down the rest of the rock herself, thawing all that was left frozen in me, and exposing me to the light of a new world—a world where I can give all I have to a woman I love without the constraints of the past holding me back. I can feel a part of myself return that I didn't know I lost.

My mother squeezes my hand. "You interrupted my time with Maddy before. I need to know the woman who is going to give me grandbabies."

"Mamma!" My face flushes the most embarrassing shade of scarlet. Maddy and I haven't talked about kids, for good reason. With everything else going on, it hardly feels appropriate. We haven't been together long, and even though I know what I want, I can't imagine asking her now. Nor can I imagine bringing kids into a world where my brother runs rampant, hell bent on destroying everything I love.

No, there's only one way this can end, I think as I

allow my mother to drag me back to Maddy. The others have set the table and finished laying the food out, and greet us with large smiles.

If I want to keep this little life I've built, then Malik needs to disappear.

I need to kill my brother.

CHAPTER 25
MADDY

It's been a week since Riven and his mother reunited and I have never seen him happier. I thought I knew happiness before, but what I felt then is only a fraction of what I feel now. I thought Riven would be more guarded and cautious with his mother back in town, but if anything, he has been the opposite. He smiles freely, and wakes me up with coffee the way I like it—which isn't new, but he has the brightest smile on his face now, no hint of sorrow anywhere. He's a man filled with determination, and while for some it might be considered a red flag that this determination stems from the desire to kill his brother, I find him dreamy.

This morning, we invited Cecile to my apartment, which is slowly becoming *our* apartment. Reece is so happy to have a new visitor and bounds over excitedly, her tail flapping side to side like a windshield wiper. Cecile is enamored with her, which leads to stories of Riven begging for a puppy as a kid. She almost caved, and said she still regrets never getting him one.

Riven brushes it off with embarrassment and says

he's perfectly content now. Reece likes the sound of that, her oversized paws creating thunderous footsteps as she runs and launches herself at him. She's noticed the shift in his demeanor, too, these days. He takes her for runs with him, sneaks her extra treats when he thinks I'm not looking, and all around has been in a better mood.

I loved him before, but I love him even more with this softer side now exposed.

Later in the morning, Riven has to go work on a lead with Natalia. He mentioned something under his breath to me about hearing about a property Malik bought off the coast, close enough to a harbor to cause trouble. It could just be for importing, but Riven is uneasy, and said they wanted to check it out anyway.

It isn't a problem. Addie already invited Cecile and I to grab brunch and go over wedding plans anyhow. My heart clenches at the thought of my best friend getting married in two months. I can't help it—I am just so damn happy for her.

Riven drops us off on his way out, but not before telling me in a low voice that a few of Natalia's guards are stationed around and in the building. His mom thinks all the security is nonsense, and so we've opted to keep it under wraps for now. I nod, and with a kiss on his cheek, wish him luck.

Now we sit in a booth with what might be the most comfortable cushions I've ever sat on, far enough in to be out of the direct sunlight of the large windows.

We chose the venue for Cecile, given that it's been a longtime favorite of ours. With Monet-esque paintings lining the walls and a pastel interior, the whole place screams comfort. Not to mention their Japanese-style pancakes might literally be to die for.

"What are we planning today?" Cecile asks, settling in on the other side across from Addie. I sit in the vacant spot next to my best friend and smile. Cecile looks absolutely adorable in a lilac sweater today, bundled despite the warm weather.

I've grown to love the woman in the past week that I've known her. She's kind and witty in an unsuspecting way, and she makes even better food than Riven. I almost feel bad taking her to this place, knowing it can't compare to her own cooking, but her eyes light up at the menu anyway.

"I can't remember the last time I had a waffle," she says like she's deep in thought. "But eggs are good too. It's good to start the day off with protein."

Addie lays her hand on the other woman's arm warmly. "Order whatever you want, Cecile. It's Natalia's treat."

Cecile scoffs playfully. "That girl spoils us."

"It's her specialty," Addie responds with a grin. I personally enjoy this so-called specialty.

Today, we are planning Addie's bachelorette party. It won't be anything wild. No strippers or the usual phallic paraphernalia that seems to have taken over—that's kind of hard to incorporate when your best friend is a lesbian. She wants to do a picnic in the park with everyone from Tella's, that way she can have them all there since her wedding is going to be so intimate. It's close family only, meaning our group of four and Cecile.

"What did Daryl say when he got the invite to a bachelorette party?" I ask, playfully wiggling my eyebrows.

My best friend laughs, almost spitting out her coffee. "Oh, he was horrified until I explained. I don't know if he'll come, but it would be nice."

Our boss most definitely will not be coming, but I allow myself the mental image of him arriving and the joy it brings me. One day when my dreams take off and I follow Addie out the exit, I'll miss that coffee shop and the man who runs it. He's seen me through more phases of my life and angst than my parents have, and given he has the personality of drying cement, that's saying something.

Addie officially left Tella's a few days ago, and I'd be lying if I said I didn't cry at the end of our last shift together. I am so incredibly proud of her, but also a tad bit heartbroken as this chapter of our life comes to a close. I knew it isn't permanent, but life seems to have changed so quickly I don't know what to think of it. It used to be just us against the world in our little apartment with our Tella's aprons. We're growing up, and the thought is as exciting as it is terrifying.

Addie seems to notice it too. Where she used to be all excitement and bubbly giggles, I sometimes spot her with a faraway look in her eye, like she's remembering simpler times—times where our biggest concern was paying rent on time, going out, and living life just the two of us, the city bending around our bodies as we walked through it arm in arm. But for her, that was a life without the love of her life, and when she blinks, that look is gone.

Nostalgia's a two-faced bitch.

I tune back in to the conversation, listening to Addie walk Cecile through the details of her engagement, then she invites her to come with to pick up her wedding dress tonight.

Cecile agrees with the widest smile I've seen her wear yet, aside from when she reunited with Riven.

Addie turns that bright gaze to me next. "You're coming, too, right?"

"Of course," I assure her with an easy grin. "I can't wait to see it again, especially with all the alterations."

"You've seen it?" Cecile asks.

It's still sometimes odd to be sitting at a table with Riven's mother, and I fight the urge to shy away. Instead, I return her kind gaze, my hands folded in my lap. "I was there when she tried it on. Me, Riven, and Marco, actually," I clarify. "Natalia wasn't allowed to come, so she's not too happy to be the only one who hasn't seen it yet."

"But tradition is tradition, and we've had enough bad luck to last a life time," Addie adds. "Anyway, I have to run to the bathroom. Mads, can you order for me if they come by while I'm gone?"

"Of course."

Addie always gets the same thing, just like I do, then we split it in half and swap plates. We just work like that.

She nods and heads off, leaving me alone with Cecile. The older woman is exquisite, and I can only hope to age like she has. I don't mean her lack of wrinkles, but the youthful energy she exudes. She's stunning, nearly glowing.

"I'm sure you were ecstatic when Addie and Natalia got engaged," she tries for our first one-on-one conversation. Addie is easy middle ground, a familiar tether between us. There is always Riven, but that seems more sensitive.

"I was, once I woke up and learned we were all still alive," I say, not bitterly, but still not meaning to sour the mood. It's supposed to be a joke, but it fails spectacularly.

Cecile frowns, and it takes me a moment to realize it is not in displeasure, but confusion. "You managed to sleep through that?"

"I— Not exactly."

Then realization dawns on her face all at once. "You're *her*."

"Excuse me?"

"Natalia told me that Addie's stalker had a girlfriend that he attempted to kill the night he took her. That was you," she says softly, the pieces now clicking almost visibly behind her eyes. "She never told me your name for your privacy, but oh, Maddy..."

It's been a while since I've cried over that night. The nightmares have all but stopped now, and its rare I think back on what unfolded these days. Still, tears burn the backs of my eyes and I blink furiously. Maybe it's the gentleness in her tone, or the fact that it's been a year now since Addie started getting those texts. It's been so long, and so much has happened, yet where my own parents pushed me to heal quickly, there's no such force in Cecile's tone. She's not pitying, but genuinely sorry for me, gentle, like a mother should be.

"It's alright. It's in the past now."

"The past can still hurt," Cecile reminds me.

"It can," I admit, "but it doesn't now."

And it's the truth. When I think of Donovan, his greased-back brown hair, crooked smile, and dry-cleaned suits, all I can think of is rage, but it's duller now. I used to direct all my fury towards myself, in an attempt to justify why he did those things to me. Why did *I* have to go through all that when all I ever gave him was my everything?

Then Riven came along and I learned that I didn't deserve it. That realization should have come earlier, but my heart had been so thoroughly bruised that I couldn't see that it didn't matter what I did or who I was. Donovan was deranged, a fucking stain of a man, if I could even call him that.

He deserved worse than he got, but in a way, he found the perfect ending. Right as he was losing his grip on the only thing he ever wanted, he died. Now, his two last victims get to live—and not just live, but thrive. We've found love and happiness that his bitter heart could never understand.

I truly don't think he knew how to love, and if I was a better person, maybe I would have pitied him for it, but I'm not a better person. I'm a healed one.

"I'm glad," Cecile says in earnest, her smaller hands clasping mine tightly.

Addie returns from the bathroom at that moment. "Sorry about that, the line was crazy. Wait, are you okay?" She was looking at me now, worry creasing her face.

I smile, broad and genuine. "Perfect. Now, were we stopping for champagne on the way to get your dress?"

"Obviously."

That settles the discussion as a light warmth floods my body. The waitress comes by to take our order, and we spend the rest of the brunch talking and laughing. Things are good now, and I want them to always stay this way. I know life doesn't work like that, but for a fleeting moment, I want it to. I want to hold on to this warmth and this family I've found without any of the accompanying sorrow.

By the end, it feels as though Cecile has adopted both Addie and I, and it's nice, feeling wanted. I know I'm wanted by my friends, but it's a different type of shy blush rising in my cheeks at the thought of being wanted by a parental figure. It's a familial love, like gentle guidance and protection. Maybe my parents loved me like that once, but I can't remember them ever speaking to me the way Cecile does.

The bridal shop is only a few blocks away so we walk, Addie and I acting as tour guides for Cecile, pointing out everything from our old apartment to Tella's. We promise to stop by on the way home from the shop, already running a bit late because we did, in fact, stop at the corner liquor store for a bottle of champagne.

When we enter, the consultant takes us back to a private room and fetches a bucket of ice for our bottle. Addie changes into a robe, and I slip a disposable camera from my purse, taking candid photos of her and Cecile with champagne flutes, sometimes slipping in for a cheesy selfie.

Only a few moments later, the consultant comes back and brings Addie into the dressing room, garment bag in hand.

Cecile, cheeks flushed, takes the time to turn to me and pull a ring off of her finger. She takes my hand and slips in on my ring finger, and my jaw drops.

"Cecile, you know you're lovely, but I'm with your son," I tease, trying to calm my frantically beating heart.

The older woman grins. "I know. Just making sure it fits. I plan to give it to Riven in hopes that you invite me back for *your* dress fitting." She winks.

I freeze, trying not to picture it. The ring is beautiful, a large oval diamond set on a sapphire-crusted silver band, but I doubt Riven wants anything from his father.

As if catching where my mind is going, Cecile shakes her head. "It's my mother's wedding ring. She gave it to me when I was a girl. I sold my wedding ring the minute my bastard husband died."

Hearing Cecile use foul language is like being splashed in the face with water. I never thought she was capable of it, but I laugh, regardless, then hand the ring back. She thanks me, and I think she has half the thought to call her son and tell him to get the marriage license ready now, but she doesn't. Instead, she fidgets with the ring while I get lost in her daydream—me, married to her son.

And for a moment, I can see it—me, standing on that platform with Addie, Natalia, Marco, and Cecile settled on these plush couches, maybe my mother would even be there if we could ever work our differences out. I'd try on nearly a hundred gowns before finding the one. Something simple, classic, and timeless with just a touch of modern elegance. It will be a shock at first, given that I usually choose to opt for the extravagant choice, but they'll all smile and understand. It would be like it was made for me, and even my mother will like it. It just might be the first thing we've ever agreed upon, and despite fighting passive aggressively the rest of the fitting, we will both be happy. Cecile's ring will be on my finger, and Addie will be wearing a wedding band. We will drink champagne until the bubbles have rotted our brain, and Natalia will drive us home, ever the watchful guard dog. I'll stumble home into Riven's arms, my heart beating a countdown until he's mine forever.

I can see it happen.

I *want* it to happen.

Cecile has a touch of motherly adoration lingering in her eyes as she watches me, almost as if she can see the fantasy I'm weaving in my own mind.

Addie steps out from behind the curtains then, her robe now replaced with a beautiful wedding dress. I found the gown stunning when I first saw it, but now that it's tailored to her body, it's beyond gorgeous.

Every step she takes has the ballgown swishing around her ankles. The skirt itself is tulle, pearls cascading from the small of her waist in a waterfall. It has a slight train, and while I would call it a ballgown, it doesn't have as much volume as I remember it having originally. Addie asked them to cut some layers down, to make the skirt flow out around her, but not be so wide she can't move.

The top of the dress is fitted to her skin like it has been painted on, crusted with the same pearls as on the skirt. They stretch up towards her collarbones, tapering off to melt into her flesh like a gradient of a neckline. The sleeves are mesh and skin colored, but look invisible save for the pearls dotting her arms, unless you look very closely.

Addie's wild curls are pulled halfway back from her face, a long veil pinned to the crown of her head. She's ethereal as she walks towards us, the broadest smile on her face.

"Please tell me you still love it, because, Addie..."

She beams. "I love it."

Cecile gives a watery inhale beside me, breathing, "Beautiful," underneath her breath.

I capture another picture with the disposable. Addie didn't ask me to take photos. She didn't have to. I know she wants to document the whole wedding-planning process, but is too kind to ask me to work during these excursions. So instead, I've opted to do it on my own, creating a joint photo album in the cloud that I've been uploading all my images to. I'll have to kick Natalia off of it before I upload these photos, or maybe just send them to Addie.

Addie walks back to change before risking spilling anything on the dress.

Natalia has already paid for everything, so we bag the dress, then walk out the door. I text Riven to meet us at Tella's instead of the dress shop, filling him in on the promise we made to his mom.

> Hey, change of plans. Can you pick us up from Tella's? Taking your mom for the best coffee of her life.

RIVEN:

> She's Italian. She won't be swayed by American coffee.

> Rude!

> Tella's is a culture in and of itself.

> You've offended my way of life.

I can live with that.

> Prick.

Marco is going to come get you. We are held up.

I frown at that. Riven said they were looking into Malik's new place, but does that mean they went to the warehouse?

> Everything okay?

Yeah

We were right. Something isn't right here. There's access to a harbor but no sign of moving equipment.

I don't know much about the drug trade, but I figure the international shipments would be hefty. Wouldn't they need some way to move things off the ship? I ask just to be safe.

> Would you need that?

> Yes. This is likely a cover for something else

>> Or a distraction so you split your resources

> You're starting to think like us

> But yes, I agree. We are camping out for a bit to see if they do make a move. I'll be home tonight for dinner.

A few minutes pass then,

> I love you.

>> Love you too.
>> Don't die.

Riven doesn't respond to that, but I can imagine him doing that silent laugh-slash-smirk thing he does when he's on duty but I've said something amusing. My humor is crude and juvenile half the time, but hey, if it works, it works.

The doorbell chimes and Liam waves wildly as we walk in. Daryl is behind the counter, saying something to Kelsey when he spots us. Addie is carrying her wedding dress, stuffed in a garment bag, and I carry the half-drank bottle of champagne in the other.

I bow at the waist and extend it before me to the middle-aged man. "A sacrifice to the god of the coffee beans," I say.

Daryl scoffs. "You can get a fine for walking around with an open container in public and I *will* fire you."

"That's why I'm giving it to you. You can celebrate!"

"Celebrate what?"

"I don't know, being alive?"

Daryl sighs and accepts the bottle, stashing it behind the bar before fixing Addie with a glare that I think is teasing, but I'm never sure. "You quit. You're dead to me."

"I didn't quit, I resigned," Addie says like it makes all the difference. "But don't worry, I still plan to haunt your door."

Daryl groans something under his breath that sounds like "Great," but then I notice a new drawing and drink on the chalkboard behind the counter.

A steaming purple cup with sprigs of lavender coming out of it is drawn on in chalk against the blackboard, "The Maddy" written in swirling cursive beneath it.

I gape at Daryl when I recognize my drink on the seasonal menu. "You put it on the menu!"

"I'm *trying* it on the menu," Daryl corrects.

"You're going soft, man."

He grunts and shuffles back to his office, bottle in hand, and shuts the door.

Liam frowns at the closed door. "He could have shared."

"You're like, a baby," Addie says, leaning across the counter to ruffle the teen's hair. "No alcohol for you."

"Yeah, yeah. What can I get you?"

We give Cecile our recommendations, and in the end, she orders an iced latte with a sprinkle of cinnamon on it. It's better than Riven and Natalia's soul-crushing orders of plain black coffee, no cream, no sugar. Disgusting.

I, of course, order the Maddy, and Addie gets an iced caramel latte. At the last second, we grab a cappuccino for Marco, who comes through the door a moment later, taking Addie's dress in his hand to stash in the car before one of us spills something on it. Which, honestly, is fair—that does sound like something we would do.

We let Cecile take the front seat as we pile into the back, and Marco accepts his drink with a kiss to the backs of our hands. We are used to not being allowed in the passenger seat on public outings, given that windshields are apparently easy to shoot someone through. Not that Malik or any of our enemies ever took such an impersonal approach. Using a gun? Fine. Using a gun when we can't see the threat in front of us? Absolutely not. Even with the drive-by that night in the park, they squealed their tires, letting us know we were in the presence of a threat, and the man Riven killed only shot at me once I'd killed Cas. It's more about the terror than the efficiency for them.

"You're such a charmer, Marco," Addie says with a sly look. "Is there someone we don't know about that you're practicing these moves for?"

"The only ladies in my life are the ones in this car," he responds with equal cunning.

Cecile laughs at that, and I ask, "What about Natalia?"

"I said ladies, not nightmares."

Addie blushes at that and I can't tell if she's agreeing or disagreeing with him.

I settle comfortably against the back of the leather seats, half giddy from a good day and half content to take a nap, feeling wholly safe in this moment. I never realized how much I took that feeling for granted before now. I stopped feeling safe the first time Donovan hit me. Every time I didn't see him was simply space between, and then once he was gone, Malik was quick to replace him. It's been well over a year since my body has completely been able to relax, but I can now. Even with Malik at large, in this car right now, surrounded by people who would die for me, I drive home to a man who would kill for me, and I have never felt safer.

CHAPTER 26
RIVEN

Malik's warehouse is exactly as I expected it to be and yet not at the same time. It's every cliché, and Malik knows it too. It's why he hides in plain sight. Malik's pride is too easily bruised for him to let anyone underestimate him, which would make anyone else think that this location is just too easy. If the cops showed up, they could easily say he is just another dumb criminal, an insult Malik would never allow himself to suffer. No, he's garnered his reputation and planted the building so that if authorities show up, it will look too clichéd for them to even bother investigating. I'm still not sure how that logic works or if it works at all, but knowing Malik, I know how his twisted brain works.

Natalia has her flashlight out, scanning the empty warehouse for anything we could have missed. Her frustrated face tells me everything I need to know.

"Is there any chance he just hasn't moved everything in yet?"

"He's been sitting on the property for days. If he was

going to, then he would have already. Besides, he doesn't have anyone stationed here, just that one camera." Natalia points her flashlight towards the blinking camera we disabled before entering. That itself is odd. Of course, it isn't one of Natalia's, but Malik doesn't like to leave cameras, or any trace of evidence, really. There's also the other question Natalia posed. If Malik plans to use this warehouse for shipments, he would have men stationed here from the moment he bought the property, but there was no one inside or out when we broke our way in.

Something isn't right, but I can't figure out what.

"He could be using it for a cover for something else? To throw us off his trail," I offer, coming to stand beside her.

The look Natalia shoots over her shoulder tells me she already knows as much. "Thank you for catching up," she murmurs. "But what is he hiding then?"

"If there was an answer to that, you'd know before me."

Natalia hums, then traces the beam of light down the wall. No loose boards to be seen, nothing in the warehouse at all. It's been cleaned spotless, the only proof that anyone has even been here. There's not a single speck of dust or cobweb to be seen as we search the entire span of the property. Something went down here, something Malik wanted to hide any trace of. What that is, I don't know.

"Any chance if we took that camera home, we could see what happened here, before everything was cleaned up? You could have someone hack it."

Natalia shakes her head, and even though I know it was a long shot, the disappointment still settles heavily in my stomach. "It was installed after whatever happened went down. Malik knows better. The camera is here for whatever is to come, not what has happened."

"Then we should take it down with us."

"Then he'll put another one up. The camera isn't worth our time."

I know she's right, but still I glance up at it, like there's a tether between me and the damn thing. I want to destroy it then burn this goddamn building to the ground, if only to piss my brother off. This place is our only lead, and I can't do that, I know, but the urge to strike out against my brother is strong, even if he'll just see it as petty and petulant.

In my mind, I know this is why Natalia is our leader. She is able to keep her head level and thoroughly evaluate both the strengths and the losses each situation might bring. As much as I'm sure she'd love to watch Malik's empire burst into flames, we can't burn anything, not yet. All it would do is piss him off and send him after our weaknesses.

In me, there is instead this thrashing violence that demands to be released. I want to destroy everything if only to satiate my own rage. It's why I know deep down I never would have been a good family head. I have Malik's wits and Cas's violence, but I have my own rage that I can barely keep contained some days. The Barone family was destined for ruin regardless of who took the throne, and it's time to let it be a relic of a bygone era in this city.

"We should head back. We aren't going to get anything from staring at an empty building," Natalia groans.

This stalemate we've been stuck in has been pressing

on her as heavily as it has been me. The Natalia I knew a year ago would have razed this city to the ground, my brother still inside it, and it might have even ended in some dramatic gun fight to the death between them. But that Natalia didn't have something to lose. She didn't have someone to pull her from the flames. Killing Malik like that would be killing herself, and now she has someone to live for.

Would I have wanted it to end that way before I met Maddy? Would I have been content to destroy the world if it meant destroying him?

If I'm being honest with myself, I don't know. Unlike Natalia, I had one person left, even if she thought I was dead already. I don't know if I could have said goodbye to her like that. Maybe that's the reason I put off dealing with Malik. I was scared. Where the old Natalia was bold and brash, the old Riven was a coward. I never had that person to come along and push me. Where Addie would pull Natalia from the flames, Maddy would push me into them, then follow me into the brightest of the blaze.

"Should we be planning an old-fashioned assassination attempt?" I ask.

It's not unheard of, but killing my brother that way would be cheap and dishonorable, and probably suicide.

"I don't want to resort to that, but the next time he shows his face, I won't hesitate to blow it off."

"He deserves worse."

Natalia hums, then fixes me with a stern look. "Riven."

"What?"

"Don't take your time killing him," she says. "He

deserves worse, but he's not some low-profile underling. Every second you spend torturing him is another second he has to scheme and escape. Kill him quick before he can hurt anyone else. Don't let your pride be the reason someone else dies."

Her words sluice over me like lava, burning straight through until all that's left is the hollow sting that tells me what she says is right. As badly as I *want* to make my brother hurt, I *need* to make sure he can't hurt anyone else. To make sure he can't hurt Maddy ever again.

She deserves better than a man who would throw away her life for his pride, and I promised myself the night I told her I loved her that I would be that man. I will be anyone she needs me to be, and Natalia is only reminding me.

I set my jaw against the furious retort rising in my throat. In the end, I nod, not trusting myself to say anything.

Addie and Maddy's laughter carries from the top of the stairs down into the atrium when Natalia and I arrive home. Marco texted to let us know that he escorted Cecile back to Natalia's old apartment, and he'd stay outside to guard the door tonight. The extra security he provides isn't exactly necessary, given that I think Natalia's apartment is more secure than Area 51, but I feel better knowing he's there with her, regardless.

I know trusting Marco with my mother means more to him than he lets on. He was the one standing outside

Addie and Maddy's old apartment the night Donovan broke in. Donovan used some chemical to gas the entire complex, knocking everyone out, including Marco. There was no way for him to have expected Donovan to have access to anything like that, and no one saw it coming.

I never blamed Marco, but I know Marco has been blaming himself since it happened. Extending this olive branch feels like the first step towards his own healing journey, as the rest of us start to complete ours.

"Let's not bring this up to the girls," Natalia says slowly.

"You want me to lie to them?" I ask. Incredulousness lines my tone and I don't bother to keep the bite from it. Addie and Mads have never been excluded from our jobs, despite how gruesome it may be. Keeping secrets is what nearly tore Addie and Natalia apart months ago, and I don't want Maddy and I to follow the same path.

"No, but listen."

I do as she says, hearing them, laughing still. Not a single tremor of worry or hesitation taints their voices. Maddy shouts something, there's a crash, then even more laughter, which I didn't even know was possible. Reece barks along, and it's now that I realize they must have made a stop to bring her home with them.

Natalia continues once she watches the realization on my face. "They're happy. They've had a good day. Do you realize how rarely we hear this sound now? Let's just let them have this day." The "and carry this burden for them" is implied.

I keep my mouth shut in silent agreement. I'll carry whatever weight the world throws at me if it means she can still have moments where she feels untethered and happy. I know she tries to do the same, in her own ways. A gentle touch, a kind word. Maddy tells me she loves me with her words often, but she shows it with her actions even more.

"You look like you need a drink."

Natalia rolls her eyes. "I need a swift kick to the head."

"I'm sure my brother could help you out with that one."

"I'll call him up."

I walk to their liquor cabinet, pulling out a bottle of whiskey. I'm not much of a fan, but I know Nat is.

"To fucked-up family lines," she says.

"To getting married in two months," I respond pointedly.

She clinks her glass against mine with a low chuckle. "I'll drink to that."

I bite back against the burn of the alcohol, shaking my head when Natalia offers me a second glass. "I have to drive home still," I offer as explanation.

"What, you don't want to stay for girls' night?"

"No, but I will go say good night before I head out," I say, placing my glass in the sink.

Nat nods, settling onto one of her couches, already flicking the TV on. She has the faintest smile tugging the corners of her lips up when I pass by her to make my way up the stairs.

I follow the noise to the master bedroom, right as the sound of a chair scraping across the floor sounds. I step into the doorway, crossing my arms and leaning against the frame to watch the scene unfold.

Maddy sits cross-legged on Addie's bed, giggling like

a mad woman with a wine glass in her hand. Reece is laying at her feet, her front paws splayed and taking up a position that is both relaxed and defensive, ready to protect her mom at any given moment. Addie, meanwhile, is balanced on a stool with a sticky note in her hand that says "Ian" while asking, "Higher?"

I notice the rest of the wall is littered with other various sticky notes, all with male names on them. I see mine at the top, then notice the rest begin to form a triangle of sorts. Addie has to step down from the stool because she's laughing too hard, and Maddy tells her to put it near the middle.

"Do I even want to know what is happening?" I ask, still from the spot I occupy in the doorway.

Maddy doubles over laughing, nearly spilling her white wine on the duvet. Addie sits next to her, her own glass abandoned on the floor so she can hold her best friend with both hands while they laugh.

They're both wine drunk. Great.

"We're rating the guys Maddy's slept with pyramid style, like that one dance show did," Addie explains between bouts of laughter.

Seeing my name at the top makes a lot more sense now, and has a smug smirk lifting the corners of my lips. I spot that guy from the apartment I got Maddy from at the bottom of the list.

"And you put me at the top, baby?"

"Best dick of my life," she swears solemnly with a hand over her chest like she's pledging to some flag.

Addie pulls a face with a whiny, "Ew," but moves off the bed to grab another sticky note. "How about Lucas?"

"Hmmm, third row."

"I'll leave you two to it," I say with a small wave.

It's nice seeing them both carefree and together again, even if it is aided by a little girls' night drinking. They haven't had a chance to just be two best friends in a while. For the past year now, it's been danger after danger for them, and it's nice to see them just be a pair of twenty-something-year-olds having fun again.

"Wait, you can't leave without kissing me. It's like, the law."

"The law?" I ask, trying and failing to keep the humor from my voice.

"Yes, the law. Don't make me punish you," she says, and I can't help it. I laugh, which only makes her face go even redder.

Before she can go off on another tangent, I stalk forward, placing a kiss on her lips. She tastes like sweet wine and hums into my mouth before I pull away, her eyes still half closed.

"I'll see you in the morning. I love you."

She smiles, and suddenly, all feels right in this twisted world once more. "I love you too."

The drive back to the apartment feels empty. No girlfriend, no dog. For the first time in weeks, I'm completely alone as I go home. The weight of the fact settles over me like smoke, clinging to my clothes and choking me. God, I've gone soft. So fucking soft.

To distract myself, I let my mind wander back to the

warehouse. Natalia warned me to let it rest for tonight and we'll revisit it tomorrow, but Natalia has a home full of joy right now, and I have a cold apartment. I could go visit my mom, but there's something about the warehouse that I can't put my finger on.

Malik had it cleaned for a reason, but why? Was it to hide the traces of something that he did already, or something he is about to do?

The Barones deal in narcotics mainly, while we hold the majority of the weapons trade on the black market. That eliminates any ghost gun shipments. Narcotics would be obvious, as we thought of that already, but there's still the variable of there being no equipment to unload it. It's possible they could have unloaded shipments by hand, but that's tedious and menial work for an organized crime group of this caliber.

We're missing something, but what?

Headlights illuminate the road behind me. I pay them no mind, continuing my mental murder board of the predicament.

The camera.

Could it be that they aren't hiding traces of something, but the purpose of the warehouse itself? The camera was there not for surveillance against unwanted visitors, but planned ones.

The headlights illuminate my car, and before I can think about the sudden shift, the driver slams into the back of my car.

Shit.

Shit, shit, shit.

I swerve to the side, drifting in preparation to turn off an old road, away from the lights of the city, when they ram into me again, hitting the side of the car now and sending us careening into a tree.

The last thing I see before the world fades to black is my car reading a text from Maddy.

MADDY:
Text me when you get home safe.

CHAPTER 27
MADDY

I'm not sure what year it is when I wake up, still dressed in my clothes from yesterday. The darkness outside tells me it's still night, and Addie lays next to me softly snoring. Reece is curled at the foot of the bed, her ears droopy as her tail wags in her sleep.

I'd like to be sleeping right now, too, but alas my bladder is screaming. Picking my way to the bathroom adjacent to the master, I do my best to avoid waking both my dog and best friend. Addie remains asleep, but I notice when I come back that Reece is awake, those ears now pricked and alert.

"Hey, Reecey girl," I murmur, patting the top of her head fondly.

Her tail thumps as it windshields between my legs and Addie's, the latter now drooling open-mouthed onto the duvet. I snap a quick picture, swearing when the flash goes off, but it doesn't wake her, nonetheless.

My phone vibrates just as I'm about to set it down. It's late, like, one a.m. I frown, pulling up the message.

UNKNOWN:

Meet me at this address or Riven dies.
Come alone.

UNKNOWN SENT LOCATION.

My heart thuds to a skidding halt in my chest. This has to be a prank, some sick joke being pulled by Marco or someone. The message itself is clichéd enough to be a joke, but then I see the address sent. It matches the warehouse address that Riven sent me earlier today when he and Natalia went to investigate it.

This isn't a malicious joke—it's a threat.

Malik has Riven, and if I don't do what he wants, then he will kill him.

Icy fear floods my veins and I jump back to my feet. The only consolation I have is knowing that Malik hasn't killed him yet. He'd have no use for me if he had. I don't think Malik actually hates me or wants me dead. He just wants to hurt his brother. If Riven were dead, he'd leave me be. I wouldn't be a threat. I'd be nothing to him. But if Riven is alive, then there's still plenty of ways to hurt him by hurting me.

It's one of the easiest choices of my life, slipping on my shoes where I've discarded them next to the bed. I look out through the door, noticing Natalia isn't downstairs. Her car keys are on the counter, one of her many cars that hopefully I can learn to drive before she wakes up and comes to find me.

Reece picks her head up, ready to come with me after reading the tension in my body.

I point back to the bed where Addie is sleeping. "Stay. Keep her safe."

There's no way in hell I'm walking into a death trap and bringing my dog. If I'm going to die, then I'll die alone, but she does not deserve, nor did she ever ask for that fate, even if I would feel better with her comforting presence pushing into my side.

Reece heels, ever the good girl, despite not looking pleased about it.

I slip downstairs, pocketing the keys, and head to the garage. I plug the directions for the warehouse into the GPS, then pause.

The warehouse was empty. That's what Riven texted, anyway, and he'd have no reason to lie. It's too easy. If Riven is there and Natalia is to wake up and notice he's missing, that would be the first place she'd send someone to look. It's too simple and out in the open for Malik, and he's someone who should know better than to underestimate her.

Riven isn't there—I know it in my gut. But where is he?

I'm thinking with startling clarity for the middle of the night, fear sharpening the edges of my mind. Then I remember.

I did something once, something out of fear that I thought was stupid until now. Riven wears the same pair of boots to work every day, and once, while he was in the shower, I took a pocket knife and jimmied the sole up before carving a shallow hole in the space beneath where I inserted a tracker. It was probably a creep's move, but it was one of those days where he came home late and bloody. I didn't know where he was that day, if he was safe and alive or dead and I'd never find his body. So I did what any caring girlfriend would do—I chipped him.

I don't look at the tracker often, if ever—that feels like a violation. No, it's for emergencies only, and this definitely constitutes as an emergency.

I pull up the tracking app and it confirms my theory. Riven isn't at the warehouse. He's somewhere in the middle of the woods on the far side of town.

My stomach clenches with something like nerves, even though nervous feels too light a description for the emotions I'm feeling right now. Something is waiting for me at that warehouse, but it's not Riven.

I put in the new coordinates and open the garage door right as a shrill ringing starts from within the house.

Fuck.

Natalia's alarm.

I peel out of the garage, tires squealing, opting to learn how to drive this European machine on the fly rather than risk both Natalia's wrath and her questions.

A few minutes later, as if on cue, I get a phone call.

"You have twenty seconds to explain why you've stolen my car and slipped out during the night before I kill you."

"You'd have to find me to kill me," I snap on instinct, before cursing at myself. "Sorry, I'm scared. Malik has Riven and I'm going to meet them now. He told me to come alone."

Natalia lets out a long string of curses. "Turn around and tell me where."

"He'll kill him and you know it."

"He'll kill you first if you go now."

"What choice do I have?" I shout into the empty car.

Natalia is silent, and I know she knows as much as I do. I don't have a choice. Riven dying is not an option either of us can accept.

"I can't let him die. I won't. I'm almost there now."

I've been pushing 100 the entire drive, and it's a miracle no cops have seen me yet. I do my best to focus on the road in front of me and not crashing, rather than the anxiety creeping up in my chest. These could be my last few moments alive, and I am driving to my own doom.

"What do you plan to do?" Natalia asks. I can hear the sound of her zipping up her boots.

"Stall him," I respond. "I'm about to pull in. I'm going to let him torture me, or do whatever the fuck he wants. He'll make it slow. He'll want Riven to see it all. You just drive like hell to get to the coordinates I'm about to send and sneak in while Malik is occupied. He expects me to go to the warehouse, so I have the element of surprise. It should buy you a few minutes."

"He could kill you, or worse," Natalia warns.

"I know."

"If he expects you to go to the warehouse, there's still time for me to get there and ambush Malik if he's not expecting anyone."

"No, there's not. He'll need to be distracted for this to work. I'm the only one who can do it. If you show up, he'll just shoot Riven, then you."

Natalia is silent as I pull into a clearing in the woods. There's the smallest shack in the middle, so small it wouldn't otherwise show up on any map. It has no address, only the coordinates I pulled up from my tracking app. I turned off the car lights a few miles back to avoid arousing suspicion, and Natalia's engine is so quiet, there's no sign of me ever arriving.

"I'm going in. Get here quick," I breathe, even though I can already hear Addie's voice. They're both in a car now, arguing over Addie's appearance. There's no time for this. I need to go. "Quickly, Natalia!"

Then I hang up.

I don't bother closing the car door once I step out, in case the sound might alert Malik of my arrival. I don't see any signs of anyone other than the three of us on the property. No cars other than Natalia's and one that I assume is Malik's. The shed is larger than I thought it was upon further inspection, and can hardly be called a shed. It's narrow but long, plenty of space for hundreds of armed Mafia men. I palm the small knife in my pocket that I grabbed at the last second, unsheathing it then hiding it up my sleeve.

If Malik has told me to come, he will wait until Riven is awake to start any true form of torture. I'll need to be prepared to defend myself should he attempt to kill me before Natalia arrives to save us both, or even just buy Riven enough time to escape.

He's going to be furious when he sees me. If I expected to walk out of this alive, I would be more scared of his reaction than Malik's. But I won't be leaving here alive. I know it deep in my soul. I'm going to die in this building, tucked in a corner of the city where no one will find me until it's too late.

I look up at the stars, shining so brightly between the tree branches, no light pollution out here to dim their glow. I'll miss seeing them. I'll miss Addie and Tella's, even my parents. I'll miss Reece and the life she gave me, all the joy she brought. I'll miss Natalia, and Marco, but most of all, I will miss Riven.

I hope someday that he can forgive me for what I'm about to do.

Then, before I can talk myself out of it, I stalk to the front of the building and throw the door open.

CHAPTER 28
RIVEN

I am going to die tonight.

I knew this was coming—everyone has to die eventually—and I thought I'd made my peace with it. I thought I had, until I realized my fucking brother would be the one to put the bullet in my head.

Malik stands opposite me, a few feet away from where I am, a door to the side between us. The first thing I noticed when I came to was that there is no one else in the room with us. The second was that my arms are bound behind my back and I'm propped up on a chair.

"You know I can break free of this in five seconds."

"Five seconds? That's sloppy, baby brother," Malik says, and I hear the unforgettable click of finger on a trigger. "It'll take me three to shoot you should you try."

I can't argue with that logic, but still, it pisses me off more than anything. Some might think I should be scared right now, begging for mercy or some other bullshit, but no. I'm furious.

"Stop glaring like that. You knew this was coming."

"What's the TV for?" I ask instead, noticing the television propped up on an old-fashioned wheeled stand. It looks as if we are about to watch some video on jump-roping and heart health in PE class rather than whatever nefarious plan my brother has.

A flicker of displeasure crosses Malik's face at my question, depriving him of the villain monologue I'm sure he has planned. It's gone in an instant, replaced instead by a coy grin. "Your last meal."

"You're really taking TV dinner to new levels, brother."

Malik's answering chuckle is dark and malicious. "You'll hold back your jokes when you see what's on the menu."

God, I'm about to be killed by a walking cliché. How embarrassing.

Still, my heart drops when I see the warehouse I was in earlier today. I force my face to stay impassive and calm as I ask, "An empty warehouse?"

"A pressure-rigged bomb set to detonate as soon as Maddy steps foot in it like I told her to about ten minutes ago. I had it rigged right before we picked you up. She should be there any second now."

Horror coils around my gut. The camera—it was never for surveillance. It was so I could watch the love of my life be blown to pieces by my sadistic brother.

The pieces click together quickly now. He had it cleaned to hide any evidence of dust settling unevenly on the floor, alerting us to the plates beneath. It was a ruse, an excuse to draw her to her own execution while I sit helpless to save her miles away.

Malik begins to count down, his voice a chill void of pure wickedness. Five seconds. Four. Three. Two...

The door between us flies open.

Maddy.

There she is, standing in the doorway, staring down my brother with all the fury of Hell.

Malik's eyebrows shoot up, like this is truly a surprise. I suppose it is, considering the warehouse camera is still on as we wait for her to stumble in and set off her explosive doom.

This is almost worse. Now, she's here instead of running, which means she knew what she was walking into and chose to come anyway.

"Maddy, *run*." I try to force all the urgency I can into the words.

She sets her jaw and doesn't let her gaze drift from Malik to me for even a second. The light catches her golden hair, setting it aflame as she steps inside.

My brother has already schooled his face back into neutral calm, as if he was expecting this. We both know he wasn't.

"You're not supposed to be here."

"I've come to collect my kid," she says calmly, then says to me without turning, "Sorry, sweetie, traffic was terrible."

"Charming," Malik coos. "You *do* realize the situation you're in right now, don't you?"

"I do."

"And yet you still chose to come."

"I did."

"Maddy, please," I beg. I try to tear the ropes around my wrists again. If I can get even just one hand free, I could buy enough time for her to run.

Malik moves his gun, now pointing it directly at

Maddy's face. "Try to break free one more time and I shoot her."

I freeze.

Maddy doesn't even flinch. "If you're done threatening him, I've come to make a deal."

That piques Malik's interest enough for him to lower his aim just a bit. I can do nothing, not while he has it pointed at her. If it was just my life hanging in the balance, I could find my way out of this with a little more time, but it's not worth risking her life. I *won't* risk her life.

"I'm listening," Malik says.

Only now does Maddy let her gaze drift from him to me. Her warm brown eyes are soft, apologetic. My heart lurches, and I already know her play.

"Kill me instead."

Every nerve in my body freezes at those words. A chill wraps itself around my lungs as I fight for breath. I am certain my words have fogged in the air.

"No." The word tears itself from my throat, no more than a guttural sound. "No."

Maddy, *my* Maddy, ignores my pleas and dares to step a foot closer. "If you really want to hurt him, then hurt me. Torture me. Kill me. Do whatever unspeakable things are in your mind to me, then cut him loose and let him live with the guilt forever," she begs.

He'd do it, I realize. He'd have his way with her here, on the filthy floor in front of me. He'd violate her in ways even the devil can't comprehend, torture her, then kill her once her screams have been etched into my bones. Then, he'd kill me next. He'd never keep his word.

Only one of us is dying today, and I won't let it be her.

"Maddy, I am begging you. Run. Natalia will protect you. Just please—"

Malik pauses for a moment, tapping the barrel of the gun against his chin as if deep in thought, then grins wickedly. "You see..." He mulls the words over his tongue as if tasting them. "I don't even care about hurting him anymore. I just want him dead."

What?

"Kill him quick," Natalia had said. Malik understands her words without ever having heard them.

Then he spins, leveling the gun straight at my chest, and pulls the trigger.

A body crashes into mine.

I look down in horror to find Maddy covering my body with her own, blood blooming across her back.

Her eyes widen and her lips part in a sharp inhale.

"Maddy!" I roar.

I thrash against my bonds as she goes limp, then I feel it. She cut the ropes as she threw her arms around me. She'd hidden a knife in her sleeve. My wickedly clever girl.

Finally free, I hold her, pressing my hands to the entry point of the bullet. They come back red. A glance down confirms a second red bloom across the front of her stomach.

Her chest shakes with each rattling breath. She clutches that knife in one hand, her knuckles white, while the other grasps for my arm, pressing bruises into my skin. I hardly notice. She's pale, so pale already, and her eyes are so wide I can see the ring of white around the brown. She's going into shock.

"You're going to be okay," I promise. "You're going to be okay."

"Riven," she gasps, pressing the blade into my hands. "I called Natalia before I came. She's almost here. Run."

"I'm not leaving you." I grit my teeth, a sob loosing itself from my chest.

"Run," she pleads again, her eyes becoming glossy.

"Touching," Malik says, then his gun clicks, "but I suppose I'll just have to live with killing you both."

He levels the gun again and something within me snaps. Like a white-hot iron, the urge to protect rages through me, even though I've already failed. Even though Maddy has already lost too much blood. Letting my rage scorch through me, I act on instinct. Maddy's knife in one hand, my other still pressed against her blood-soaked back, I whirl on him. The blade arcs perfectly in the air, then plants itself between my brother's eyes.

He falls too quietly.

Like an anticlimactic movie ending, he slumps to the ground, the blade protruding from his forehead like some still you'd see in a museum. *The hunter becomes the prey*, or something poetic like that. The crimson blood pools beneath him, the only proof that he was ever human.

Maddy whimpers in my arms just as the sirens sound from outside the warehouse. My eyes snap back to hers, to the blood that is now staining my knees and the ground beneath us.

"I need to get you up, Blondie. It's going to hurt, but I need to get you up."

"I love you."

"I know."

"I love you."

"Stop saying that like you're dying," I pant. My body flares with pain at each motion, but I lift Maddy regardless, staggering for the door.

Addie bursts in before even the paramedics, Natalia behind her, reaching for her as if she stands a chance at stopping her lover.

Addie screams, and it is the second worst sound I have ever heard, falling just behind Maddy's deathlike confessions.

The paramedics pour in soon after, taking Maddy from my arms and laying her on a stretcher. They rush her into the ambulance. Natalia holds Addie back as she sobs, still reaching for Maddy's prone body. Natalia's gaze drops to the front of my shirt and she looks like she's going to say something to me but I don't wait to hear it. I clamber into the back of the ambulance with Maddy, and it's already peeling off by the time the second one arrives. I assume it's for me, but I'm fine. Maddy is the only one I'm worried about right now.

I recognize a few of the EMTs, and realize this isn't a civilian ambulance but one of the Mancini ones. Letting myself slump forward to hold Maddy's hand, I turn my focus to feeling her pulse as they rush around her.

One EMT cuts her shirt open, peeling it back to reveal the gaping wound in her stomach, and the fact that she's not wearing a bra. I want to scream at them to cover her with something. She'd be terrified to be so vulnerable and exposed like this if she were awake, but they're too busy saving her life to notice.

Someone calls for more gauze, and I try not to focus on how much blood is coming out of her. I've tortured, maimed, and murdered countless men. I've done unspeakable things to my enemies, but I never knew the human body held so much blood before now. It's like I can see the life slipping from her with each scarlet drop.

I press a kiss to her wrist, feeling the weak pulse fluttering.

Then I can't feel it.

The monitor screams.

EMTs push me out of the way to get to both sides of her.

Her heart rate flatlines.

Someone called for a defibrillator and they pull the rest of her shirt off.

"Clear."

A pause.

"Again."

"Charging."

"Clear."

A longer pause.

A glance at me.

"Again."

"Charging."

"Clear."

Her body lurches on the stretcher, her back arching each time they lay the paddles against her bare chest and her still heart.

Come on, Maddy. Don't do this to me. Don't you dare do this to me.

The heart rate monitor beeps, weak but steady.

Alive.

She's alive.

My head falls into my hands as sobs wrack my body.

A paramedic pushes me back further, shifting to continue to check her vitals. Someone calls out that she's still breathing—somehow, she's still breathing.

We pull into the hospital shortly after, and then they're pulling her out of the ambulance and away from me. I leap up to follow them when I stagger, my hand going to my stomach where the stain of blood continues to grow. I frown. I haven't touched Maddy since before the ambulance. It shouldn't have grown.

Maddy. I need to get to Maddy.

I take another staggering step, a doctor rushing forward to take my shoulder.

"Are you with the Mancini shooting?"

"Let me go to her." I grit my teeth, even as my knees buckle.

The woman's eyes widen as she stares down at my stomach, the blood soaking me. "Maddy Yapon, shot in the abdomen, bullet went clean through." She recites the facts as she stares down at me. "Shot throwing herself over Riven Barone. Are you Riven?"

Before I can answer, I fall to my knees, and the doctor calls for another stretcher. I can faintly hear her shouting to the others something about the bullet being in me, but that's wrong. I wasn't shot, Maddy was. They need to be saving her, not me.

The world spins. Someone rips open my shirt while someone else presses something over my nose and mouth. The lights blur together, then fade out entirely.

CHAPTER 29
MADDY

Everything is hazy. Not the type of fogginess where the world blurs with sleepy eyes, or swirling beneath your feet from a night out that will definitely leave you hungover tomorrow. No, this is like viewing the world from the clouds, and each motion I try to make feels like trying to move my body through some viscous substance, too thick to be water but too thin to be blood. I can see myself try to wiggle my toes first, then lift my hand. The toes are a success, but my hand is weighed down by something.

It is only then that I notice the second person in the room. I shift my gaze to my hand, my eyes focusing like tuning an instrument, and I notice Riven, sitting in a chair beside me, his hands in mine and his head dropped towards the floor.

Riven, who is in a hospital gown.

"I—"

His head snaps up in an instant, his eyes locking on my face.

"I need a doctor," he shouts, and I wince at the sound.

"She's awake!" He turns his body to press the pager next to my bed, where IVs and monitors hang to attach to my body.

"If I had known," I croak, "that all it took to get you to wear matching pajamas was to get shot, then I would have done it sooner."

"Maddy."

"What? You refused two weeks ago."

"How?" His voice breaks. "How can you joke right now?"

I look to the second IV hooked in my other arm and take a guess. "They've got me on strong pain meds right now."

He laughs then, beautiful and light until it shatters into sobs. His shoulders are shaking, and I don't think I've seen him cry as much as he has in the past few weeks. My heart breaks within my chest, the only proof aside from the heart rate monitor that it still beats. All I've ever wanted is to make him happy, but his eyes haven't been dry since he met me.

"I'm just so fucking relieved, baby," he says, reading my mind like he always does. "I thought you died."

"I'm hard to kill. Like a cockroach."

"Fucking hell. What am I going to do with you?"

"Kiss me, hopefully," I respond. Yep, that is definitely the pain meds talking now. I am the lightest of lightweights on medication and I'm not quite down to earth enough to be embarrassed just yet.

Riven does what I say, leaning over to kiss me softly, but when I press my hand against his abdomen, he flinches. I pull back sharply, a bit too quickly, I realize, as my head begins to spin.

"What happened to you?" I ask, and Riven has the nerve to look sheepish.

"I'm fine."

I assumed he was in a matching hospital gown as a precaution, or because of all the wounds Malik inflicted, but then I spot the bed behind it. There are IVs dangling loosely, and I know he ripped them out himself.

I tug his hospital gown down so quickly it rips, leaving him standing there, shocked in his boxer briefs.

"Don't de-clothe me in the hospital, woman."

"Addie and Natalia did it once."

"What?"

"You've been shot!" I overlook his confusion to shriek. There is a thin line across his stomach, a surgical incision, I realize, that has been stitched up tightly. It's then that I feel the pain in my lower abdomen. I peer down my own gown now as Riven groans into his hands. I remember being shot in the back, but there's a long angry wound in the front of my stomach, stitched tight. The sight of my own jagged flesh sends a wave of nausea through me and before I realize it, I'm vomiting over the side of the bed.

"Easy, baby, let it out," he says soothingly, then shouts, "Can we get some fucking help in here?"

There's the pattering of sprinting feet across the tile floors from outside now as a doctor rushes in. They slide a bucket underneath me and try to get me to a sitting position rather than a twisted one, murmuring something about tearing my stitches.

"The bullet passed clean through you and into me," Riven explains once I've stopped vomiting and the doctor is checking me over. "You saved my life."

"Not very well, apparently." I moan in pain as the doctor presses on a tender area of my stomach. "You're still here twinning with me. Speaking of, Doc, can we get a new gown for him? I kind of ripped it."

"I can see that, just like I can see that you're out of the bed that you were supposed to stay in, Mr. Barone," the doctor says with a pointed look.

I would have shrunk under that glare, but Riven shrugs, matching the doctor stride for stride. "Is she okay?" he asks instead, gnawing at his bottom lip with anxiety.

The doctor nods, pulling my gown back down and writing something in my chart. "Surgical site looks good, and her vitals are stable. You'll both be here for a few days for continued treatment and monitoring, but I hope to get you home as soon as possible."

"That makes two of us," Riven mutters.

After much coaxing from me, Riven lays down in the other hospital bed with the most childish-looking pout on his face. The doctor moved it as close to mine as she could, with enough room that she can still work if an emergency should arise.

I let my head loll to the side, staring at him through my bleary gaze. I'm trying to find the courage to ask him what's been bothering me since I arrived. "Is Malik..."

"Dead," Riven says. "He's dead. I killed him."

"Oh. Good."

Riven fills me in on everything that happened since I passed out in his arms—the way he used my knife to kill his brother, the way my heart stopped in the ambulance and he thought he'd lost me, the fact that he hadn't noticed he'd been shot at all. He says he was so worried I was going to die, it was all he could think about. It never even crossed his mind that he could have been injured. He thought the blood on his shirt was mine, but it was both of ours.

Addie and Natalia are in the waiting room, apparently, and Marco is bringing Cecile over once Natalia makes sure the route and hospital are secure. We've eliminated the king, so the rest of the kingdom should crumble now, but she's ever the cautious type.

Worrying my lip with my teeth, I try to focus on the positives of the situation. We are both alive. The bad guy is dead. There's no more threat to our lives or anyone we love. We should be happy.

But the villain in our story was once a friend in Riven's, a brother, even if it is only by blood.

"Are you okay?" I ask tenderly.

Riven frowns like he doesn't know what I mean, then his face softens in recognition. "You don't have to worry about me."

"But I do."

"And I love you for it, but I'm alright. He tried to kill you. He almost did."

"But he didn't," I assure him. I'm still here, somehow. I never expected to walk out of there alive. I went in expecting the worst. Every nightmare I've ever had, every pain I have ever imagined enduring, I was ready for it, so long as it meant saving him—Riven, my Riven, who deserves so much better than what the world has offered him.

I reach over to him, breaking the space between us as I take his hand. "We're going to be okay," I assure him, and I believe it.

Every challenge life has thrown at us, every villain we've faced, we've bested them all and screamed, "Fuck you!" to the universe more times than I can count. I wouldn't go as far to think we might be immortal, but we've made it this far.

I'm no longer afraid of what comes next. I know that as long as I have this man beside me to fight for and fight with, we will be okay.

"Yeah," he murmurs, "we will."

EPILOGUE
MADDY

Two months later

Why do doctor's appointments always run late when you have somewhere to be?

Okay, I don't have somewhere to be right *now*—as in I have a few hours left before my flight—but still. The inconvenience has me gritting my teeth as I answer one more pointless question that I am almost one hundred percent sure I already answered on their pre-appointment questionnaire.

Riven texted me six minutes ago letting me know he's sitting in the car outside. A minute later, I get sent a picture of Reece with her head out the window, jowls pulled back by the wind in a smile, her tongue flying. A second photo pops up beneath it, obviously taken after the first. It's Reece in the lobby of Mancini Security, a very pale intern holding her leash with a death grip as the dog drags him towards a hall.

RIVEN:

We had to make a pit stop.

I stifle a laugh at the thought of my shepherd sprinting down the pristine corridors of Natalia's security company, bumping into some high-up politician or businessman.

She's going to be running the place by the time we get back.

I'm sure, but sadly, she's with your parents.

How was that?

Your dad loves her. Your mom loves me, so I think she'll forgive us for leaving Reece with her.

How much longer?

Forever. I think they're going to ask me for my star sign next.

Zebra, right?

Libra.

Same thing.

That's such a Virgo response.

> What did you just call me?

I pocket my phone when the doctor finally returns to direct me to the checkout. I pay, sign maybe a million more papers, then practically sprint out the door to where Riven awaits. He leans against the hood of his new car, a sleek machine with some long name that I can't be bothered to remember. He got it after his last one was totaled by Malik.

Riven looks good. He always looks good, but goddamn. He wears jeans, something he finally has taken a hint about and started to wear more often, matched with a black shirt that clings to every sculpted muscle.

"How'd it go?" he asks, wrapping his arm around my waist as I barrel into him, pressing my lips against his cheek with a resounding smack.

"Perfect. They've cleared me. My first appointment is when we get back."

I had just finished my first scar removal consultation. I have opted to have every trace of Donovan removed from my body permanently. The doctors warned me that this process will not remove them completely, and it may not work on all of them, but there's hope that over time, most could fade entirely. I trust them—after all, Riven picked them himself, meticulously scouring every source he had on each doctor. He already knew a good plastic surgeon, the one I wound up going to, but he wanted me to know I had options.

In the end, I chose to keep the two scars from being shot. One is a long, angry pink line that runs down my abdomen from where the surgeons had to cut into me in order to stop the internal bleeding and patch the organs that had been hit. It was supposedly a long and complicated surgery. I apparently died and was brought back.

The second scar is almost a perfect circle, right on my lower back, from where Malik's bullet pierced clean through. It's raised like the one in the front, and the same pink shade, with a touch more of a purple undertone.

Riven wept when he saw it the first time. Even now, I wake up sometimes to him laying awake, gently brushing over it with his fingertips. He'll have a faraway look in his eye, a devastating mix of sorrow, love, and awe. I don't think he's ever had someone actually take a bullet for him before.

After our procedures, the doctors released us both by the end of the week. I know they wanted to keep me longer, but Natalia pulled some strings. She has a doctor who knows about her... illegal endeavors. I've met the man before—he's saved Addie's life more than once. Dr. Park is a kind man who knows when to keep his mouth shut. He is only scared of one person, and he doesn't want to cross her by letting her best friends die due to negligence or malpractice. He visited the apartment a few times a day for the next few days to provide ample checkups and routine cleanings. Riven tried to help once and wound up becoming the patient again.

I settle into the passenger seat next to him, clicking my seat belt. It catches on my yellow sundress, lifting up my legs ever so slightly. I thoroughly enjoy the way Riven's gaze follows the motion.

"How much longer do we have until our flight?" I ask, doing my best to turn in my seat without bumping the freshly prodded-at skin.

Riven's answering smile is beautiful and free. He

finally looks his age, if not younger, now that he is able to put his family behind him. "Addie and Natalia are meeting us at the jet strip in two hours." Then, without missing a beat, "So we have time to stop if you want to eat before we go."

He knows me too well at this point. I haven't eaten this morning, too nervous for my first appointment. It isn't that I'll be sad to see my scars go—the opposite of that, actually—but it feels like starting something new. Maybe it's the first chapter of a new story, as Addie would say.

I struggled before this first appointment. A part of me wanted to hold on to that pain and let it fester, if only as a reminder, or a small thought that maybe I don't deserve this fresh start. The part of me that is healing told me to let the pain go, and so I listened.

I've started therapy as well. At first, it was to reconcile with all that has happened and all that I have survived. Now, my weekly sessions feel more like unwinding as I learn to manage the trauma on my own, with the support I have around me.

Riven sat in on a session once. I told him he should go more often.

The main thing I've been taught so far is that there will always be more battles in my future—maybe more violent than the average person's—but I can't fight them if I'm still fighting the ones that are already over. I'm heading to the airport to go to my best friend's wedding, the love of my life at my side. I've already won.

"Anything you had in mind?" Riven asks again, passing me his phone, the GPS open already.

"Maybe burgers?"

The small smile that he tries to fight is my reward as I correctly guess what he wants but won't ask for himself. I plug in the directions to our new favorite place, a small, family-owned grill half a block from our new apartment.

We moved in last week, and to be honest, half of our things are still in boxes. We prioritized unpacking what we need for the wedding, and let the rest sit for a while. A lot opened up next to Addie and Natalia's property, the perfect size for us to build a house with enough room for Reece to run in the back. We've held off on any official form of planning or engagement, but Riven bought the property anyway, just in case.

I have a feeling our just in case will be coming sooner rather than later, but I don't mind the wait. I know that wherever life takes me, Riven will be there for the rest of it.

Addie and Natalia are already at the runway by the time we arrive, bags in hand. I pass lunch to Natalia before embracing Addie.

I beam. "You're glowing."

"Thanks. It's the spray tan," Addie says in earnest.

Riven chokes on a laugh and Natalia rolls her eyes. She dropped us off at the spa yesterday for a girls' day, one that she didn't want to participate in, rudely enough, but still paid for, regardless. A day of pampering ended with tans and maybe a glass too much of champagne, before Marco brought us back home. Meanwhile, Riven and Natalia were on packing duty—lucky them.

"You ready?" I ask once we're seated on the jet. The

seats are comfortable, and I told Riven last night he should buy one. He asked me why he would buy one when he could just steal Natalia's from time to time for free. I couldn't argue with that logic.

"More than anything," my best friend sighs. "After everything that happened this past year, if a beautiful Italian wedding is the result, I'll take it."

The wedding is taking place at Lake Como tomorrow, with Marco already there to oversee preparation, with help from Cecile. Addie wants an intimate wedding, and without her parents there, Cecile and Marco will give her away, with me as her maid of honor and Riven as Natalia's best man. Addie didn't even try to invite her mom, doesn't even know where she is right now, but Cecile and Marco are more than thrilled to walk her down the aisle.

I can't say I'm disappointed by the wedding venue. After my first and only trip to Italy lasted less than forty-eight hours thanks to Donovan, I'm excited for the do-over. Riven and I are going to travel the country while Addie and Natalia enjoy their honeymoon in Greece. We plan to stop by his mother's house in Rome first, then the rest is a surprise, according to Riven.

"Any wedding news from you two soon?" Addie asks, with a pointed look towards Riven.

"Yes. We've secretly eloped. Surprise," Riven responds, and I toss one of my flip-flops at him. It hits his shoulder with a satisfying smack, and he feigns injury, folding over on himself.

"You should've been a quarterback, Blondie."

"And you should've been a court jester. Alas, you were born in the wrong era."

"You wound me."

"You love me."

"That," he says, pressing a kiss to the top of my head, "I do."

Addie's wedding is beautiful. The wisteria around Lake Como is in full bloom, and every inch of the pavilion has been decorated with imported florals. Addie's dress is just as beautiful as it was the first time she tried it on, and I sob from my spot next to her as I watch her exchange vows with the love of her life.

The reception takes place downtown, a truly Addie touch. She wears a shorter white dress now, her veil still pinned to her head as we head into a local bar. Natalia pays for everyone's drinks, and a cheer goes around the building as we dance and laugh.

In the middle of the celebration, all the women gather in the center for the traditional bouquet toss. I stand front and center, just as Addie instructed.

"I'm going to aim for you," she whispers with a wink.

I laugh it off—her aim is truly terrible—but a knot coils in my stomach. Where is Riven?

Before I can think too long on it, Addie has her back turned and is lining up her shot. She throws it with a glance over her shoulder, and the bouquet hits me right in my face. I spit out leaves as she doubles over and points to the side where Riven stands, camera in hand.

"Beautiful, Blondie," he calls over the music.

I blush at what I thought would happen. It's too soon for Riven and I to be engaged. That was Addie just being Addie.

"What?" he asks, a devilish smirk in his eyes once I approach. "Did you think you'd catch it and I'd propose?"

Alright, then, so we're back to playing his favorite game: Let's Read Maddy's Mind and Then Call Her Out on It.

"I would have killed you if you had. This is their night, and they deserve to have it to themselves."

Riven smiles at me, that beautiful smile that has my heart doing backflips and melting me from the inside out. "I had a feeling you'd say that, which is why I turned Addie down when she offered. I fully plan to tonight, once it's past midnight and they've had their day."

My heart pauses its backflips and lurches to my throat. "You do realize you just technically proposed already," I try to joke in a voice that is cooler than how I feel. It fails spectacularly. I can tell by the smug look on Riven's face.

"No, I'm letting you know in advance so you don't have a panic attack when you come back to the hotel room. I'm letting you decide what type of trip this will be."

I drag my tongue over my lips, wetting them as my pulse quickens. "And what are my options?"

"It can be what you planned on, a good tour of Italy, or an engagement trip."

Then he walks off, leaving me with a bouquet in my hands and a blush on my cheeks. What will I say tonight, when he gets down on one knee and asks me those four words?

I never wanted to be married while I was with Donovan. I planned on it, but only because it seemed like the natural next step. I never wanted to be his wife, not truly,

I don't think. But being Riven's wife? Coming home every day for the rest of my life to the first man to ever make me feel safe, the person I love most in the world? Having children together, if that's something he wants? I don't know. We've never discussed it. Between dodging murder attempts and blood feuds, we never stopped to think about what will happen next. I don't think either of us thought we'd get to grow old enough to make that choice.

We get to grow old together. I once used to think leaving behind my youth and wild life was the most terrifying thought, but entering into that world with Riven?

It's the easiest decision I'll ever make.

When I climb the stairs to our hotel room, Riven's hand in mine, I have one word echoing in my head. The lights are off when we get back, and when Riven flicks them on, there are roses everywhere—and I don't mean just a trail of petals.

I mean there are bouquets of them, thousands strung together to outline the entire room until the whole space is filled with their floral scent. There's champagne cooling on ice, with crystal flutes ready beside them.

Riven looks nervous. Gone is the cool and charming exterior he threw up at the reception. There is only fear on his face now, and he looks more terrified than the moment he thought I was dying.

A new emotion washes over me at the sight of the man I love most, who loves me so terribly that he's terrified at the prospect of not being able to spend his life with me.

He sinks to one knee.

"Yes."

"God, Maddy, I don't even have the ring out yet."

"I don't need it. I just need you."

"Well," he says, silver lining his eyes, "you're getting the damn ring, and every word of this speech I've been rehearsing for two months. Then, once I'm done, you get to decide."

"My answer will be the same. I need you, Riven, and I won't survive a world where you're not by my side every single day."

"Stop being the love of my life for five seconds and let me propose to you."

I laugh, not caring that there are tears streaking down my face now, ruining the last of my makeup.

Riven stays kneeling before me, and fishes out the ring box. It's his mother's ring, just as she promised me back in the wedding dress shop. He's placed it in a blue velvet box to match the sapphires crusting the band, the oval diamond shimmering in the hotel light.

"Maddy Yapon," he says, his voice trembling, "I won't lie and tell you that I loved you from the moment I met you. In fact, it was quite the opposite. I couldn't stand how easily you seemed to glide through life while I felt like I was drowning. It wasn't until I learned that you were drowning in the same sea as me but taught yourself to swim that I began to fall for you. You matched me scar for scar, and while I was content to let myself rot for years, you kept fighting, even when you didn't realize it. You are the most brave and goddamn stubborn woman I have ever met. You bring meaning to fighting fire with fire, and I've come to love the only person in this world who can beat me at my own game. You saved me, in every meaning of the word, while you were saving yourself. You're beyond incredible, Maddy. I promise to work every day to deserve your love and to keep you safe. I won't let you want for anything as long as we both live, and if I have to kill the devil himself with my own hands to ensure your happiness, I will. Will you marry me?"

I take his face in my hands, smashing my lips against his. One arm reaches out to support me, wrapping around my middle as I push us both backwards.

Riven stands then, holding my body against his, his tears mixing with mine.

"*You* saved *me*, Riven. I was so lost in the pain, I couldn't find my way out. I wasn't swimming, I was floating. And my answer is still the same—yes. A million, trillion times, yes."

It's with trembling hands that he slips the ring onto my finger. It's a perfect fit, just like it was when Cecile had me try it on all those months ago.

My back hits the bed, Riven already pushing my dress up past my hips. I take his face in my hands, kissing him soft and slow, like we have all the time in the world.

For the first time in my life, I can see a future past today. I've always planned for what I want, content to work rather than wait. Even as I took baby steps towards my dreams, they've never felt real or tangible, but I can see them now.

I can see myself walking down the aisle, towards the rest of my life with the man of my dreams. I see us building a house and moving onto that property he bought. Our friends will come over to *our* house for dinner now, trading off weekends and recipes. Addie and

I will travel the world, her a bestselling author and me an award-winning photographer. Reece will live the best life money can buy a dog, loved like a human child by both her parents. One day, Riven and I will have another type of family, or maybe we won't. I'll be happy either way.

In what feels like the first time in forever, I sigh and take the first step towards tomorrow, leaving the past in my shadow where it belongs.

ACKNOWLEDGMENTS

I would like to start this off by thanking my parents for always supporting my writing, regardless of whether or not I allow them to read it. Burning Heaven and Freezing Hell both all under the "please do no read this, oh my god" category, and as far as first time author parents go, they've taken it all in stride.

I'd also like to thank my dear friend Kailyn, the inspiration behind one of Riven's sassy quips. Thank you for letting me use your "I'll throw a dollar at it" line on another character (rather than you using it on me this time HAHA). I officially bestow you with the title of #1 Freezing Hell fan.

I couldn't have done any of this without the support of some of my amazing author friends, Celaena and Sara. You both mean the world to me, even if you like leaving me in emotional distress from your beautiful writing.

As always thank you to my wonderful editor, Jess. Jess takes my characters and their story and polishes them to perfection every time. There's no one else I could ever imagine entrusting my book babies to.

Last but not least, thank you to the Smoke and Ice Duology for giving me a place to explore new parts of my author identity. This is a genre that I did not see myself writing, and it has been a thrilling ride that has opened so many new doors for me.

I can't wait to see where we go next.

Just kidding. I know exactly what is coming next. Muahahaha!

<3

H

ABOUT THE AUTHOR

Haydn Hubbard is a North Carolina native who spends most of her time daydreaming of worlds filled with love, magic, and occasionally dragons. The King's Queen is her debut fantasy series and the first of many to come. When Haydn is not writing she can be found competing with her horses, in any local coffee shop, or anywhere where there is a dog.

ALSO BY HAYDN HUBBARD

The King's Queen Series

The King's Queen

Oracle of Ruin

Smoke and Ice Duology

Burning Heaven

Freezing Hell

Printed in Dunstable, United Kingdom